THE AVENGERS

MIGHTY MARVELS

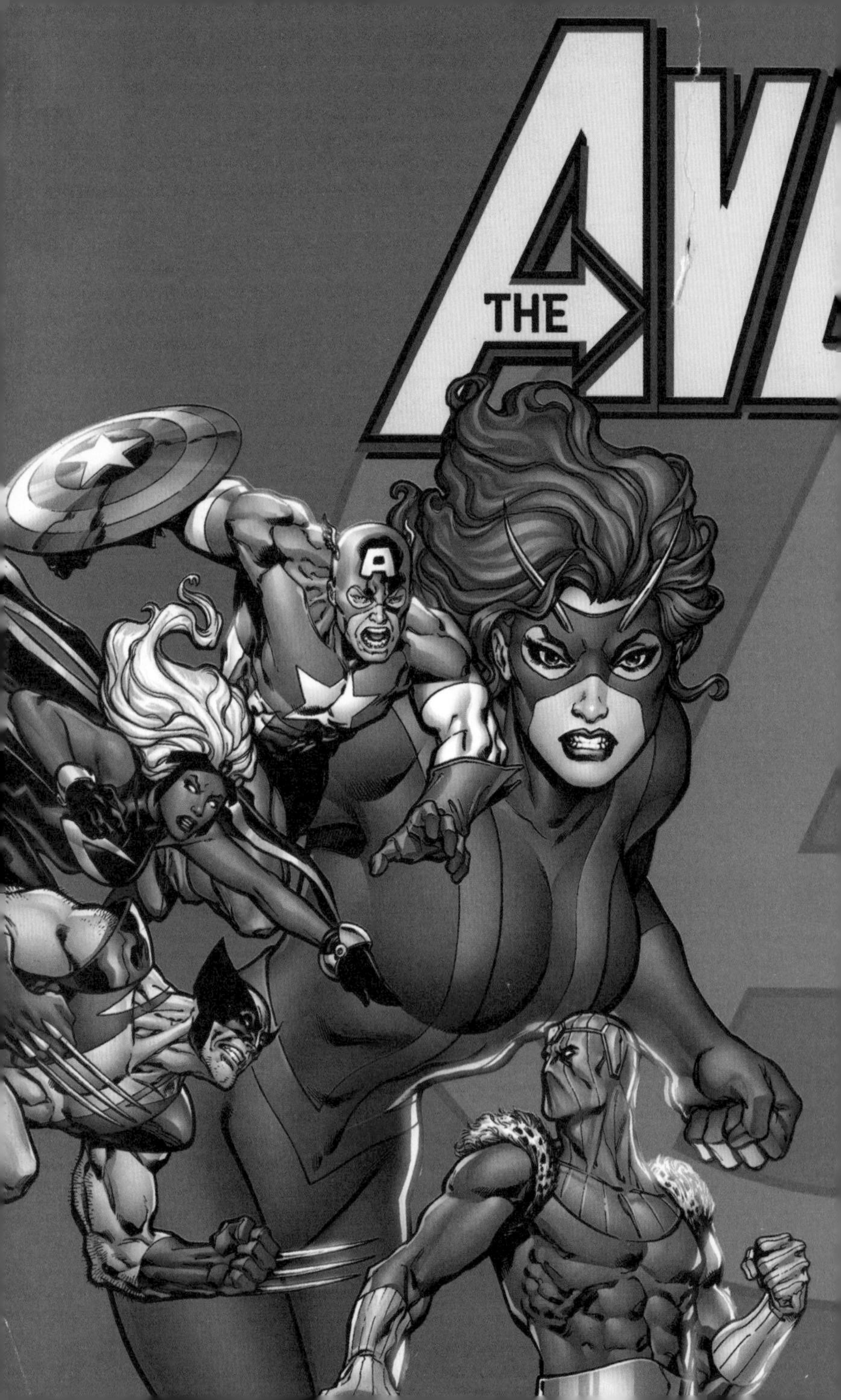
THE

NGERS

MIGHTY MARVELS

Writer: **Marc Sumerak**
Pencils: **Ig Guara & Kevin Sharpe**
Inks: **Norman Lee & Jay Leisten**

Colors: **Ulises Arreola**
Letters: **Dave Sharpe**
Cover Art: **Leonard Kirk, Terry Pallot & Val Staples**
Assistant Editor: **Nathan Cosby**
Editor: **Mark Paniccia**

Captain America created by Joe Simon & Jack Kirby

Collection Editor: **Jennifer Grünwald**
Assistant Editors: **Cory Levine & John Denning**
Editor, Special Projects: **Mark D. Beazley**
Senior Editor, Special Projects: **Jeff Youngquist**
Senior Vice President of Sales: **David Gabriel**
Vice President of Creative: **Tom Marvelli**

Editor in Chief: **Joe Quesada**
Publisher: **Dan Buckley**

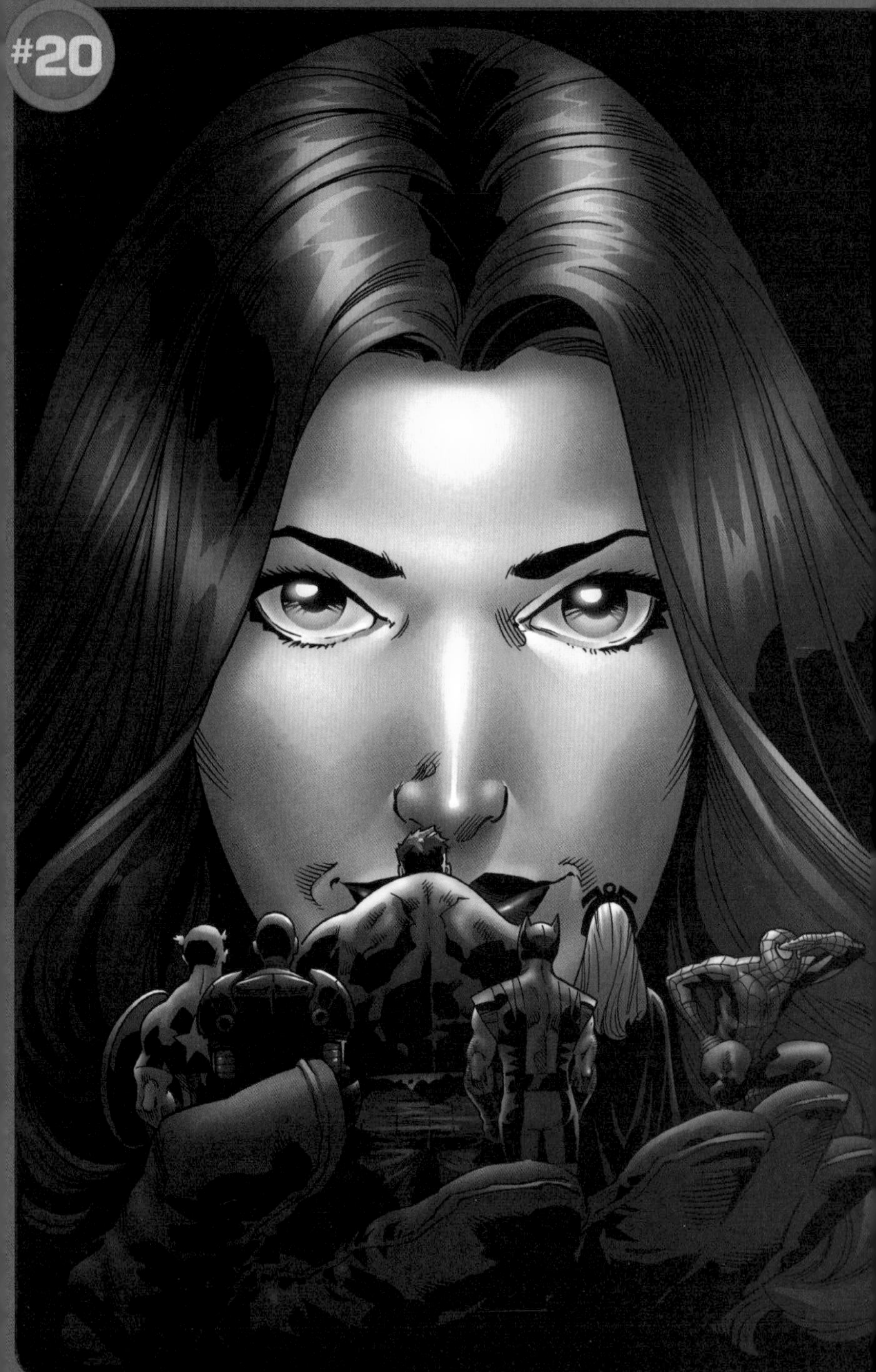
#20

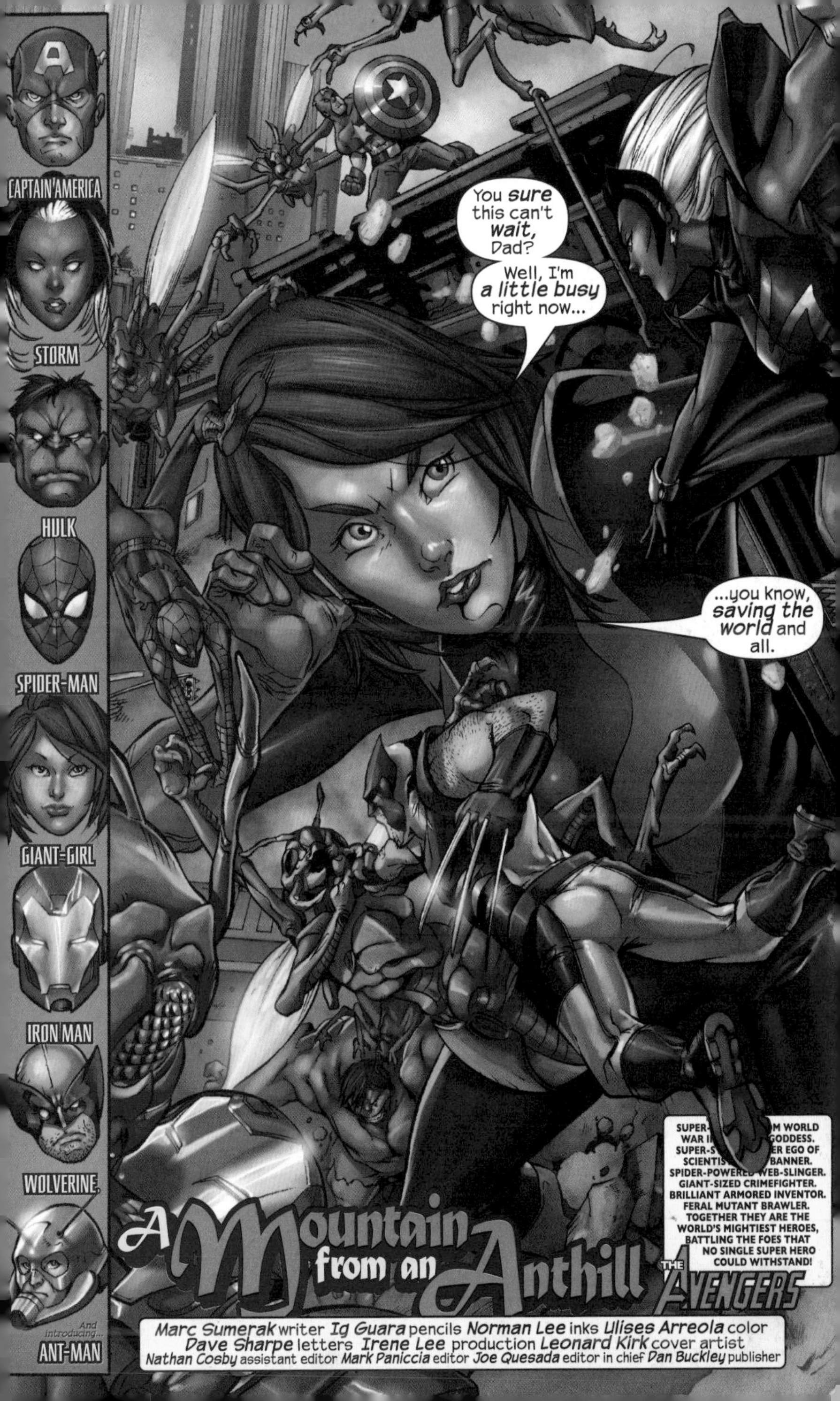

CAPTAIN AMERICA
STORM
HULK
SPIDER-MAN
GIANT-GIRL
IRON MAN
WOLVERINE
And introducing...
ANT-MAN
You sure this can't wait, Dad?
Well, I'm a little busy right now...
...you know, saving the world and all.
SUPER- M WORLD WAR I GODDESS. SUPER-S ER EGO OF SCIENTIS BANNER. SPIDER-POWER WEB-SLINGER. GIANT-SIZED CRIMEFIGHTER. BRILLIANT ARMORED INVENTOR. FERAL MUTANT BRAWLER. TOGETHER THEY ARE THE WORLD'S MIGHTIEST HEROES, BATTLING THE FOES THAT NO SINGLE SUPER HERO COULD WITHSTAND!
A Mountain from an Anthill
THE AVENGERS
Marc Sumerak writer Ig Guara pencils Norman Lee inks Ulises Arreola color
Dave Sharpe letters Irene Lee production Leonard Kirk cover artist
Nathan Cosby assistant editor Mark Paniccia editor Joe Quesada editor in chief Dan Buckley publisher

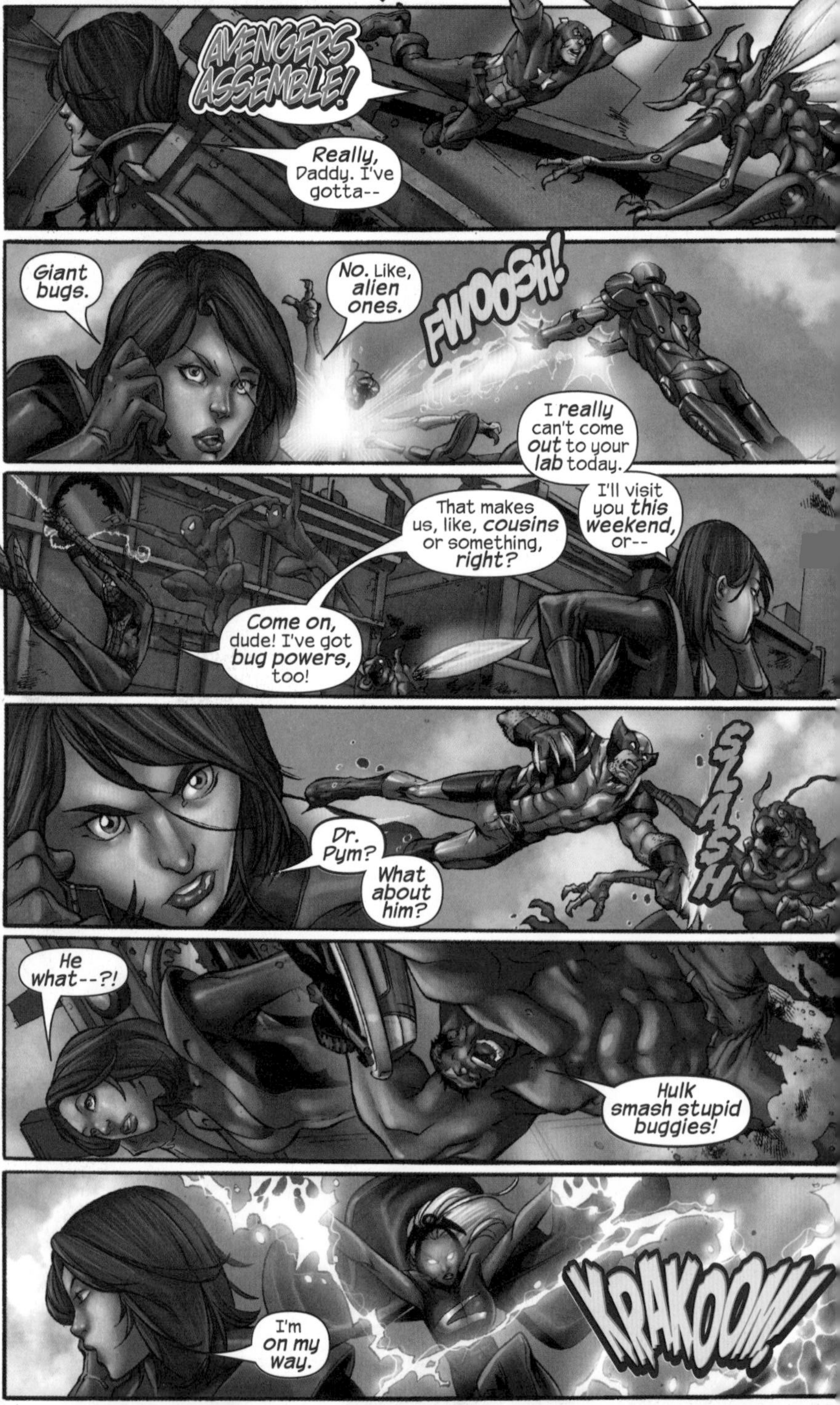
AVENGERS ASSEMBLE!
Really, Daddy. I've gotta--
Giant bugs.
No. Like, alien ones.
FWOOSH!
I really can't come out to your lab today.
I'll visit you this weekend, or--
That makes us, like, cousins or something, right?
Come on, dude! I've got bug powers, too!
Dr. Pym?
What about him?
SLASH
He what--?!
Hulk smash stupid buggies!
I'm on my way.
KRAKOOM!

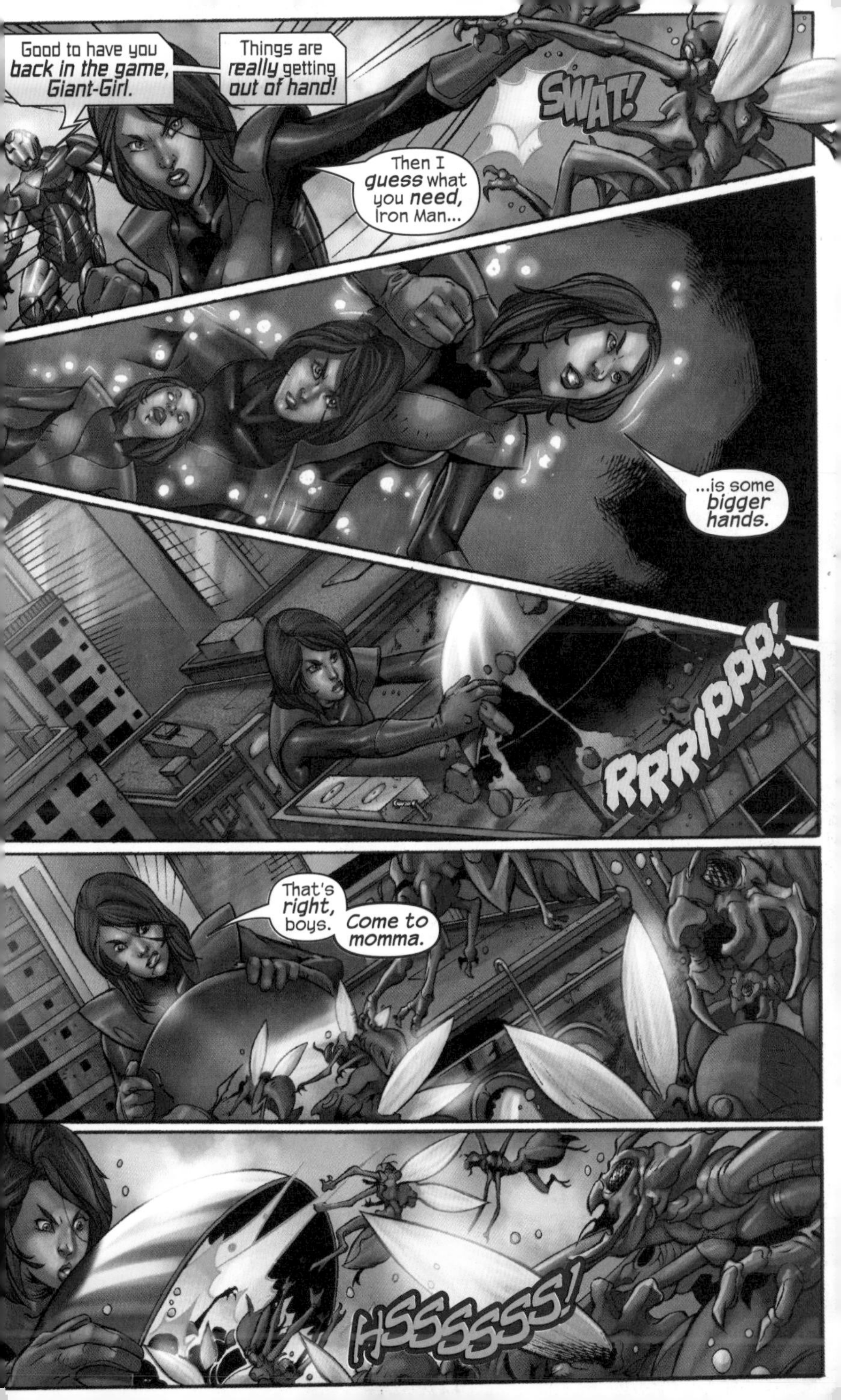
Good to have you back in the game, Giant-Girl.
Things are really getting out of hand!
SWAT!
Then I guess what you need, Iron Man...
...is some bigger hands.
RRRIPPP!
That's right, boys.
Come to momma.
HSSSSSS!

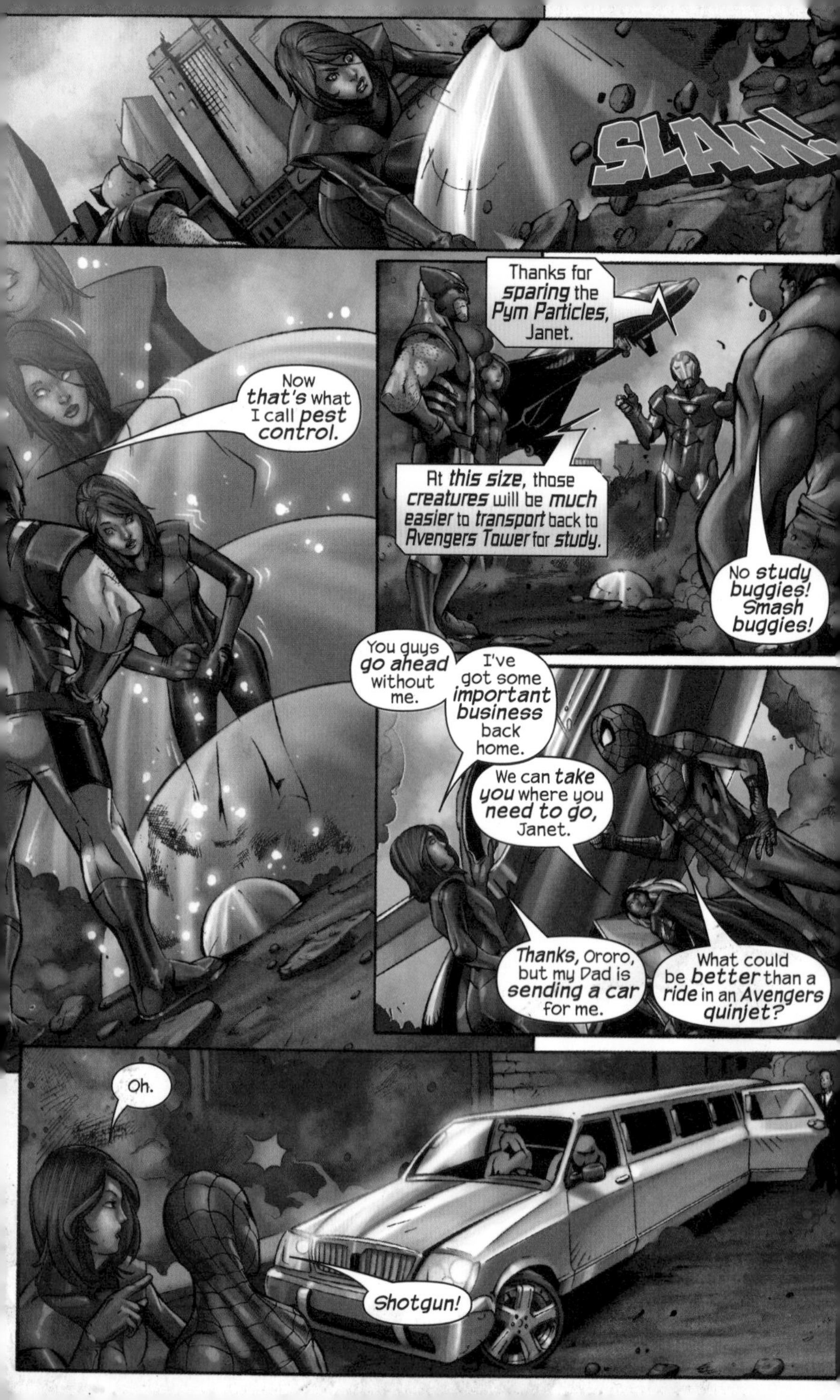
SLAM!
Now that's what I call pest control.
Thanks for sparing the Pym Particles, Janet.
At this size, those creatures will be much easier to transport back to Avengers Tower for study.
No study buggies! Smash buggies!
You guys go ahead without me.
I've got some important business back home.
We can take you where you need to go, Janet.
Thanks, Ororo, but my Dad is sending a car for me.
What could be better than a ride in an Avengers quinjet?
Oh.
Shotgun!

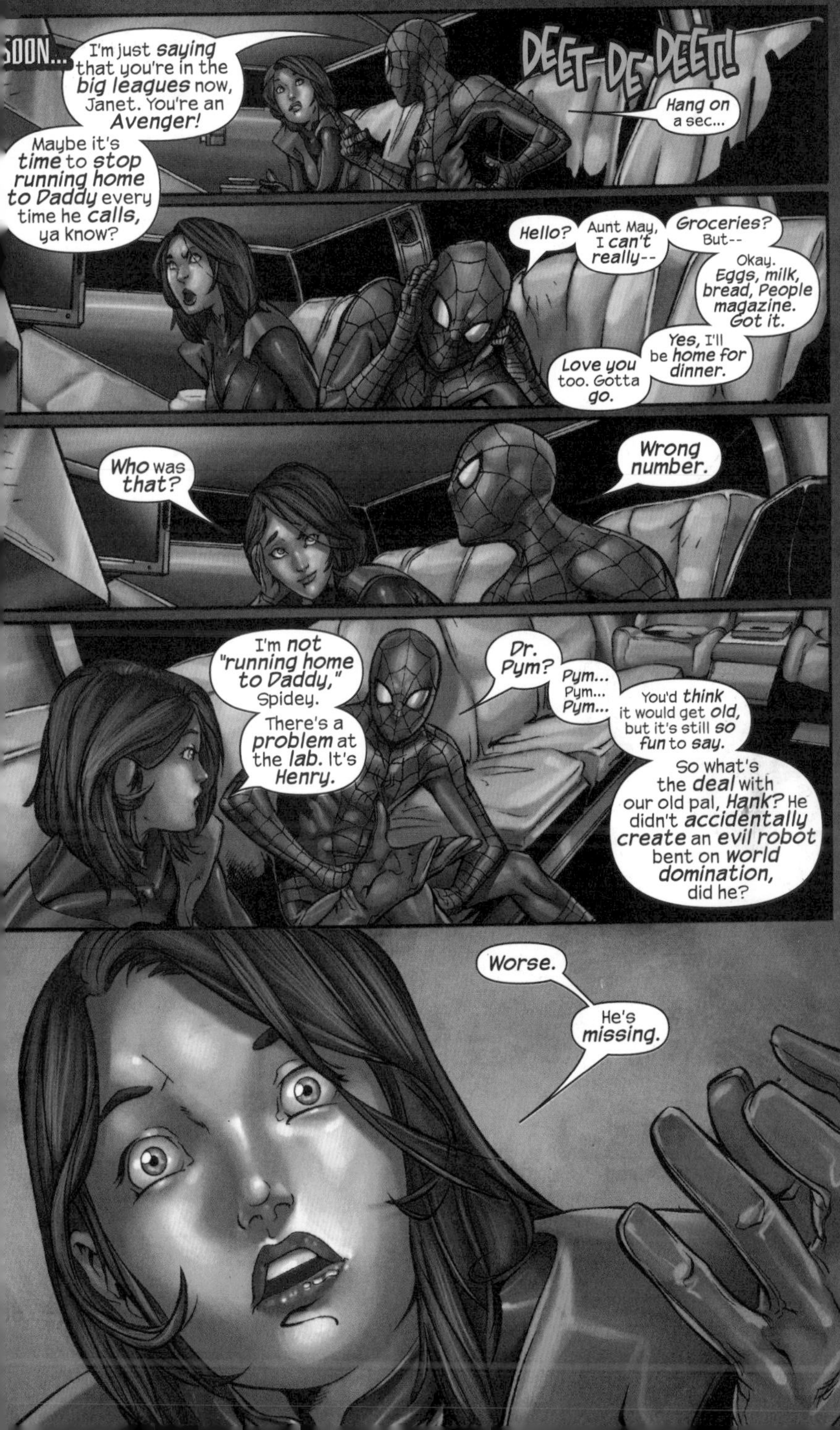
SOON...
I'm just saying that you're in the big leagues now, Janet. You're an Avenger!
Maybe it's time to stop running home to Daddy every time he calls, ya know?
DEET-DE-DEET!
Hang on a sec...
Hello?
Aunt May, I can't really--
Groceries? But--
Okay. Eggs, milk, bread, People magazine. Got it.
Yes, I'll be home for dinner.
Love you too. Gotta go.
Who was that?
Wrong number.
I'm not "running home to Daddy," Spidey.
There's a problem at the lab. It's Henry.
Dr. Pym?
Pym... Pym... Pym...
You'd think it would get old, but it's still so fun to say.
So what's the deal with our old pal, Hank? He didn't accidentally create an evil robot bent on world domination, did he?
Worse.
He's missing.

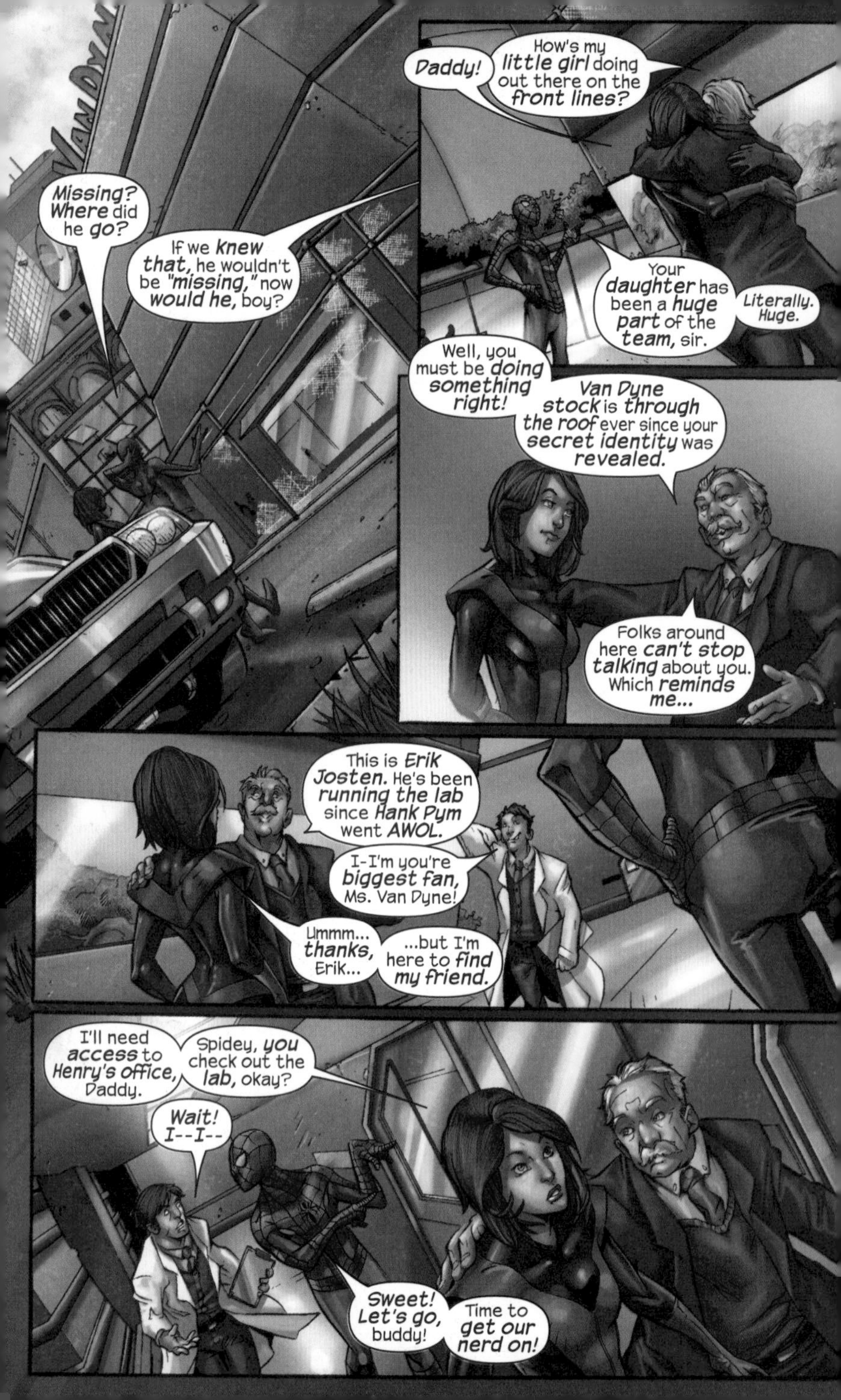

VAN DYN
Missing? Where did he go?
If we knew that, he wouldn't be "missing," now would he, boy?
Daddy!
How's my little girl doing out there on the front lines?
Your daughter has been a huge part of the team, sir.
Literally. Huge.
Well, you must be doing something right!
Van Dyne stock is through the roof ever since your secret identity was revealed.
Folks around here can't stop talking about you. Which reminds me...
This is Erik Josten. He's been running the lab since Hank Pym went AWOL.
I-I'm you're biggest fan, Ms. Van Dyne!
Ummm... thanks, Erik...
...but I'm here to find my friend.
I'll need access to Henry's office, Daddy.
Spidey, you check out the lab, okay?
Wait! I--I--
Sweet! Let's go, buddy!
Time to get our nerd on!

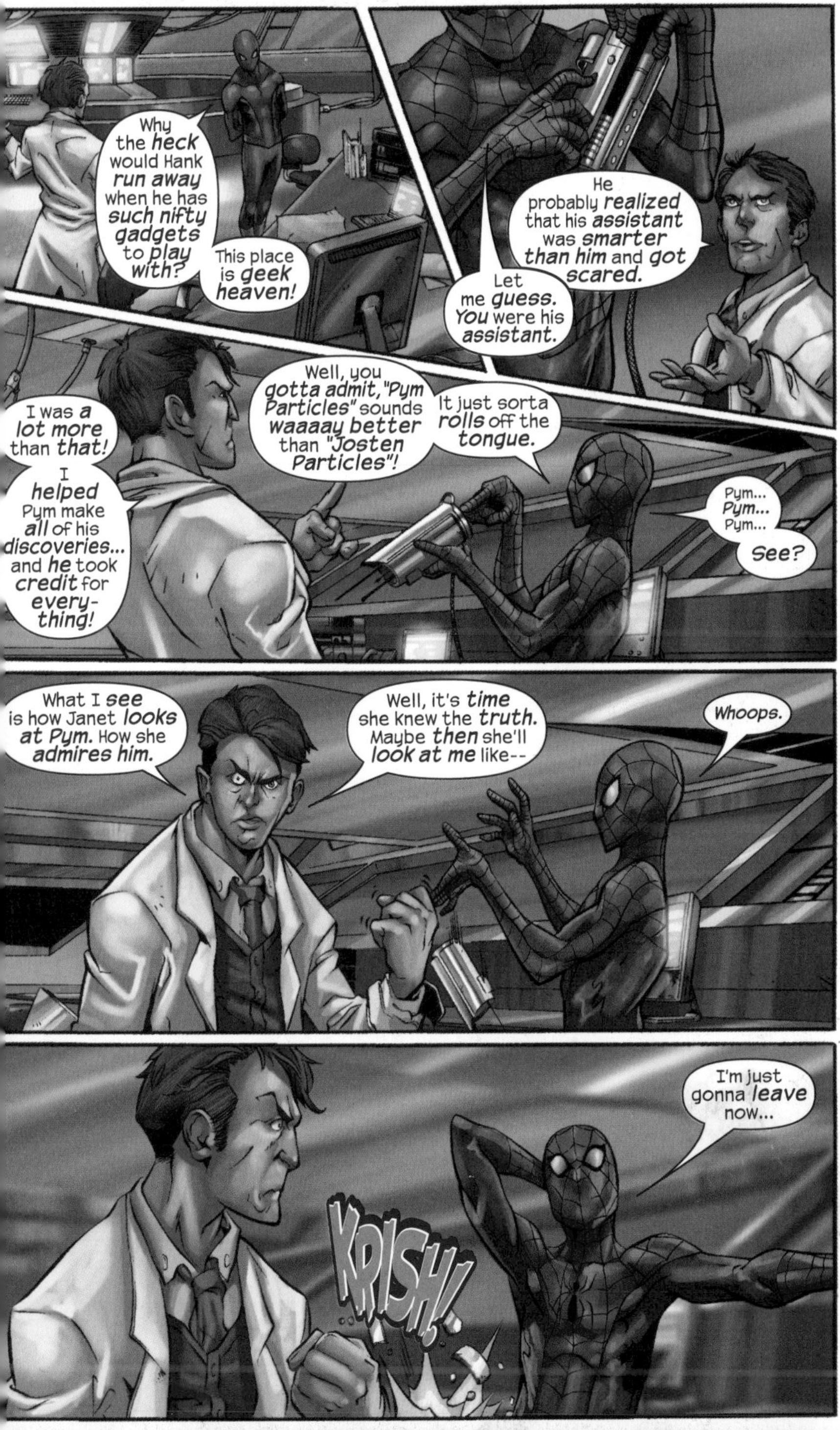
Why the heck would Hank run away when he has such nifty gadgets to play with?
This place is geek heaven!
He probably realized that his assistant was smarter than him and got scared.
Let me guess. You were his assistant.
I was a lot more than that!
I helped Pym make all of his discoveries... and he took credit for every-thing!
Well, you gotta admit, "Pym Particles" sounds waaaay better than "Josten Particles"!
It just sorta rolls off the tongue.
Pym... Pym... Pym...
See?
What I see is how Janet looks at Pym. How she admires him.
Well, it's time she knew the truth. Maybe then she'll look at me like--
Whoops.
I'm just gonna leave now...
KRISH!

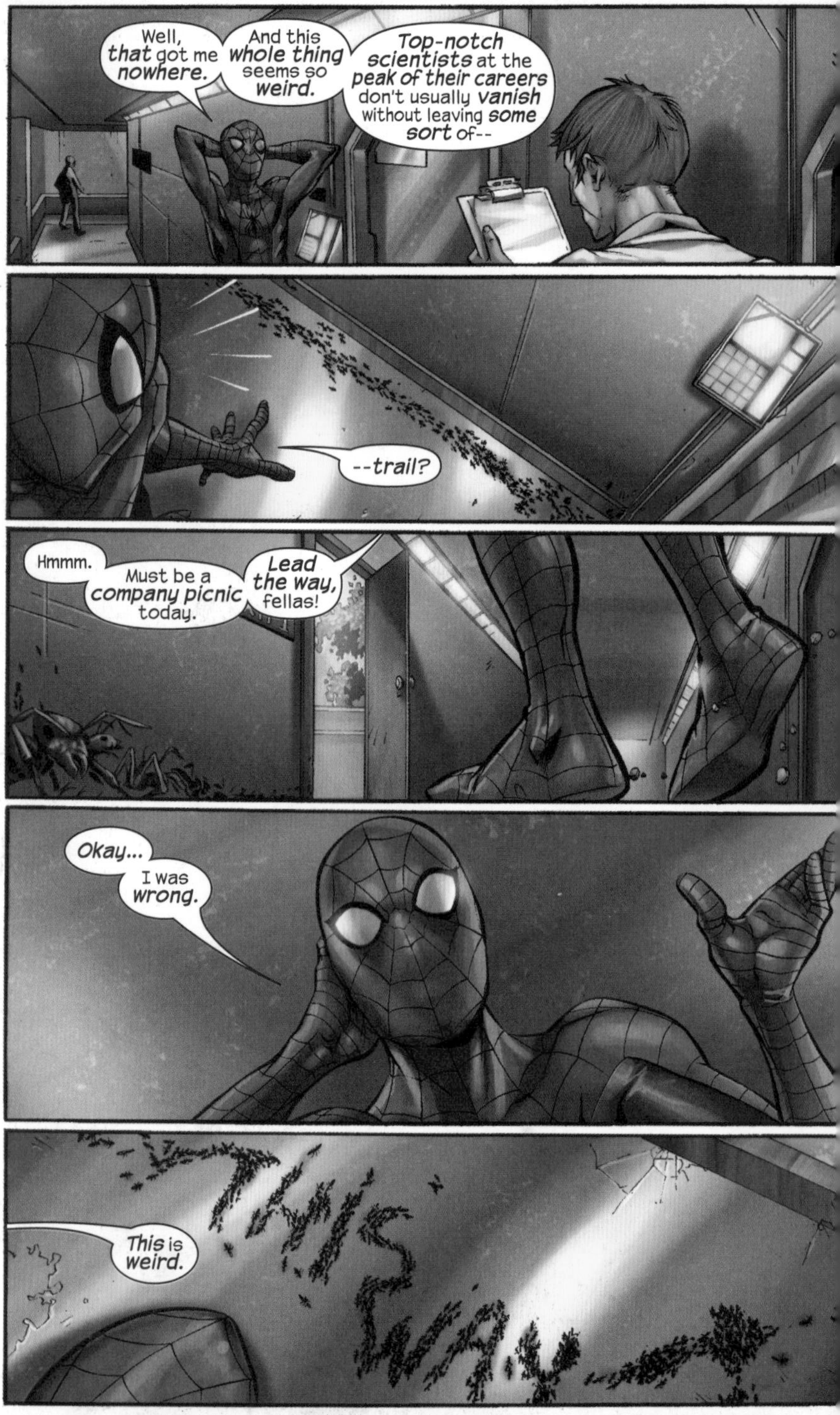
Well, *that* got me *nowhere.*
And this *whole thing* seems so *weird.*
Top-notch scientists at the *peak of their careers* don't usually *vanish* without leaving *some sort* of--
--*trail?*
Hmmm.
Must be a *company picnic* today.
Lead the way, fellas!
Okay... I was *wrong.*
THIS WAY
This is *weird.*

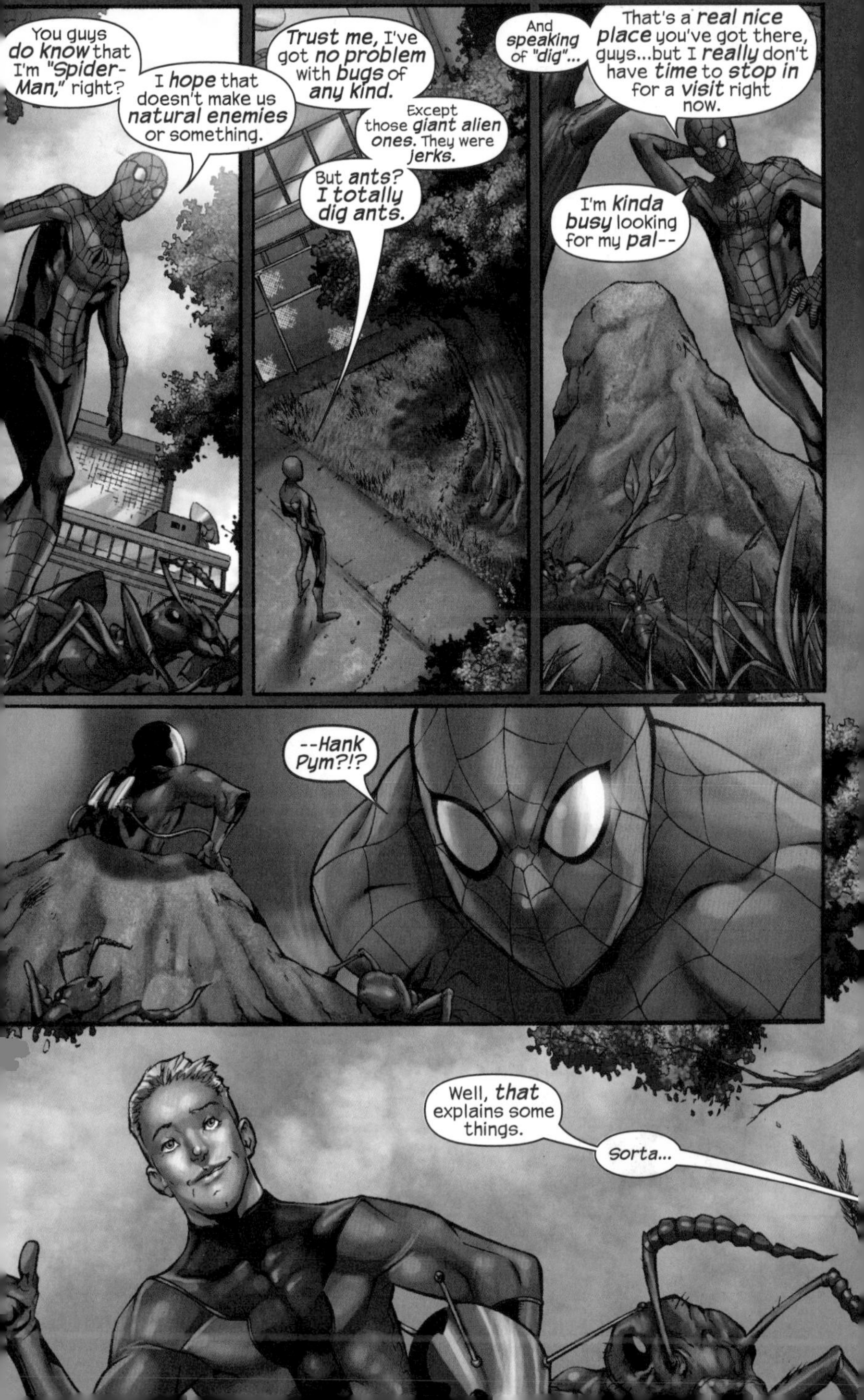
You guys do know that I'm "Spider-Man," right?
I hope that doesn't make us natural enemies or something.
Trust me, I've got no problem with bugs of any kind.
Except those giant alien ones. They were jerks.
But ants? I totally dig ants.
And speaking of "dig"...
That's a real nice place you've got there, guys...but I really don't have time to stop in for a visit right now.
I'm kinda busy looking for my pal--
--Hank Pym?!?
Well, that explains some things.
Sorta...

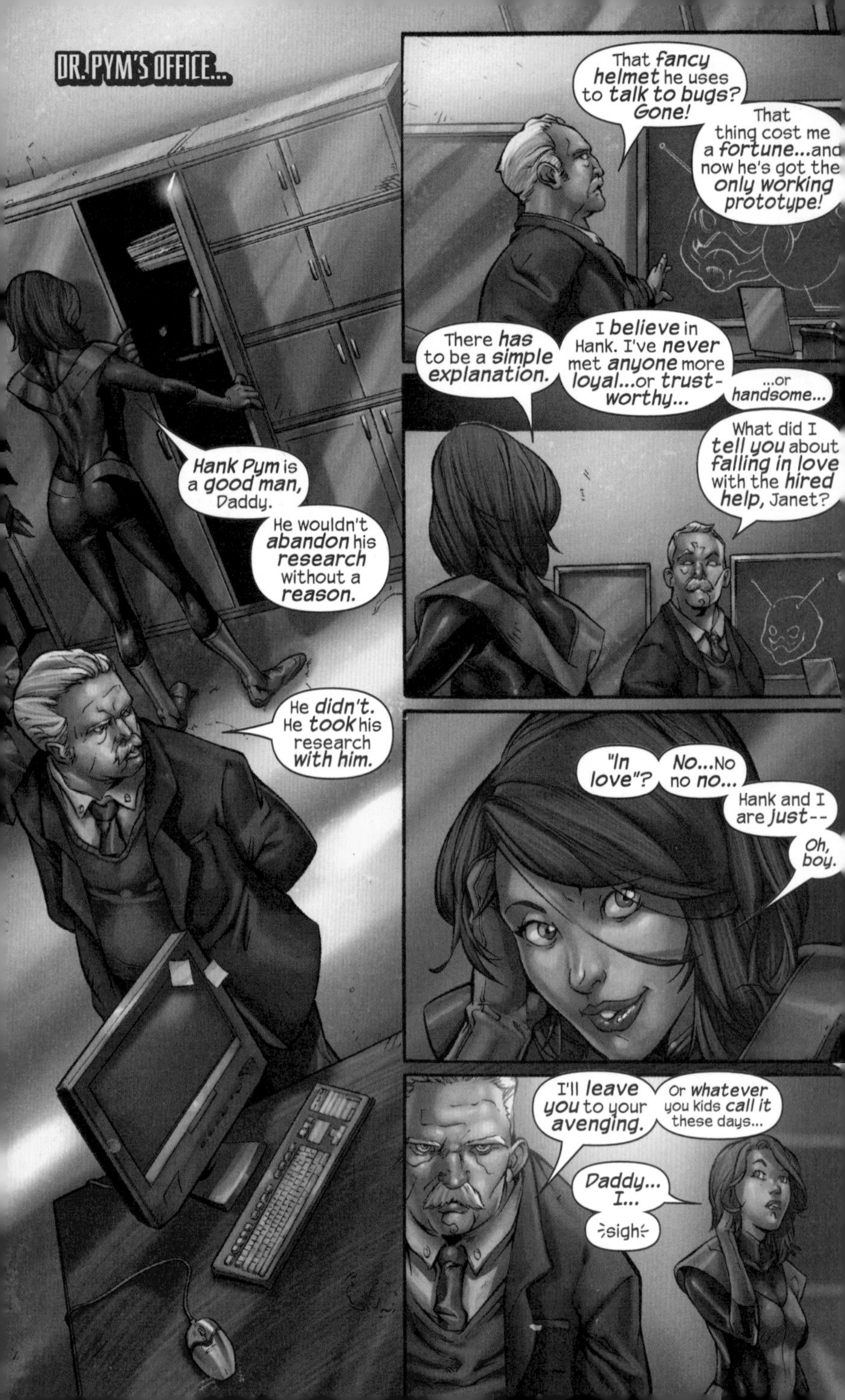
DR. PYM'S OFFICE...
Hank Pym is a good man, Daddy.
He wouldn't abandon his research without a reason.
He didn't. He took his research with him.
That fancy helmet he uses to talk to bugs? Gone!
That thing cost me a fortune...and now he's got the only working prototype!
There has to be a simple explanation.
I believe in Hank. I've never met anyone more loyal...or trust-worthy...
...or handsome...
What did I tell you about falling in love with the hired help, Janet?
"In love"?
No...No no no...
Hank and I are just--
Oh, boy.
I'll leave you to your avenging.
Or whatever you kids call it these days...
Daddy... I...
sigh

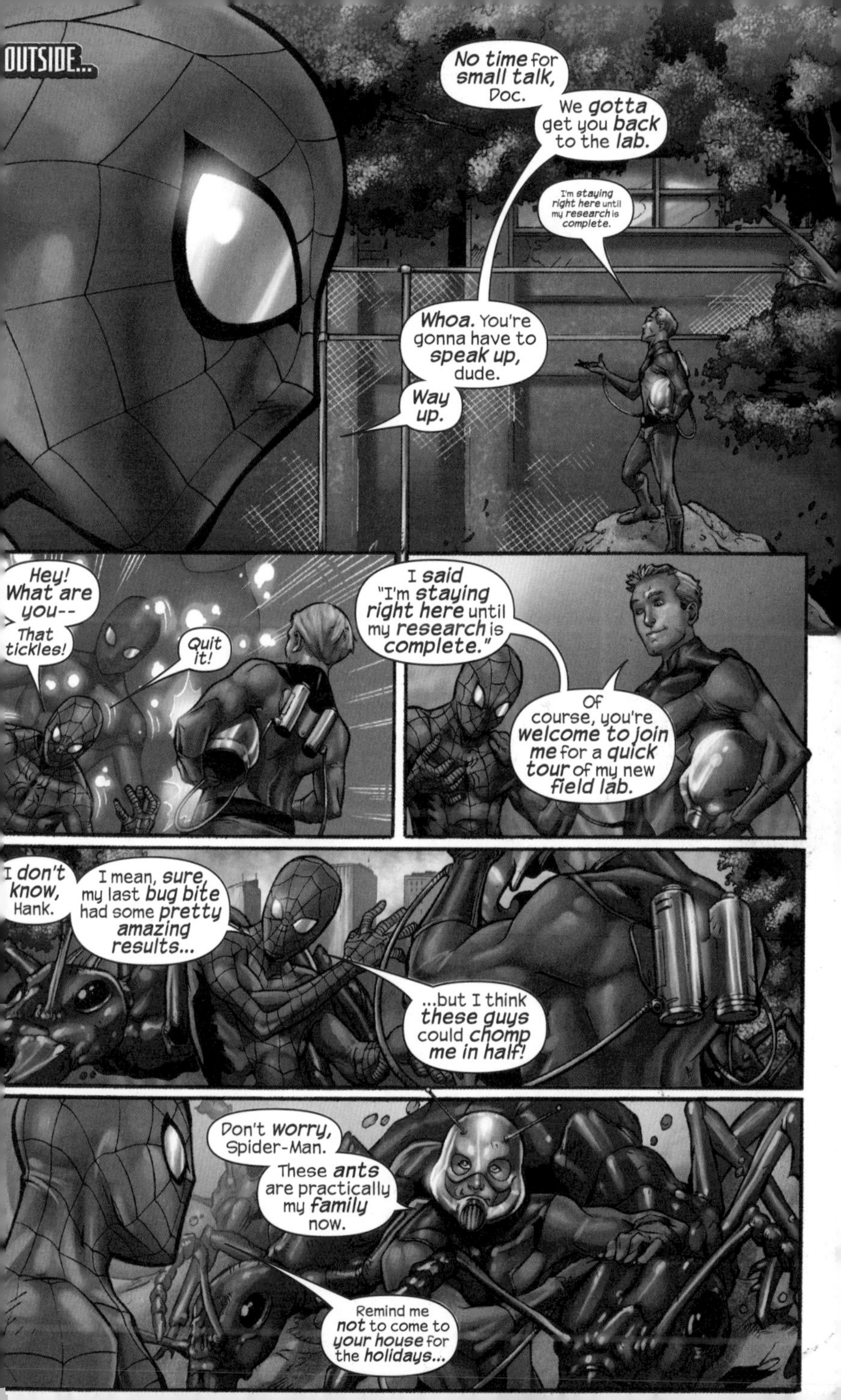

OUTSIDE...
No time for small talk, Doc.
We gotta get you back to the lab.
I'm staying right here until my research is complete.
Whoa. You're gonna have to speak up, dude.
Way up.
Hey! What are you--
That tickles!
Quit it!
I said "I'm staying right here until my research is complete."
Of course, you're welcome to join me for a quick tour of my new field lab.
I don't know, Hank.
I mean, sure, my last bug bite had some pretty amazing results...
...but I think these guys could chomp me in half!
Don't worry, Spider-Man.
These ants are practically my family now.
Remind me not to come to your house for the holidays...

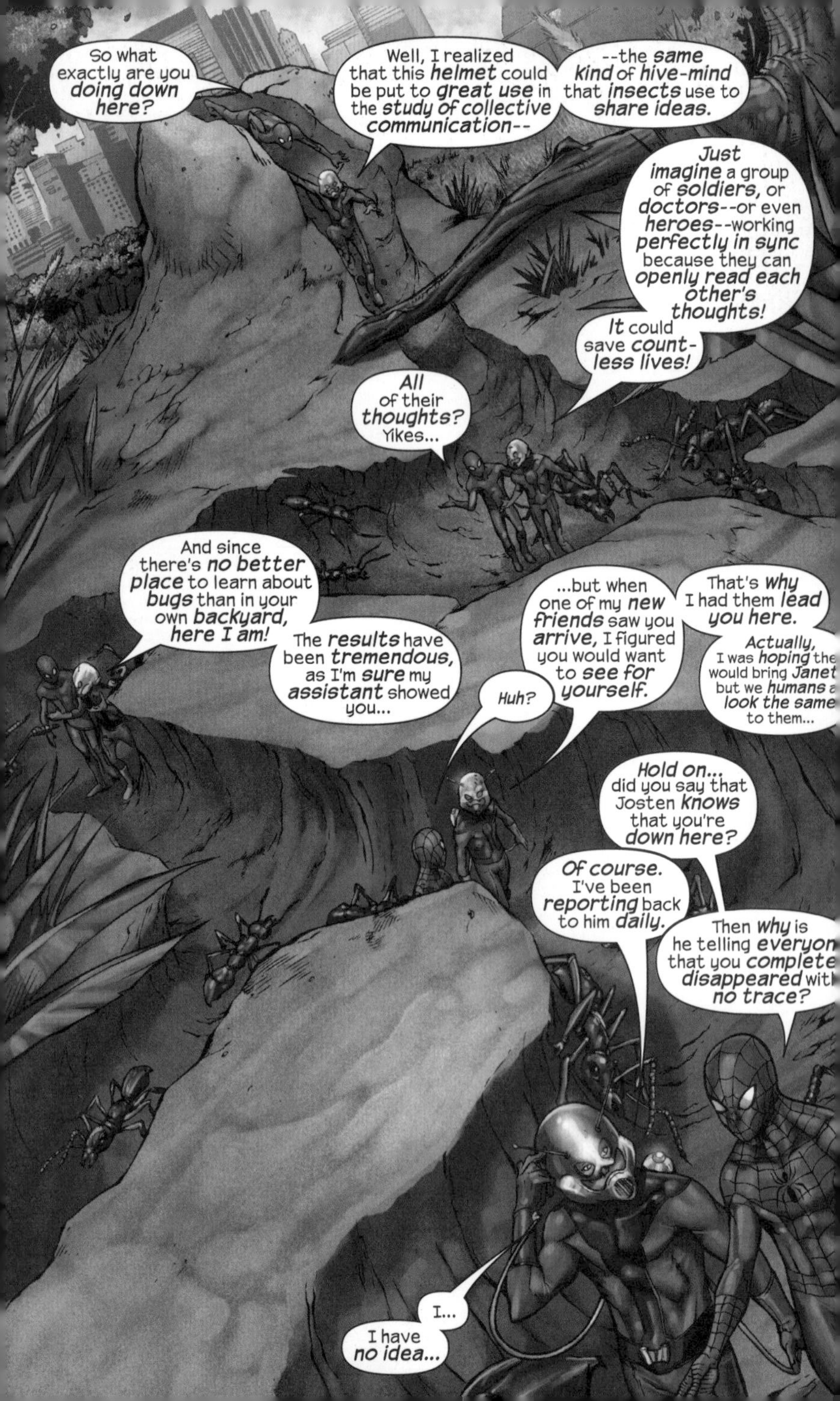
So what exactly are you doing down here?
Well, I realized that this helmet could be put to great use in the study of collective communication--
--the same kind of hive-mind that insects use to share ideas.
Just imagine a group of soldiers, or doctors--or even heroes--working perfectly in sync because they can openly read each other's thoughts!
It could save count-less lives!
All of their thoughts? Yikes...
And since there's no better place to learn about bugs than in your own backyard, here I am!
The results have been tremendous, as I'm sure my assistant showed you...
...but when one of my new friends saw you arrive, I figured you would want to see for yourself.
Huh?
That's why I had them lead you here.
Hold on... did you say that Josten knows that you're down here?
Of course. I've been reporting back to him daily.
I... I have no idea...

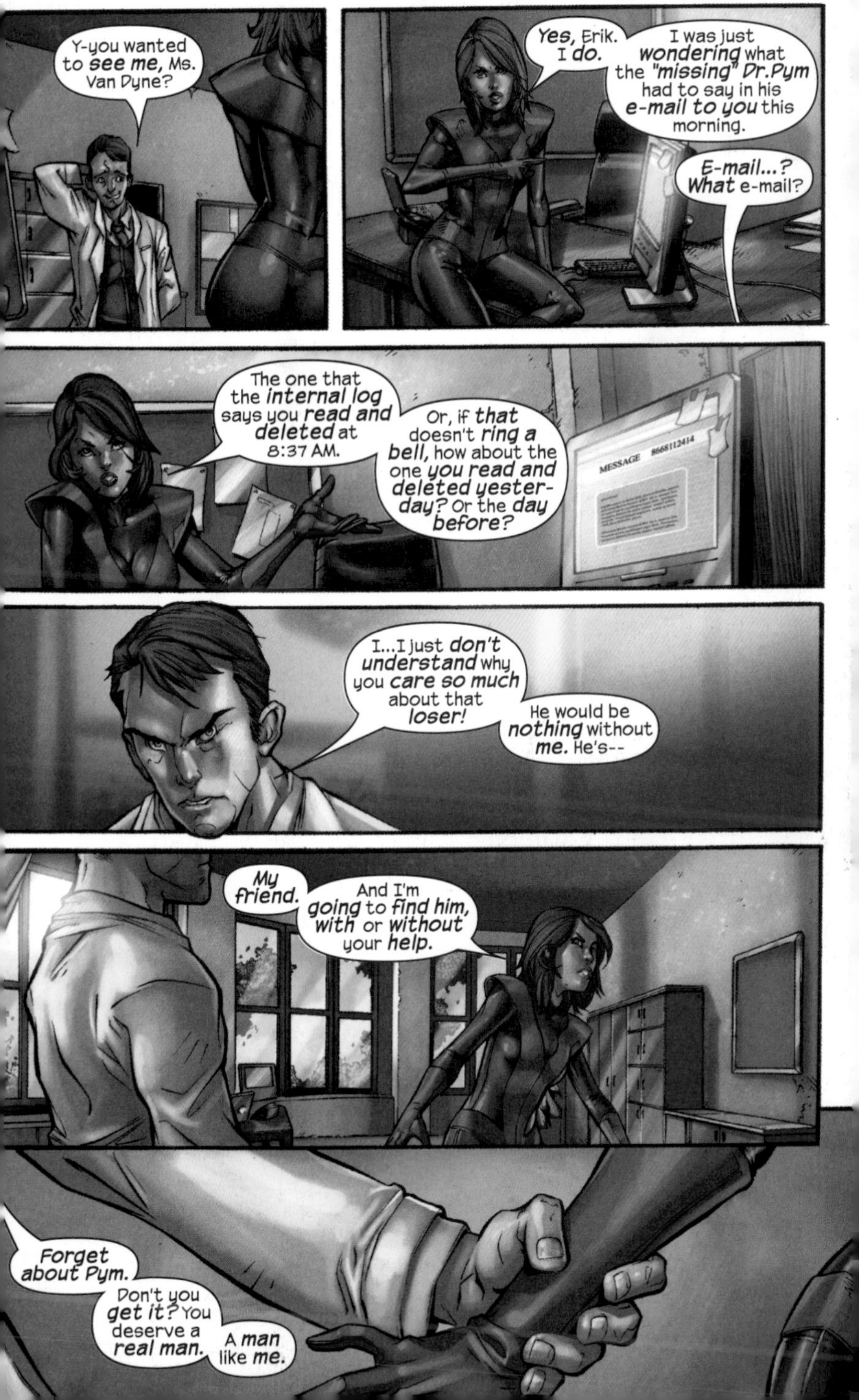

Y-you wanted to see me, Ms. Van Dyne?
Yes, Erik. I do.
I was just wondering what the "missing" Dr. Pym had to say in his e-mail to you this morning.
E-mail...? What e-mail?
The one that the internal log says you read and deleted at 8:37 AM.
Or, if that doesn't ring a bell, how about the one you read and deleted yester-day? Or the day before?
MESSAGE 8668112414
I...I just don't understand why you care so much about that loser!
He would be nothing without me. He's--
My friend.
And I'm going to find him, with or without your help.
Forget about Pym.
Don't you get it? You deserve a real man.
A man like me.

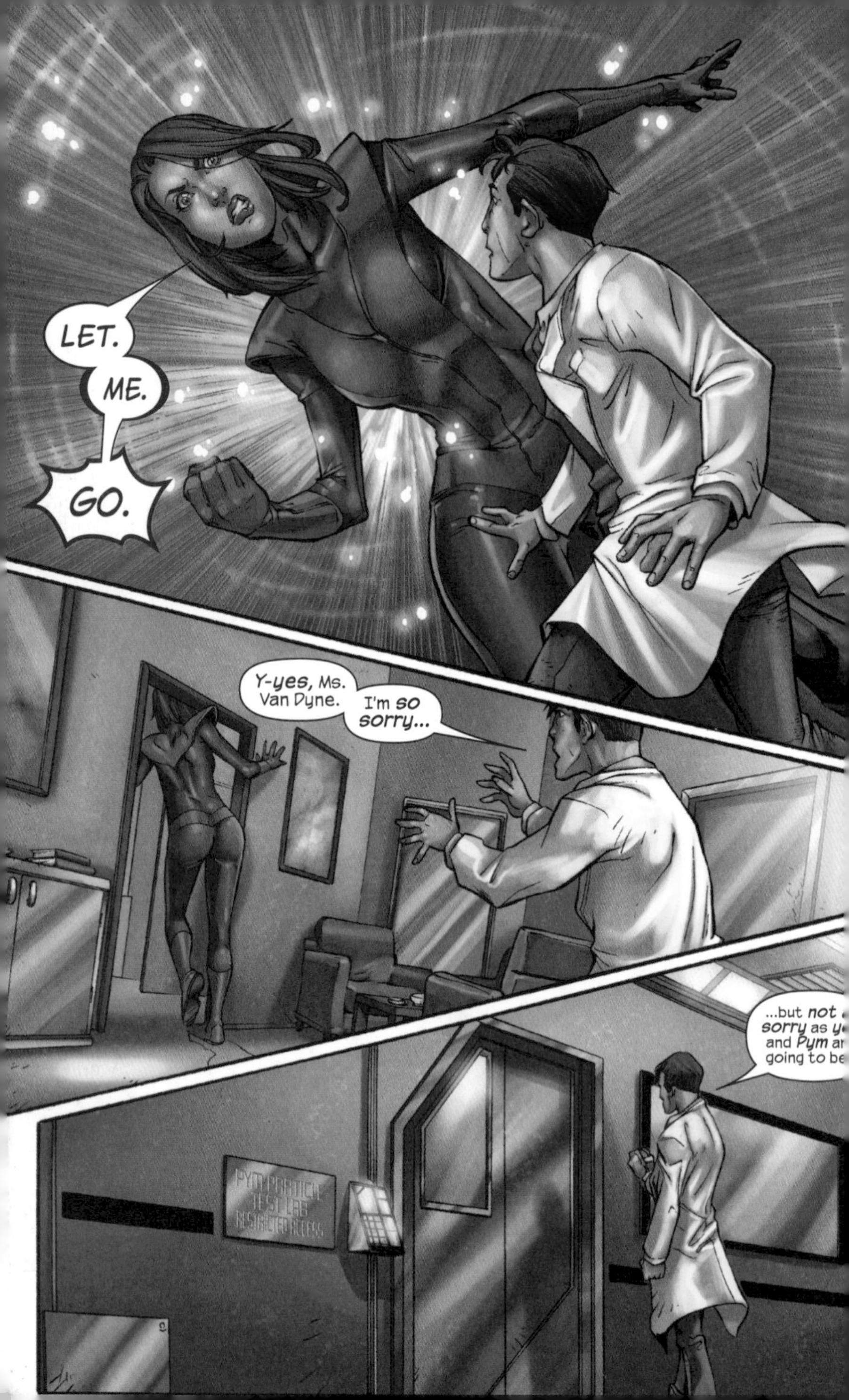
LET.
ME.
GO.
Y-yes, Ms. Van Dyne.
I'm so sorry...
...but not
sorry as
and Pym
going to be
PYM PARTICLE TEST LAB RESTRICTED ACCESS

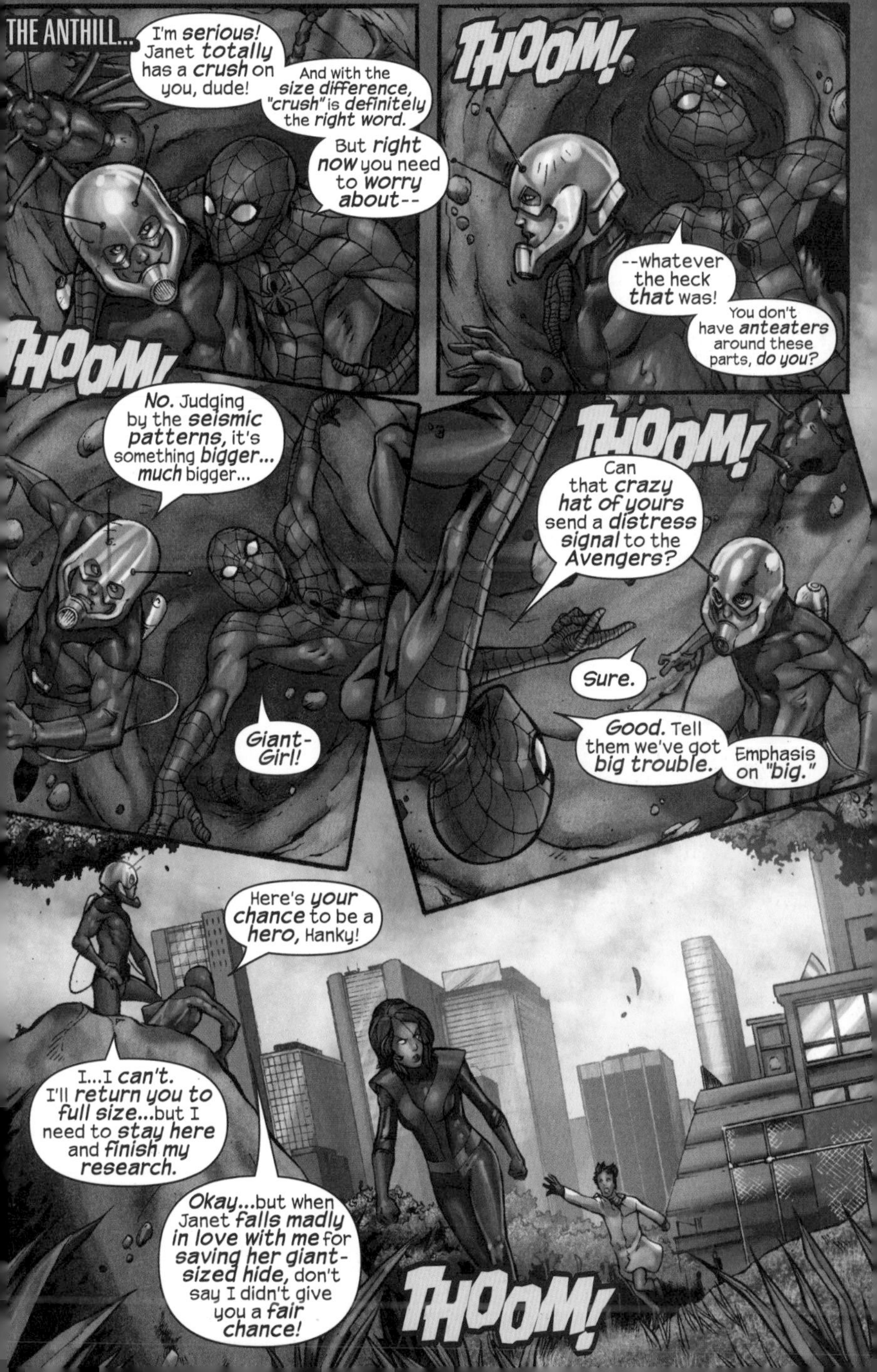
THE ANTHILL...
I'm serious! Janet totally has a crush on you, dude!
And with the size difference, "crush" is definitely the right word.
But right now you need to worry about--
THOOM!
--whatever the heck that was!
You don't have anteaters around these parts, do you?
THOOM!
No. Judging by the seismic patterns, it's something bigger... much bigger...
Giant-Girl!
THOOM!
Can that crazy hat of yours send a distress signal to the Avengers?
Sure.
Good. Tell them we've got big trouble.
Emphasis on "big."
Here's your chance to be a hero, Hanky!
I...I can't. I'll return you to full size...but I need to stay here and finish my research.
Okay...but when Janet falls madly in love with me for saving her giant-sized hide, don't say I didn't give you a fair chance!
THOOM!

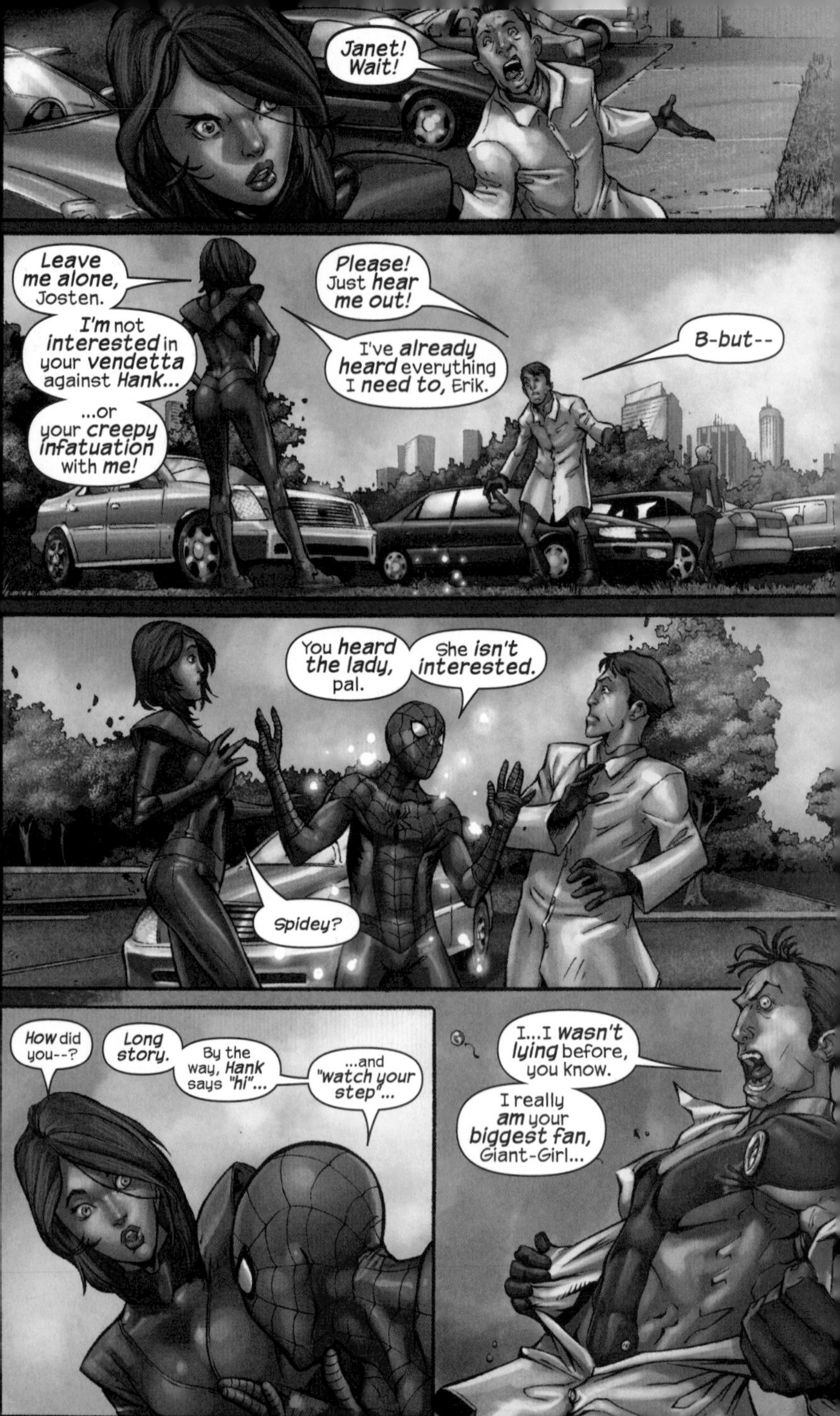
Janet! Wait!
Leave me alone, Josten.
I'm not interested in your vendetta against Hank...
...or your creepy infatuation with me!
Please! Just hear me out!
I've already heard everything I need to, Erik.
B-but--
You heard the lady, pal.
She isn't interested.
Spidey?
How did you--?
Long story.
By the way, Hank says "hi"...
...and "watch your step"...
I...I wasn't lying before, you know.
I really am your biggest fan, Giant-Girl...

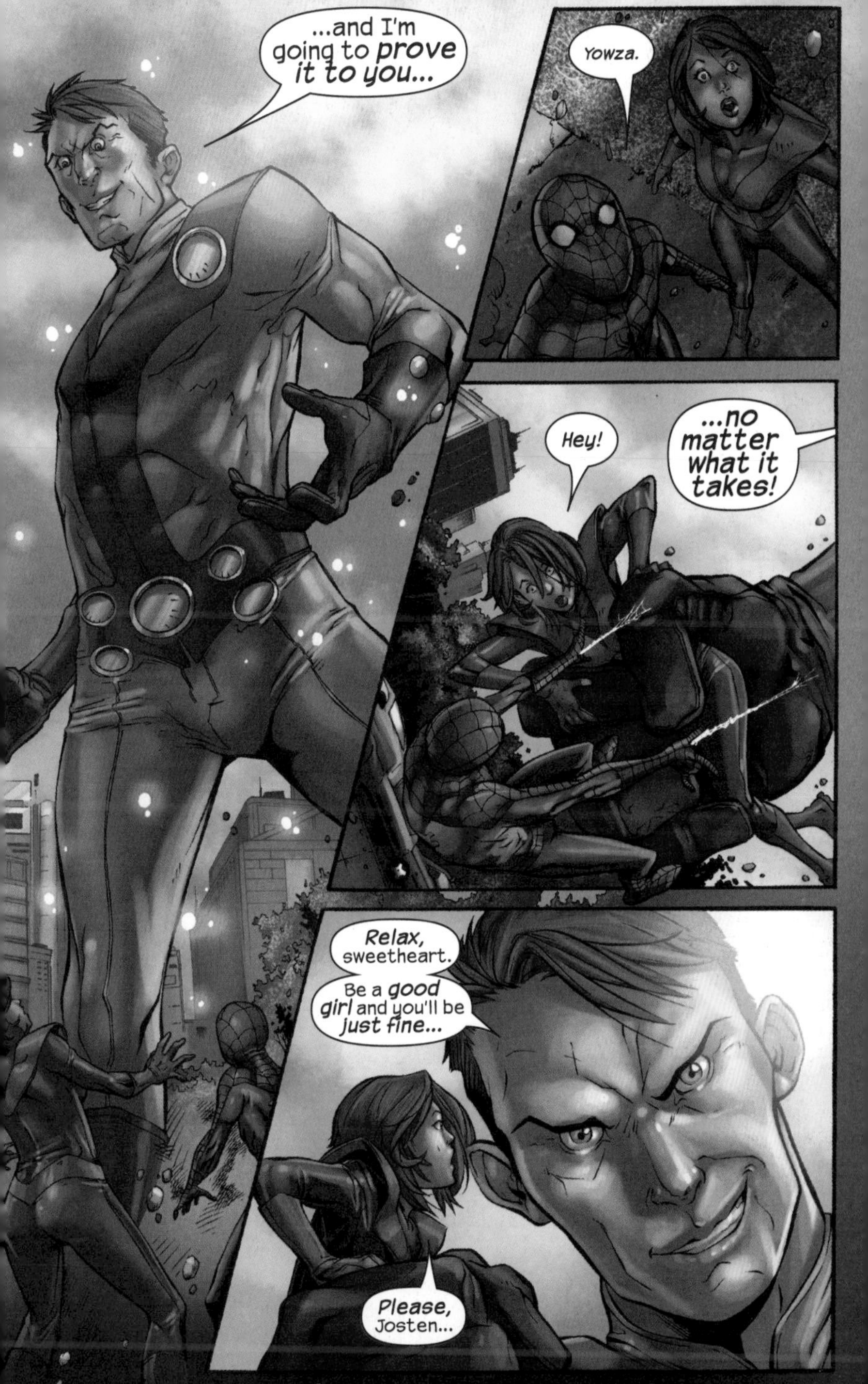
...and I'm going to prove it to you...
Yowza.
Hey!
...no matter what it takes!
Relax, sweetheart.
Be a good girl and you'll be just fine...
Please, Josten...

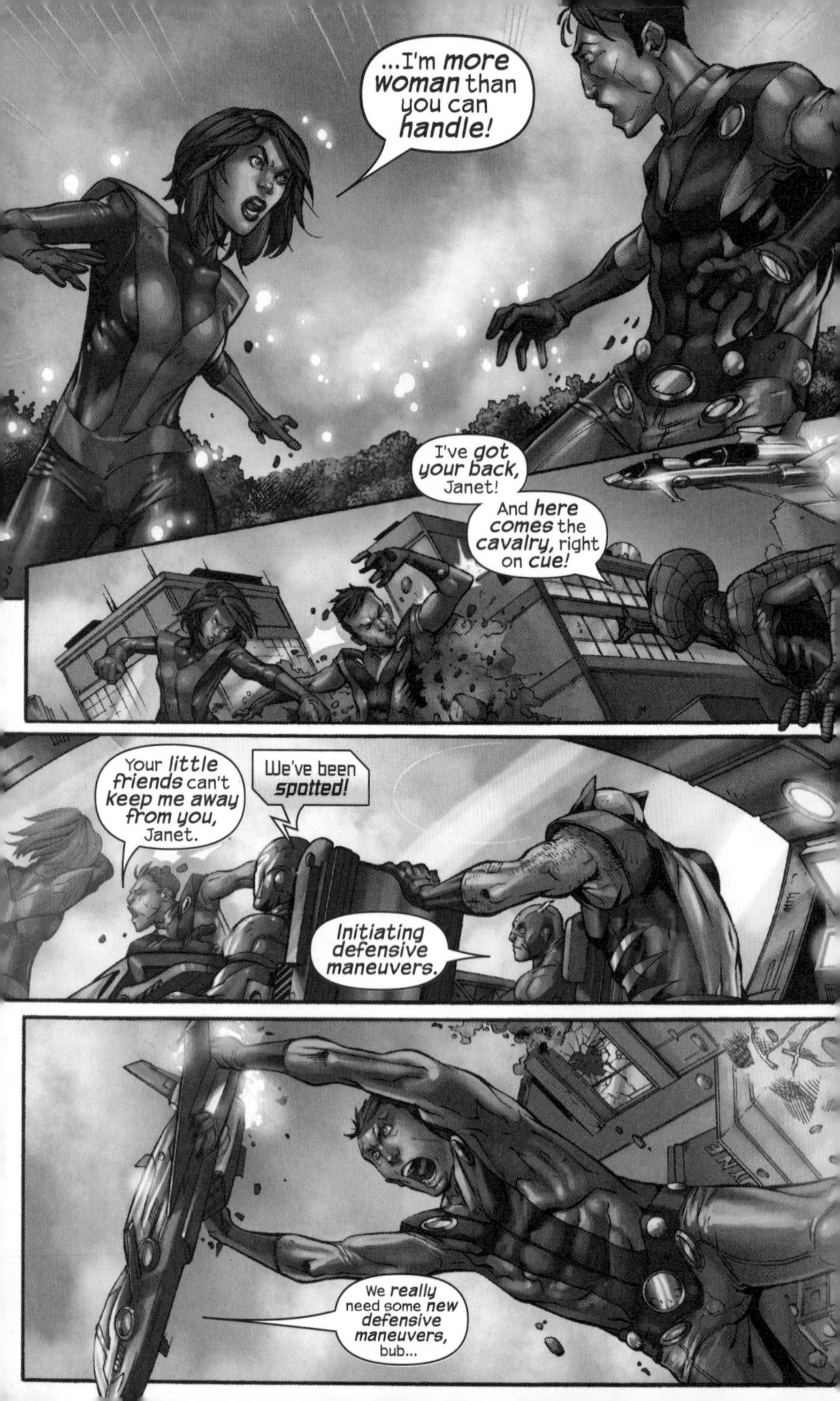
...I'm more woman than you can handle!
I've got your back, Janet!
And here comes the cavalry, right on cue!
Your little friends can't keep me away from you, Janet.
We've been spotted!
Initiating defensive maneuvers.
We really need some new defensive maneuvers, bub...

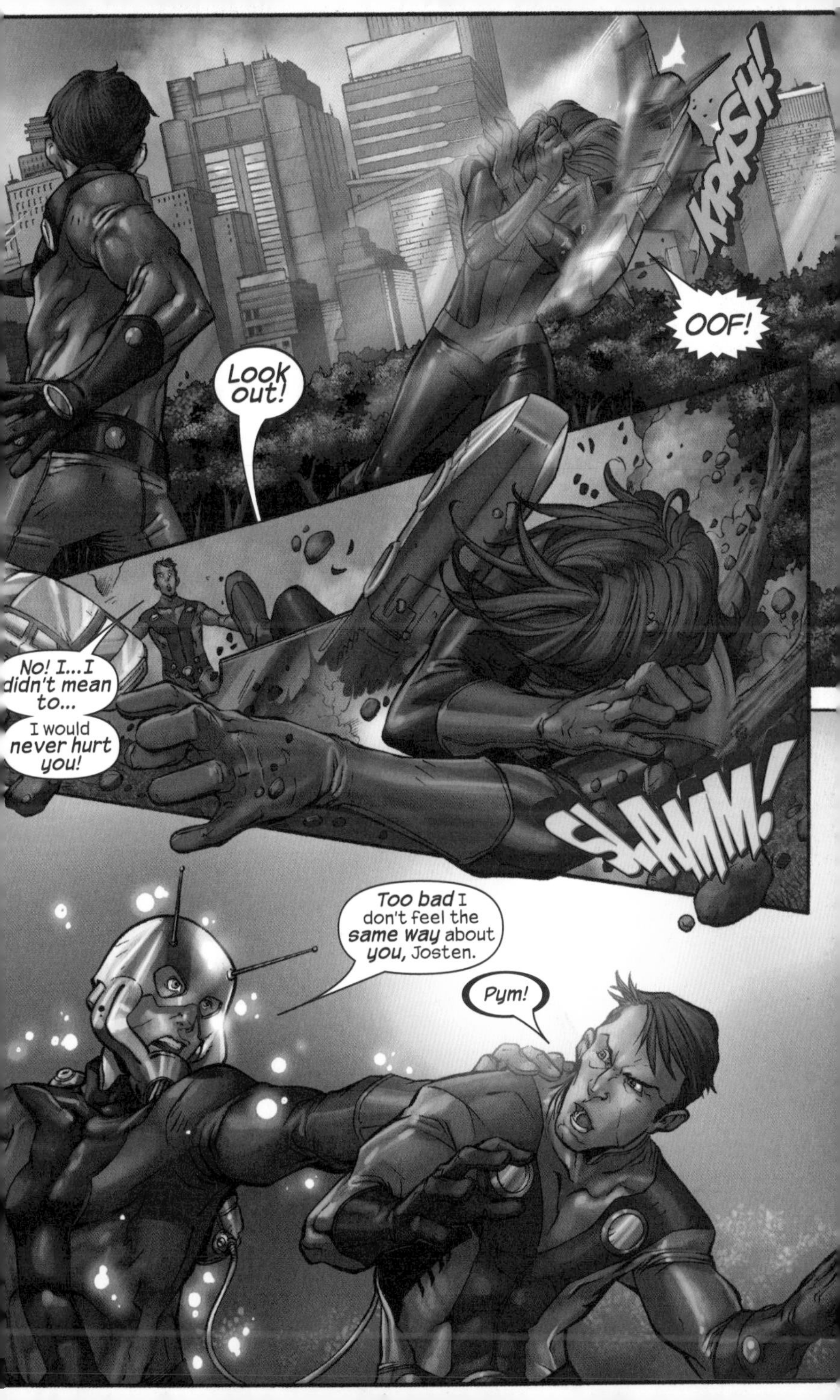

KRASH!
OOF!
Look out!
SLAMM!
No! I...I didn't mean to...
I would never hurt you!
Too bad I don't feel the same way about you, Josten.
Pym!

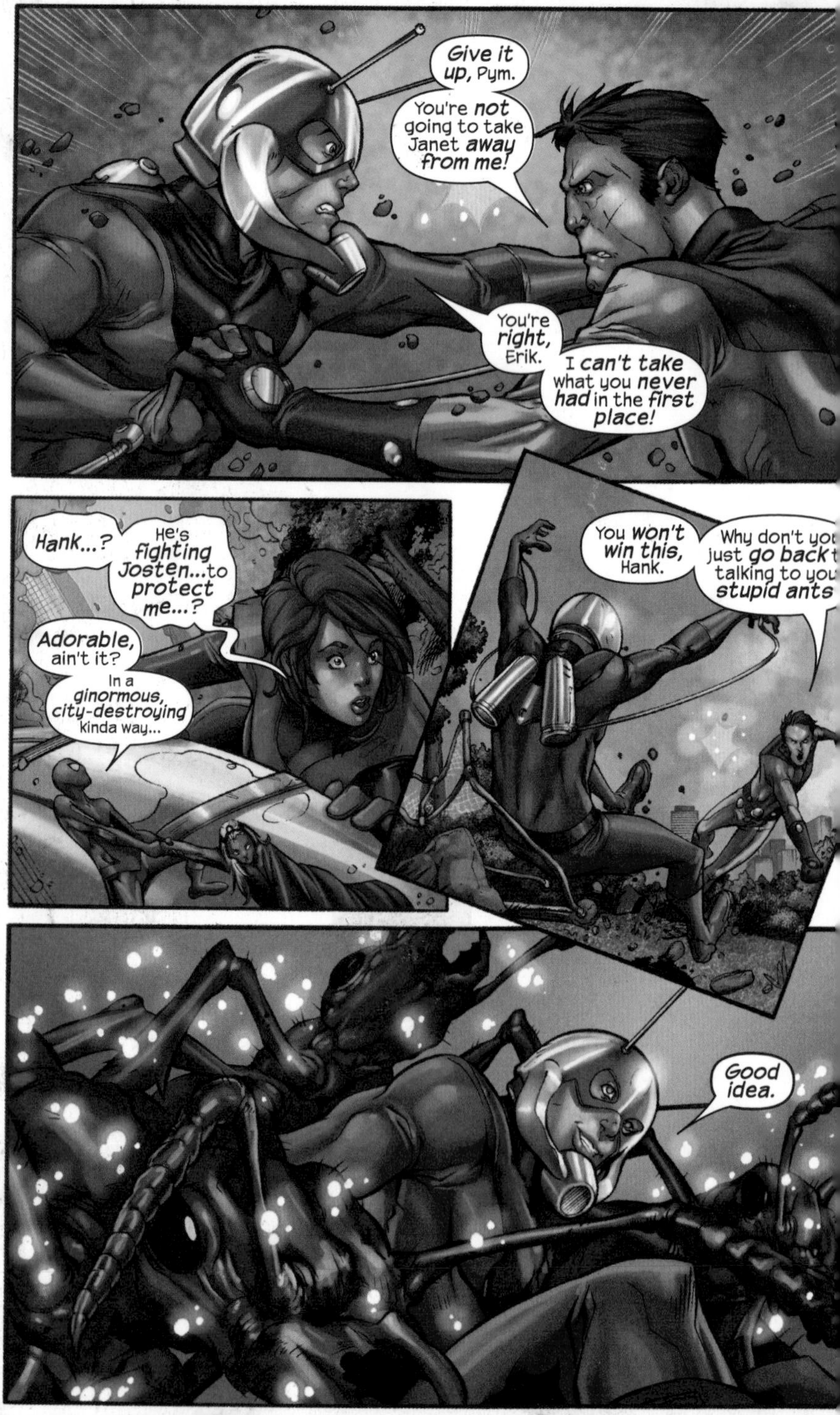
Give it up, Pym.
You're not going to take Janet away from me!
You're right, Erik.
I can't take what you never had in the first place!
Hank...?
He's fighting Josten...to protect me...?
Adorable, ain't it?
In a ginormous, city-destroying kinda way...
You won't win this, Hank.
Why don't yo just go back t talking to you stupid ants
Good idea.

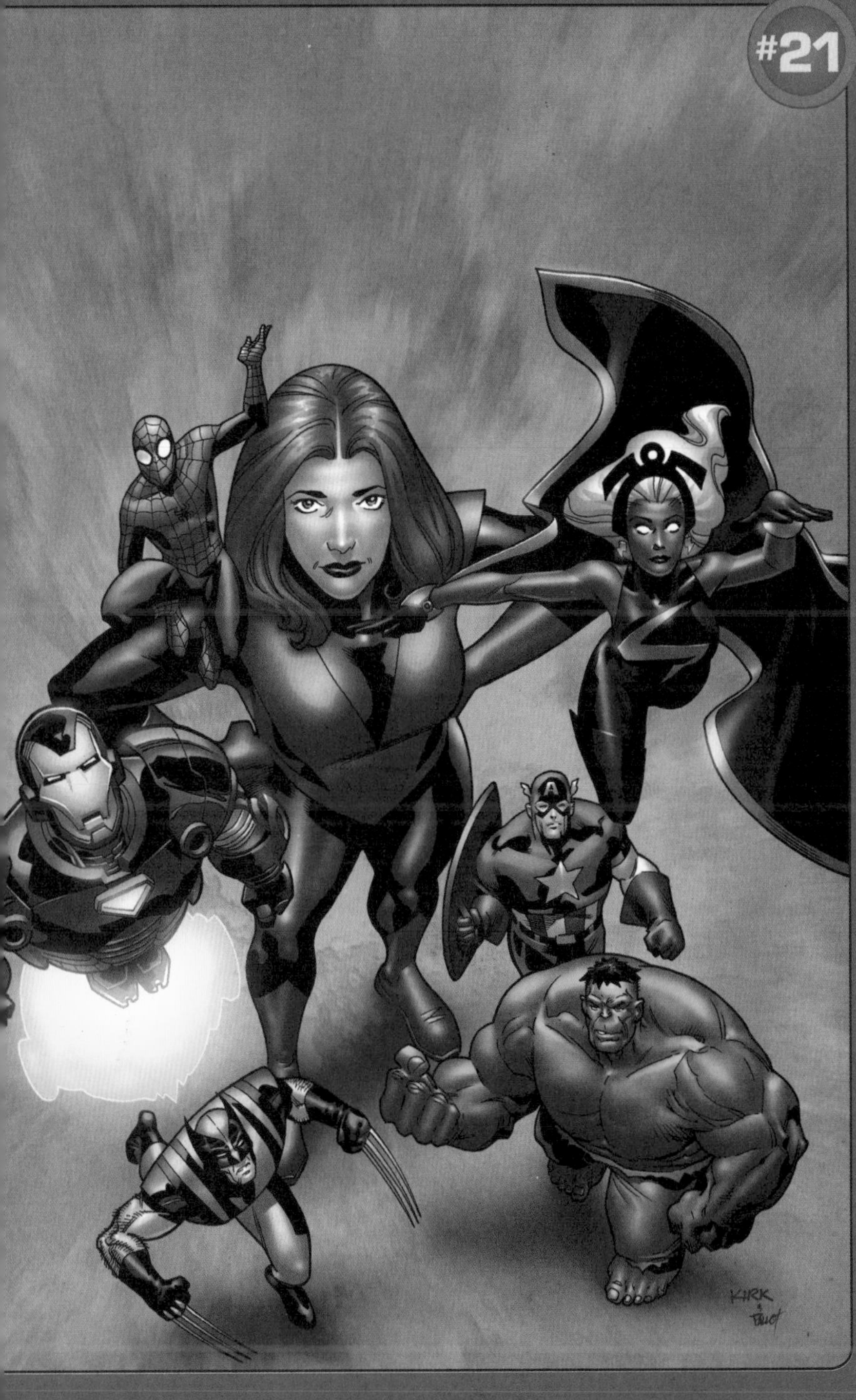
#21
KIRK

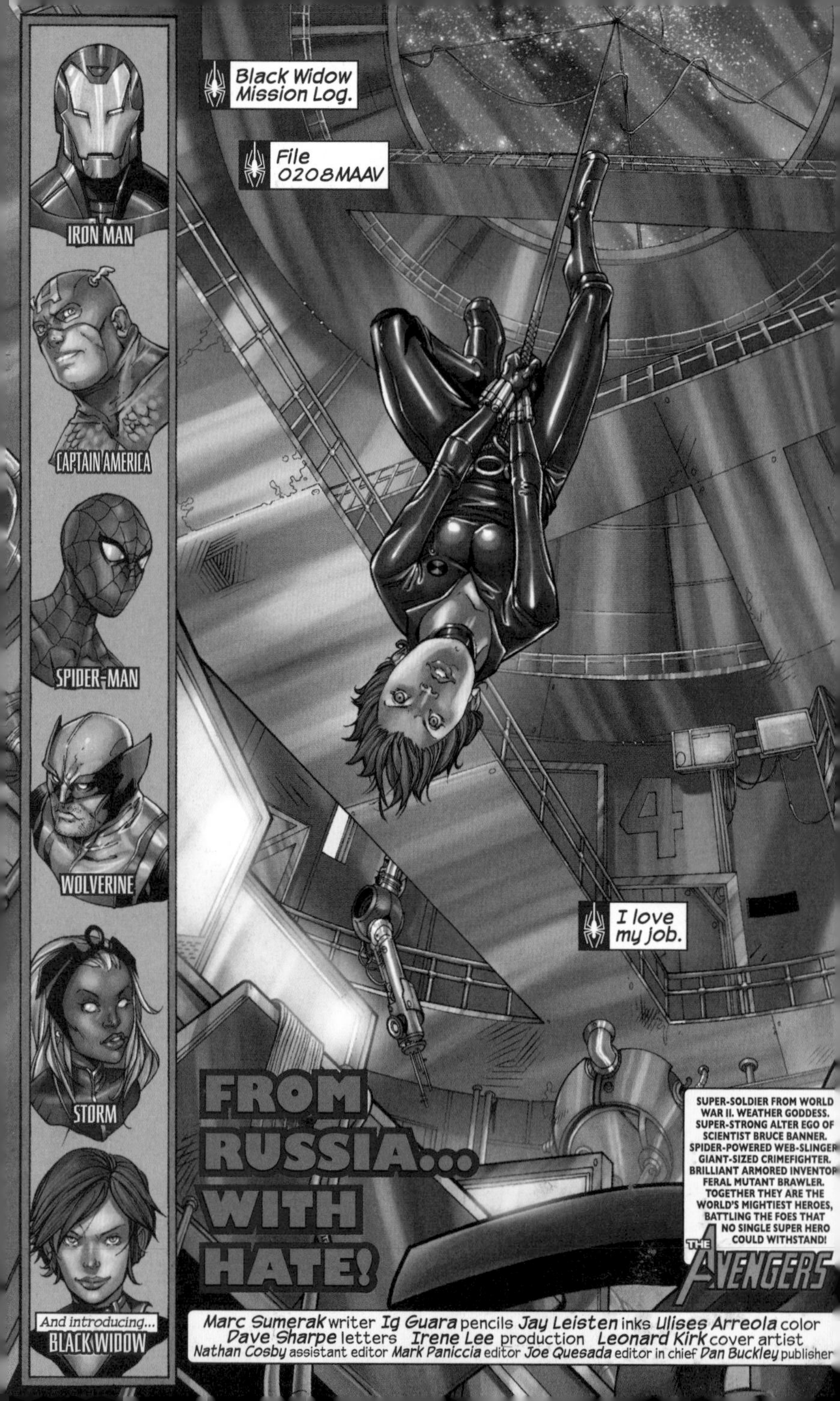

IRON MAN
CAPTAIN AMERICA
SPIDER-MAN
WOLVERINE
STORM
And introducing...
BLACK WIDOW
Black Widow Mission Log.
File 0208MAAV
I love my job.
FROM RUSSIA... WITH HATE!
SUPER-SOLDIER FROM WORLD WAR II. WEATHER GODDESS. SUPER-STRONG ALTER EGO OF SCIENTIST BRUCE BANNER. SPIDER-POWERED WEB-SLINGER GIANT-SIZED CRIMEFIGHTER. BRILLIANT ARMORED INVENTOR FERAL MUTANT BRAWLER. TOGETHER THEY ARE THE WORLD'S MIGHTIEST HEROES, BATTLING THE FOES THAT NO SINGLE SUPER HERO COULD WITHSTAND!
THE AVENGERS
Marc Sumerak writer Ig Guara pencils Jay Leisten inks Ulises Arreola color
Dave Sharpe letters Irene Lee production Leonard Kirk cover artist
Nathan Cosby assistant editor Mark Paniccia editor Joe Quesada editor in chief Dan Buckley publisher

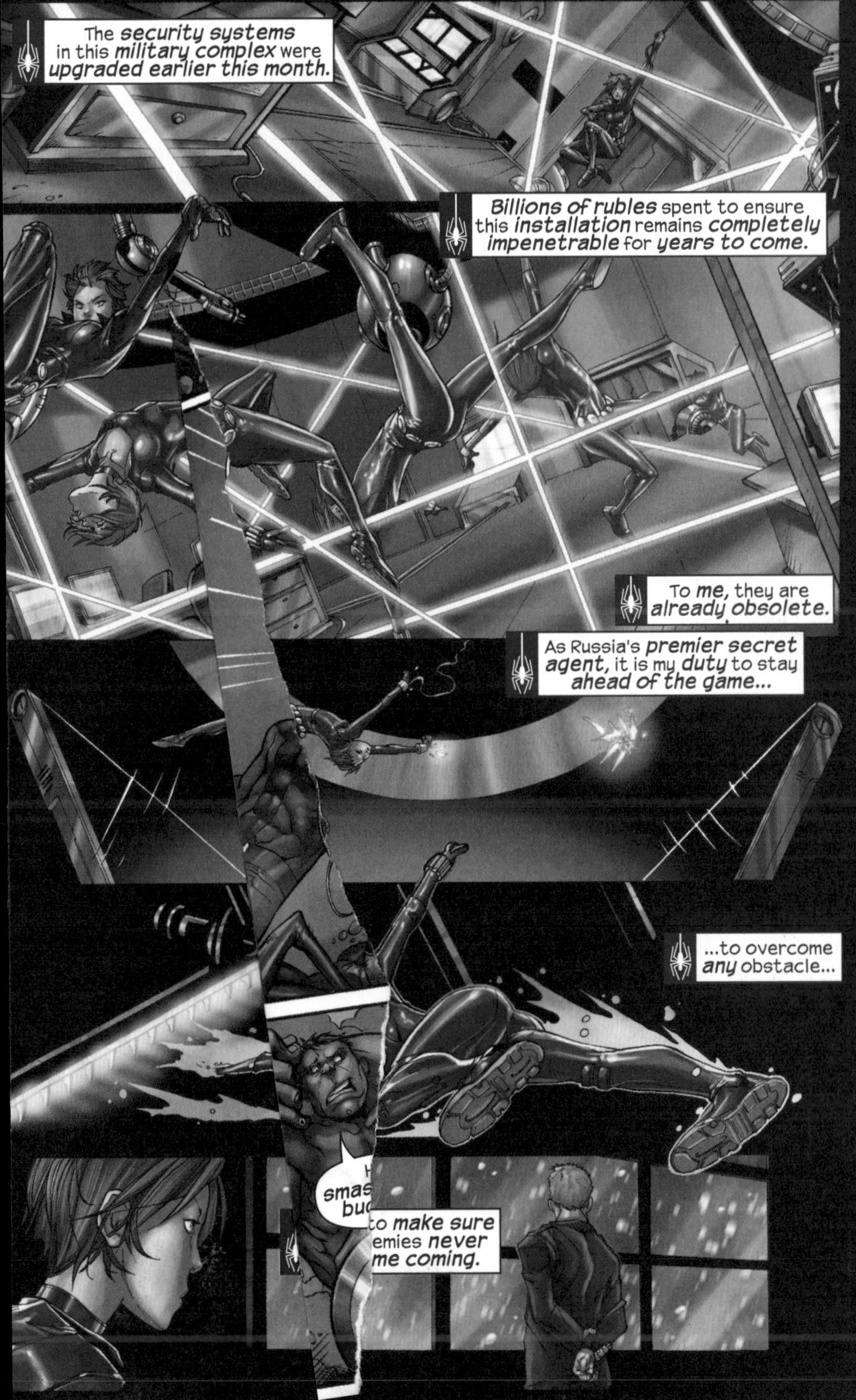
The security systems in this military complex were upgraded earlier this month.
Billions of rubles spent to ensure this installation remains completely impenetrable for years to come.
To me, they are already obsolete.
As Russia's premier secret agent, it is my duty to stay ahead of the game...
...to overcome any obstacle...
to make sure emies never me coming.

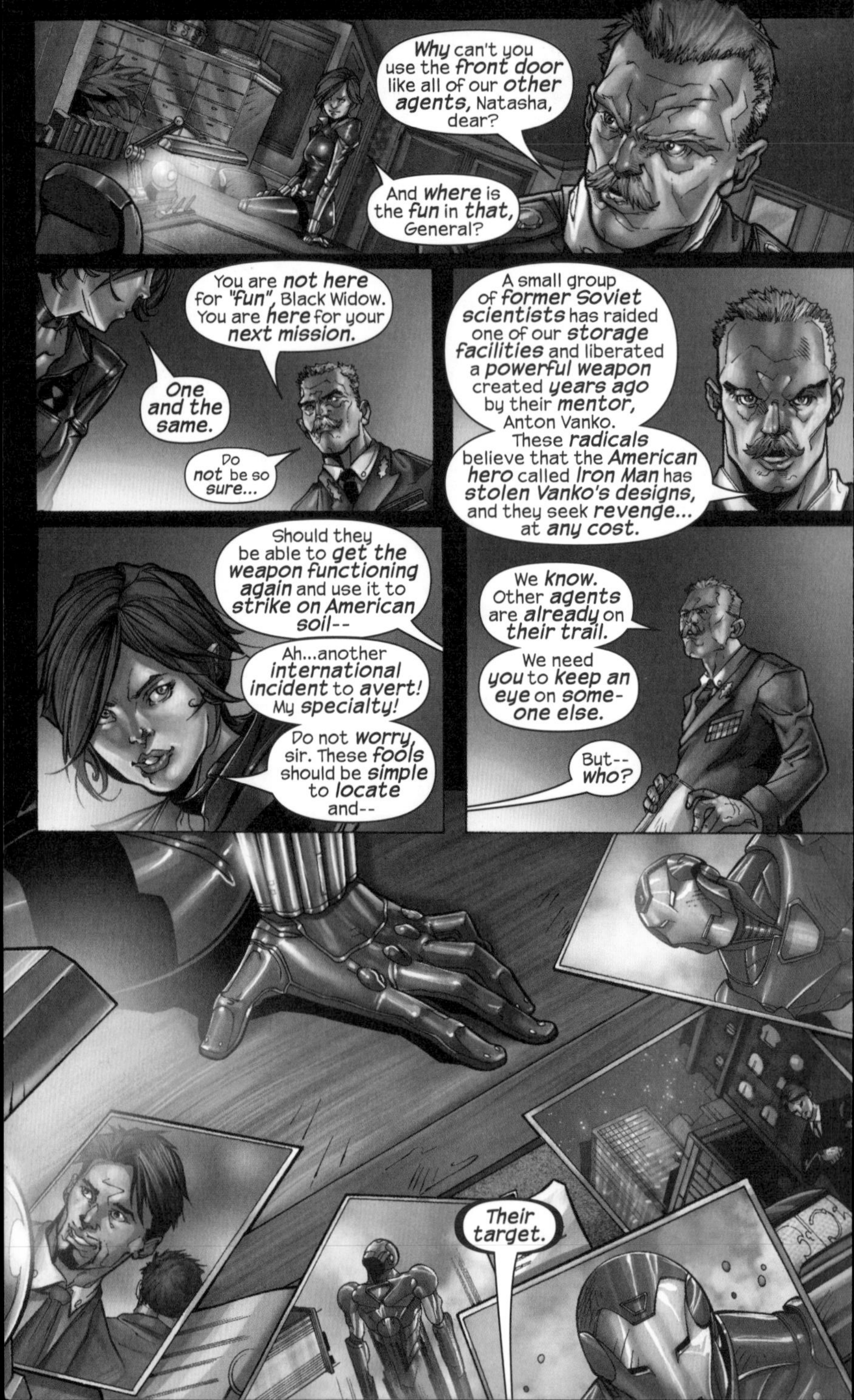

Why can't you use the front door like all of our other agents, Natasha, dear?
And where is the fun in that, General?
You are not here for "fun", Black Widow. You are here for your next mission.
One and the same.
Do not be so sure...
A small group of former Soviet scientists has raided one of our storage facilities and liberated a powerful weapon created years ago by their mentor, Anton Vanko.
These radicals believe that the American hero called Iron Man has stolen Vanko's designs, and they seek revenge... at any cost.
Should they be able to get the weapon functioning again and use it to strike on American soil--
Ah...another international incident to avert! My specialty!
Do not worry, sir. These fools should be simple to locate and--
We know. Other agents are already on their trail.
We need you to keep an eye on some-one else.
But-- who?
Their target.

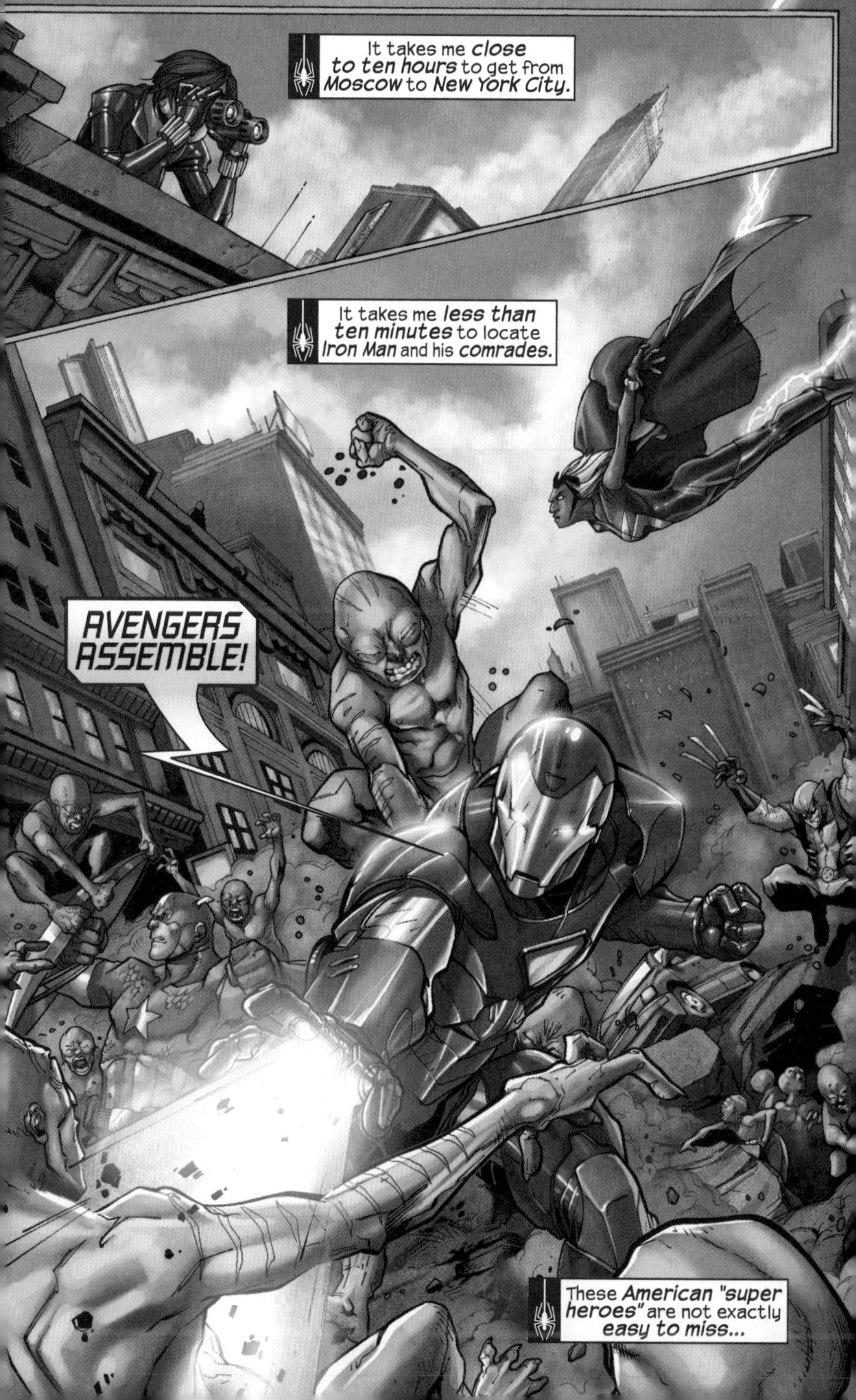
It takes me close to ten hours to get from Moscow to New York City.
It takes me less than ten minutes to locate Iron Man and his comrades.
AVENGERS ASSEMBLE!
These American "super heroes" are not exactly easy to miss...

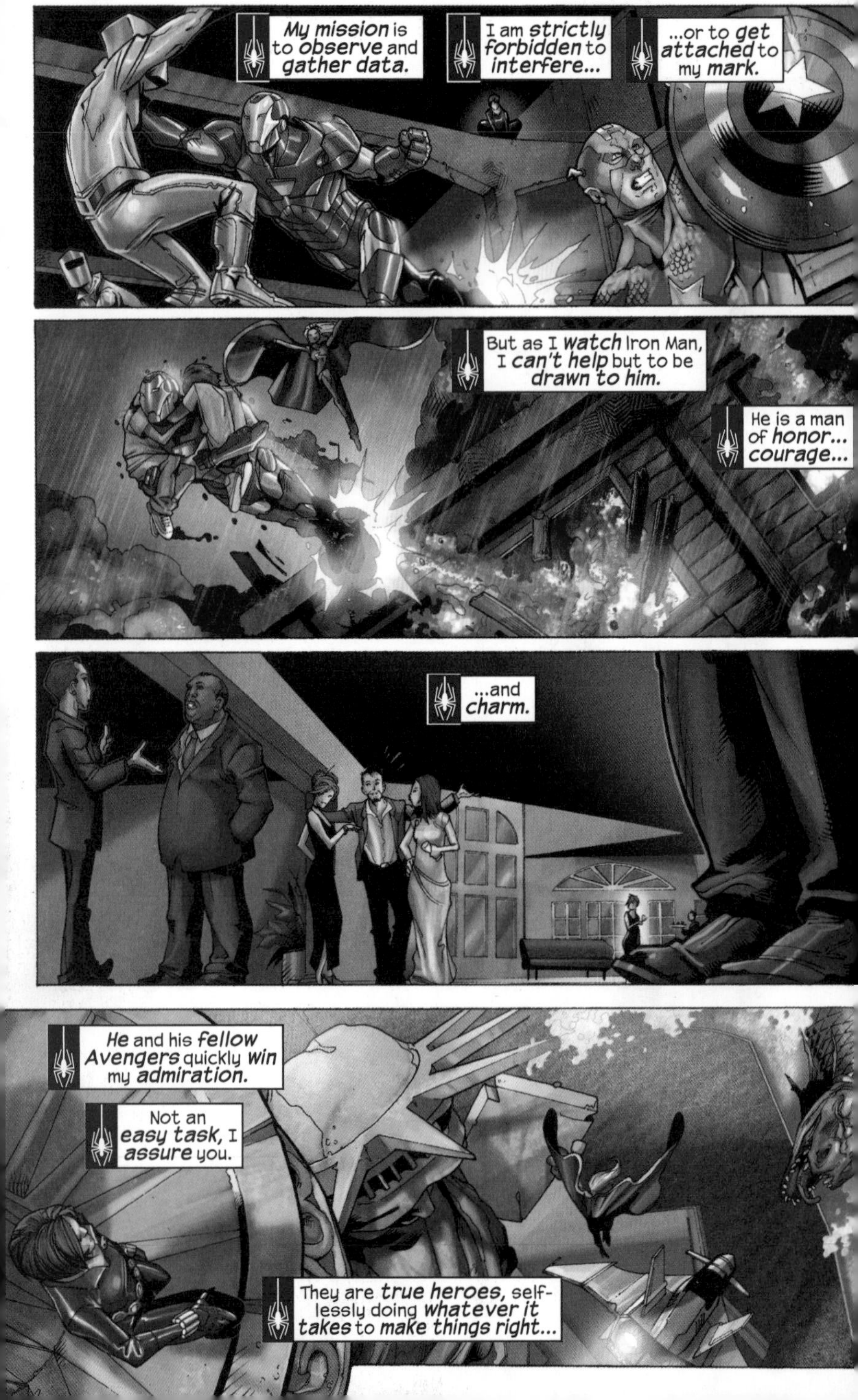

My mission is to observe and gather data.
I am strictly forbidden to interfere...
...or to get attached to my mark.
But as I watch Iron Man, I can't help but to be drawn to him.
He is a man of honor... courage...
...and charm.
He and his fellow Avengers quickly win my admiration.
Not an easy task, I assure you.
They are true heroes, self-lessly doing whatever it takes to make things right...

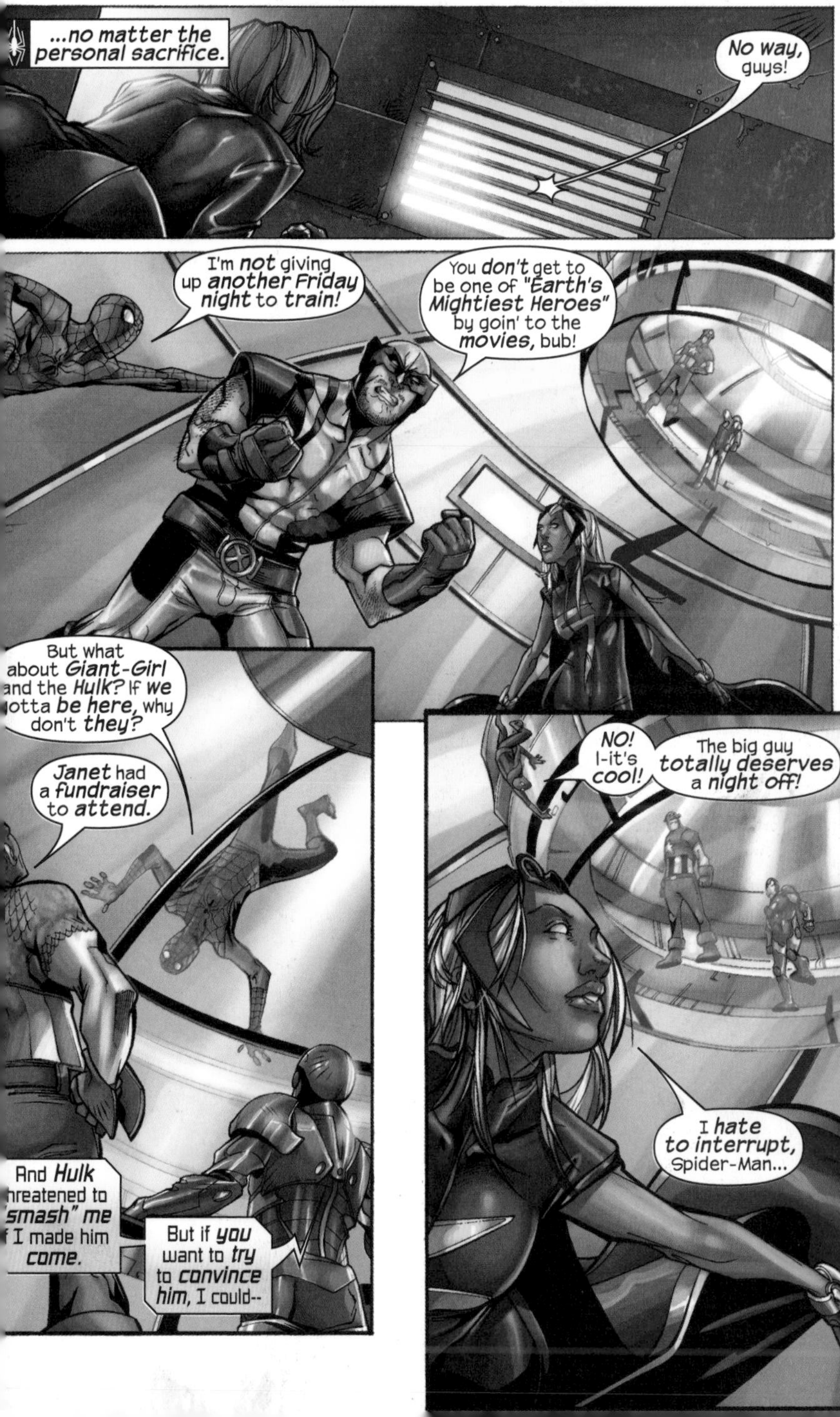

...no matter the personal sacrifice.
No way, guys!
I'm not giving up another Friday night to train!
You don't get to be one of "Earth's Mightiest Heroes" by goin' to the movies, bub!
But what about Giant-Girl and the Hulk? If we gotta be here, why don't they?
Janet had a fundraiser to attend.
And Hulk threatened to "smash" me if I made him come.
But if you want to try to convince him, I could--
NO! I-it's cool!
The big guy totally deserves a night off!
I hate to interrupt, Spider-Man...

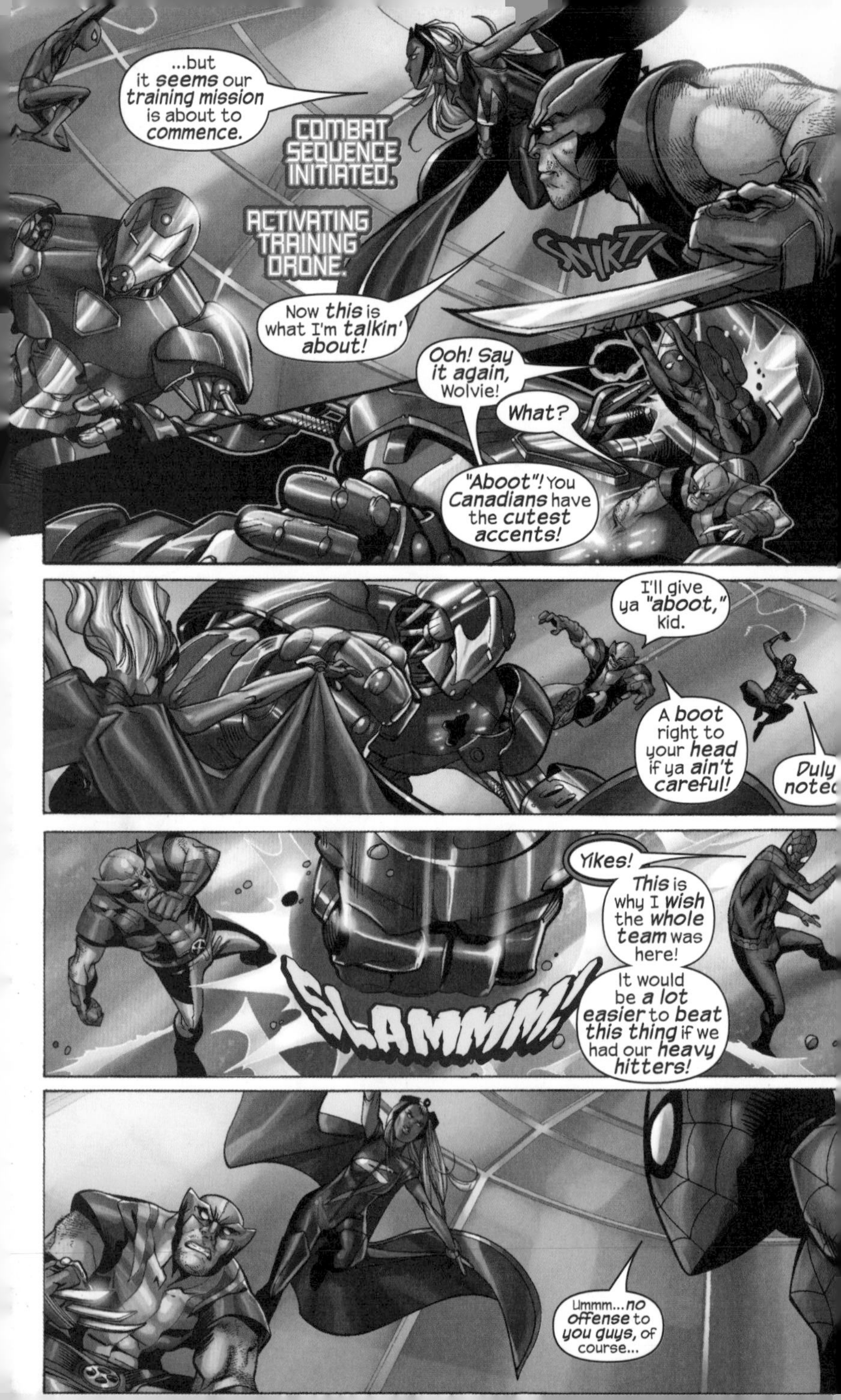
...but it seems our training mission is about to commence.
COMBAT SEQUENCE INITIATED.
ACTIVATING TRAINING DRONE.
SNIKT!
Now this is what I'm talkin' about!
Ooh! Say it again, Wolvie!
What?
"Aboot"! You Canadians have the cutest accents!
I'll give ya "aboot," kid.
A boot right to your head if ya ain't careful!
Yikes!
This is why I wish the whole team was here!
It would be a lot easier to beat this thing if we had our heavy hitters!
SLAMMM!
Ummm...no offense to you guys, of course...

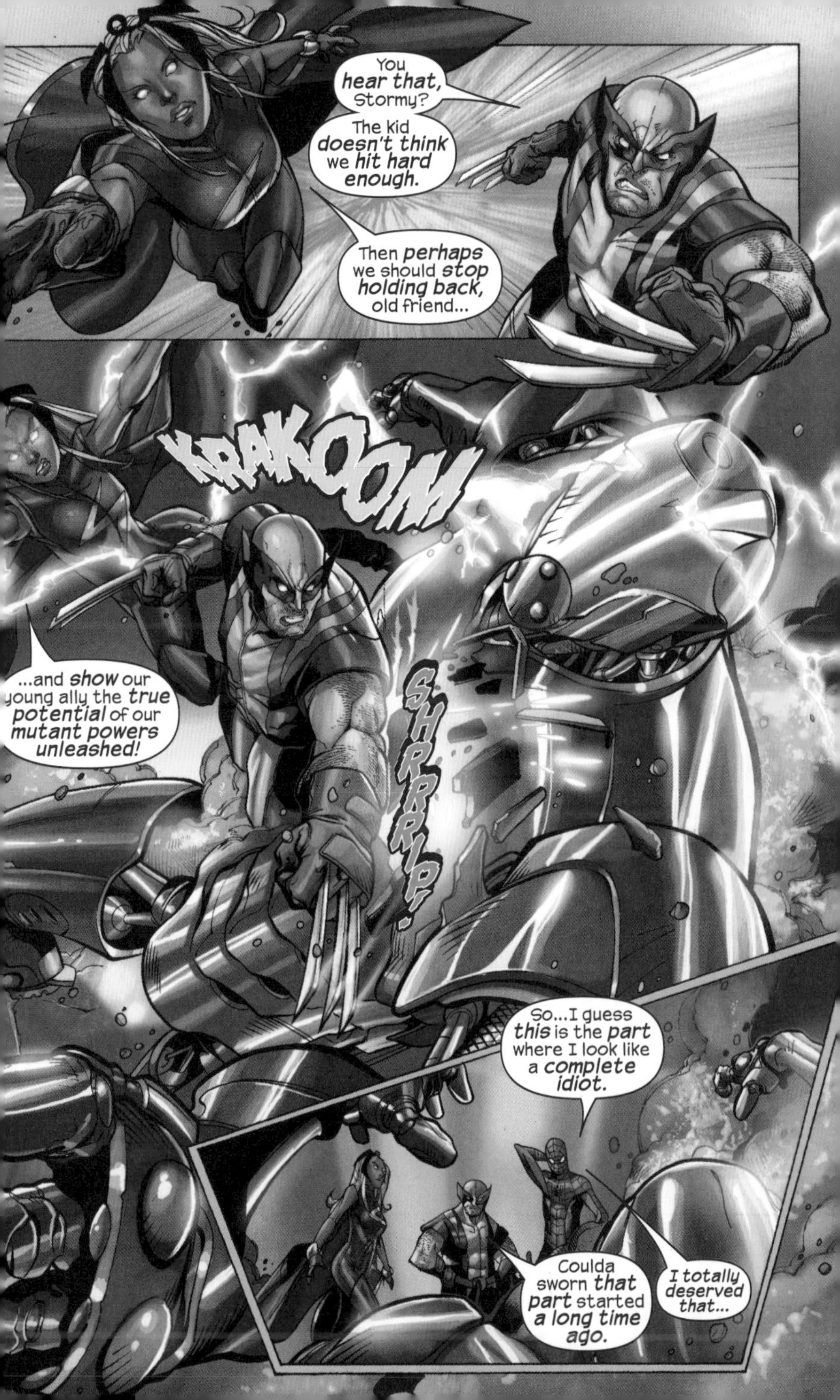

You hear that, Stormy?
The kid doesn't think we hit hard enough.
Then perhaps we should stop holding back, old friend...
KRAKOOM
...and show our young ally the true potential of our mutant powers unleashed!
SHRRRIP!
So...I guess this is the part where I look like a complete idiot.
Coulda sworn that part started a long time ago.
I totally deserved that...

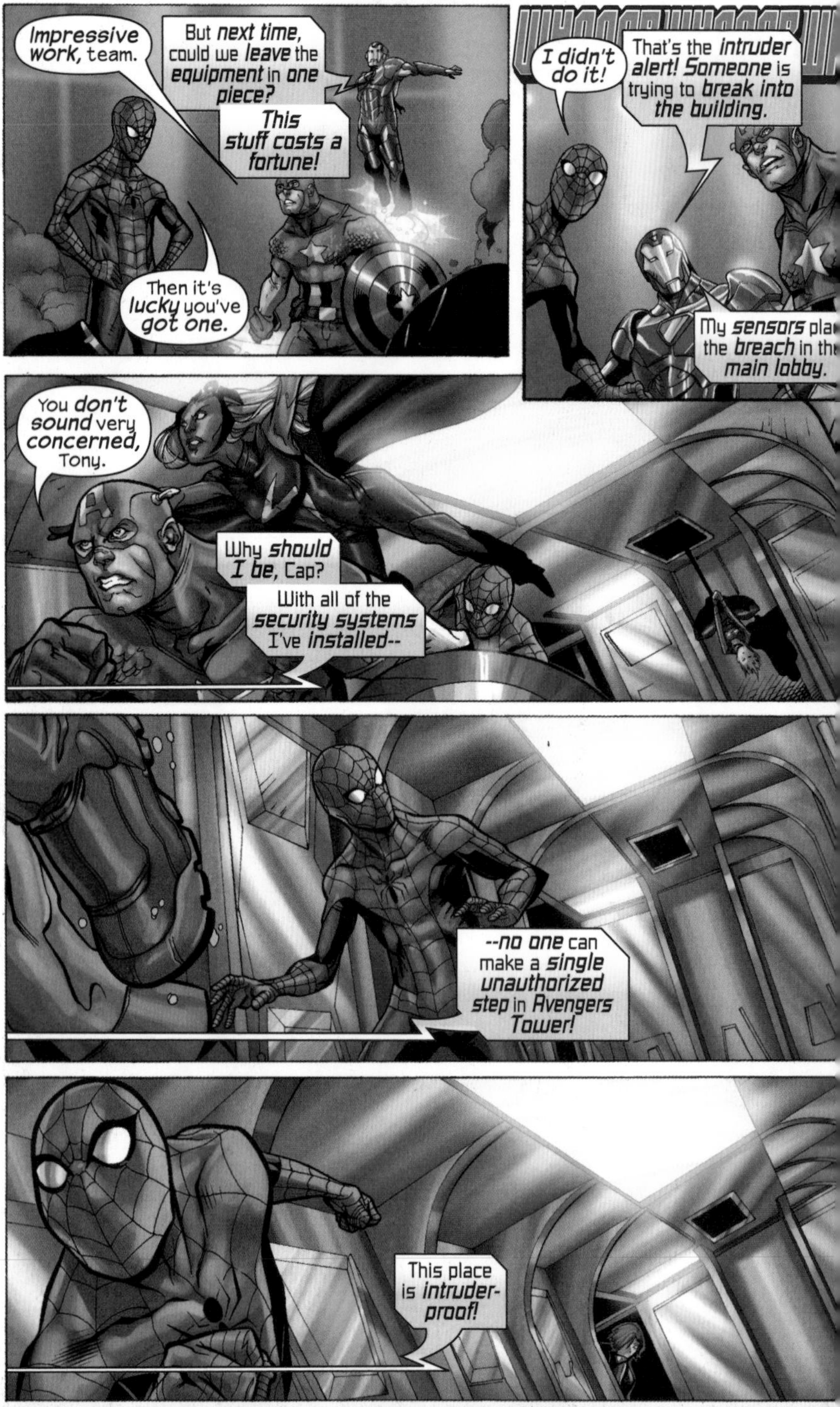

Impressive work, team.
But next time, could we leave the equipment in one piece?
This stuff costs a fortune!
Then it's lucky you've got one.
I didn't do it!
That's the intruder alert! Someone is trying to break into the building.
My sensors pla the breach in th main lobby.
You don't sound very concerned, Tony.
Why should I be, Cap?
With all of the security systems I've installed--
--no one can make a single unauthorized step in Avengers Tower!
This place is intruder-proof!

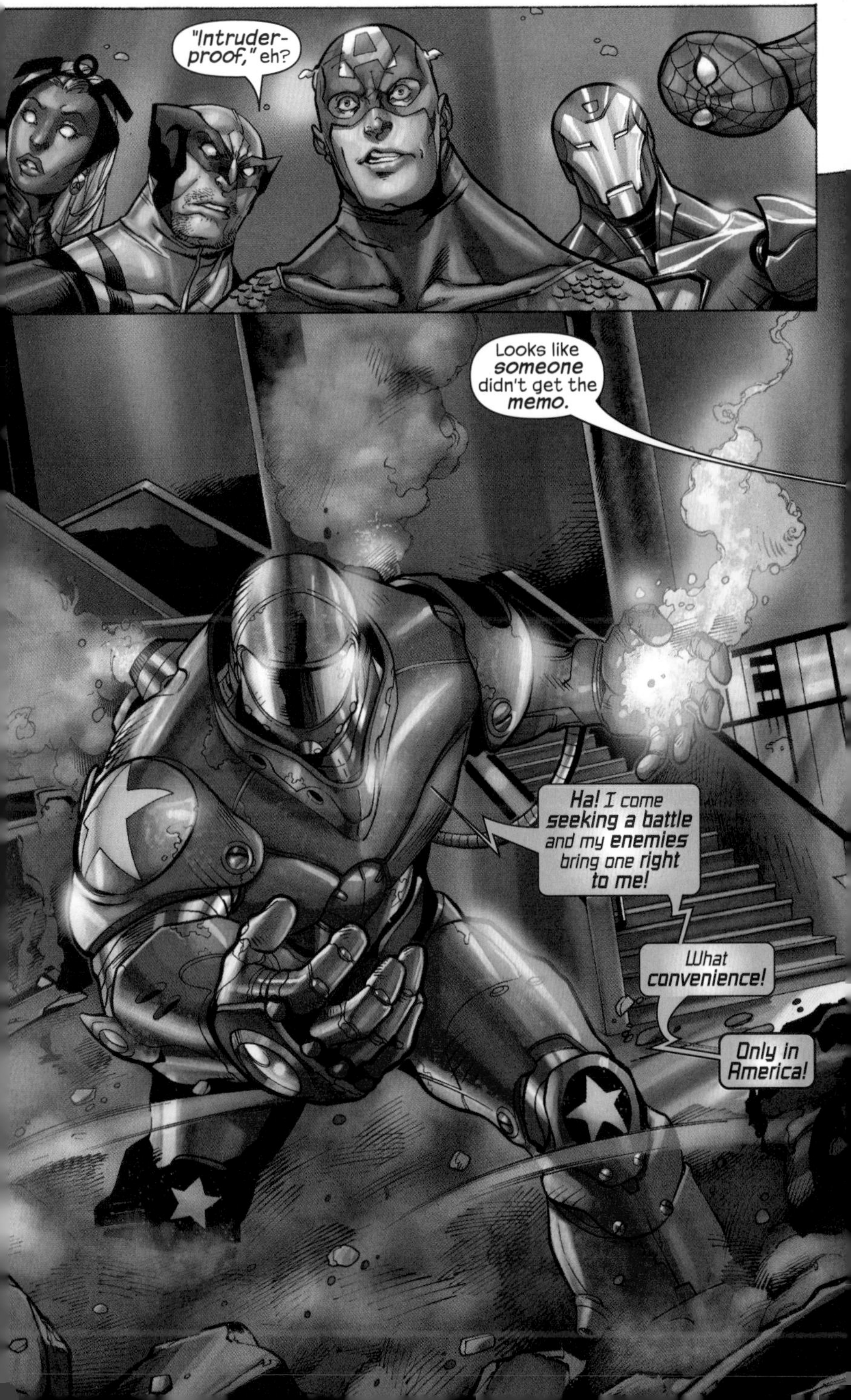
"Intruder-proof," eh?
Looks like someone didn't get the memo.
Ha! I come seeking a battle and my enemies bring one right to me!
What convenience!
Only in America!

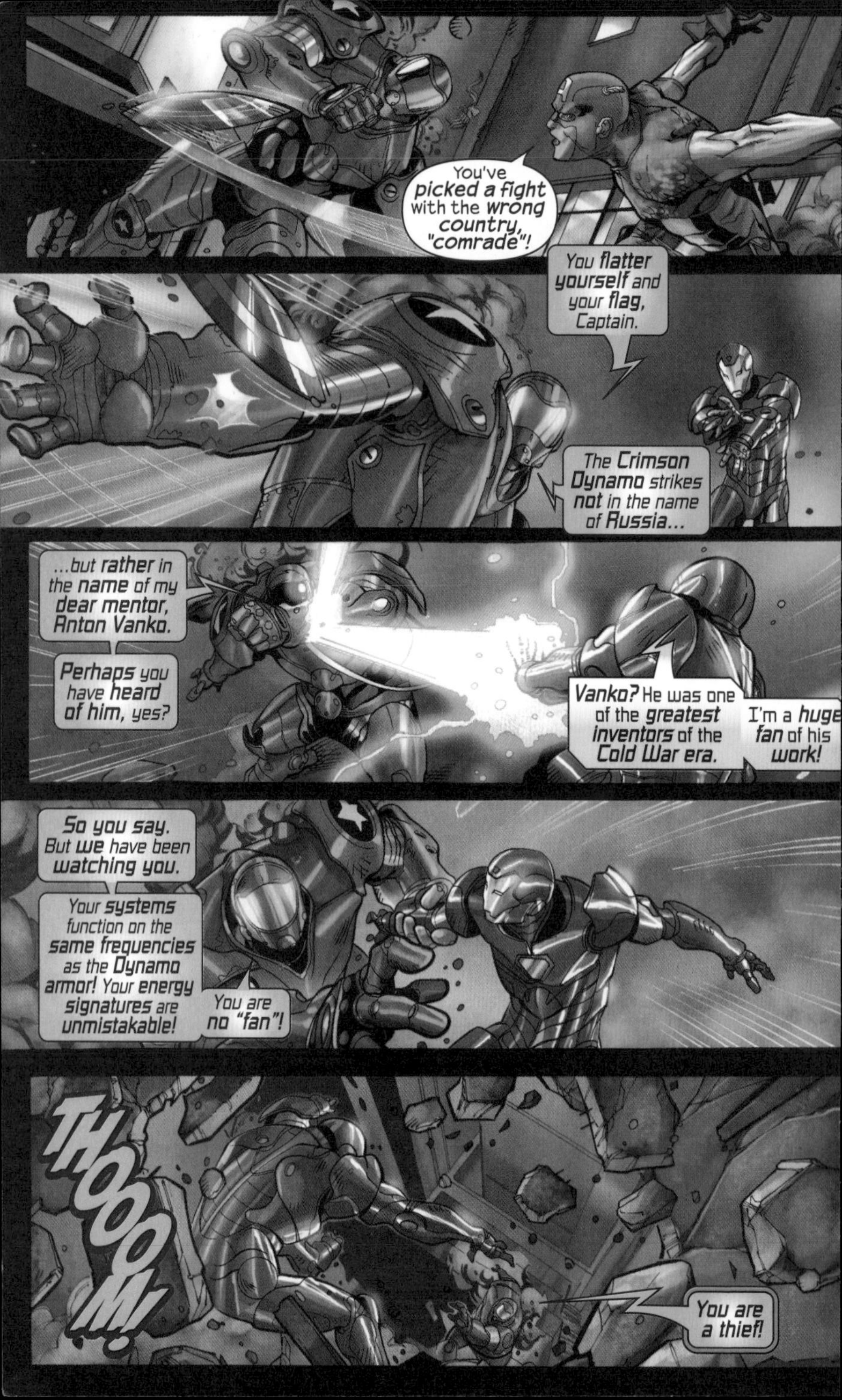

You've picked a fight with the wrong country, "comrade"!
You flatter yourself and your flag, Captain.
The Crimson Dynamo strikes not in the name of Russia...
...but rather in the name of my dear mentor, Anton Vanko.
Perhaps you have heard of him, yes?
Vanko? He was one of the greatest inventors of the Cold War era.
I'm a huge fan of his work!
So you say. But we have been watching you.
Your systems function on the same frequencies as the Dynamo armor! Your energy signatures are unmistakable!
You are no "fan"!
THOOOM!
You are a thief!

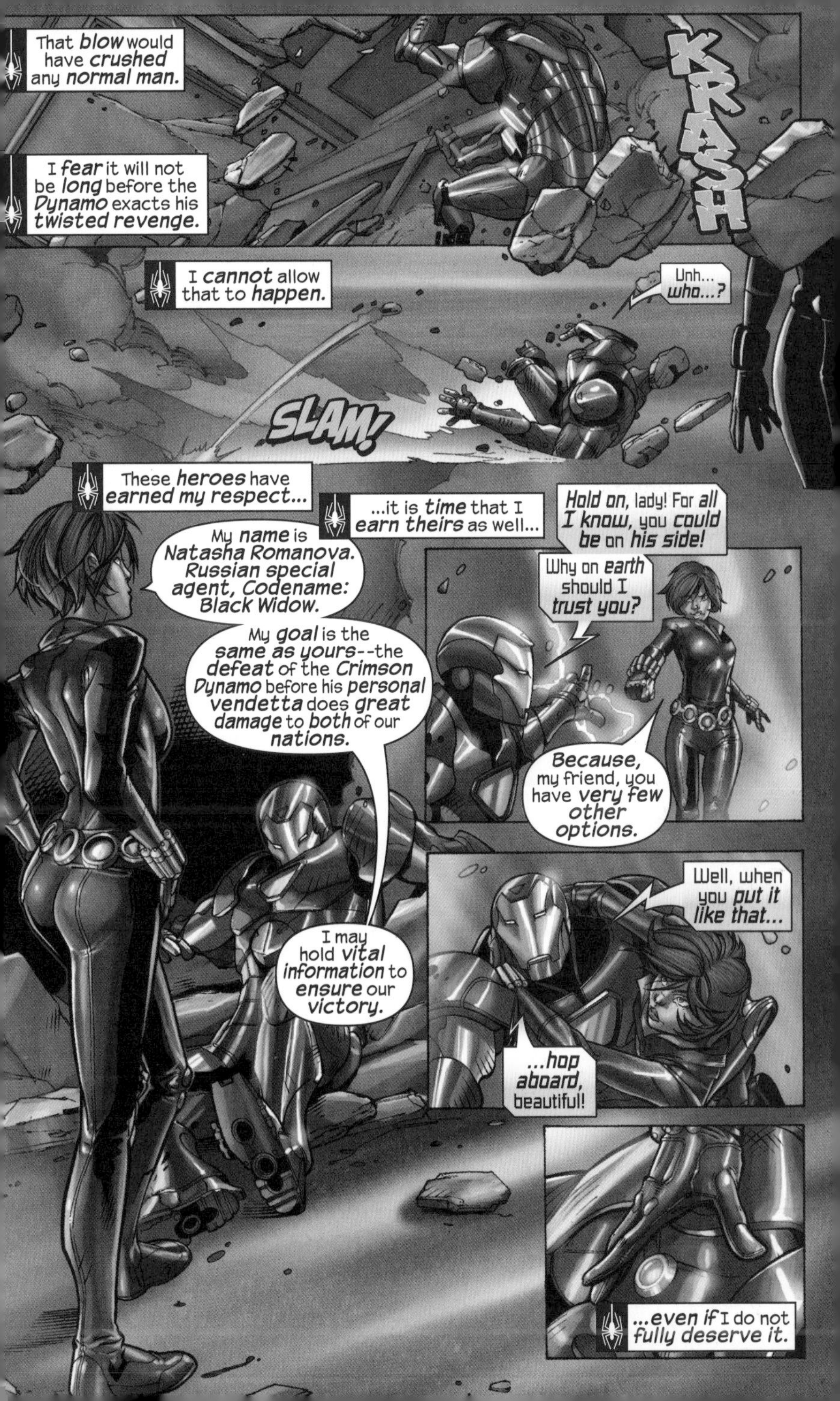

That blow would have crushed any normal man.
KRASH
I fear it will not be long before the Dynamo exacts his twisted revenge.
I cannot allow that to happen.
Unh... who...?
SLAM!
These heroes have earned my respect...
...it is time that I earn theirs as well...
My name is Natasha Romanova. Russian special agent, Codename: Black Widow.
My goal is the same as yours--the defeat of the Crimson Dynamo before his personal vendetta does great damage to both of our nations.
I may hold vital information to ensure our victory.
Hold on, lady! For all I know, you could be on his side!
Why on earth should I trust you?
Because, my friend, you have very few other options.
Well, when you put it like that...
...hop aboard, beautiful!
...even if I do not fully deserve it.

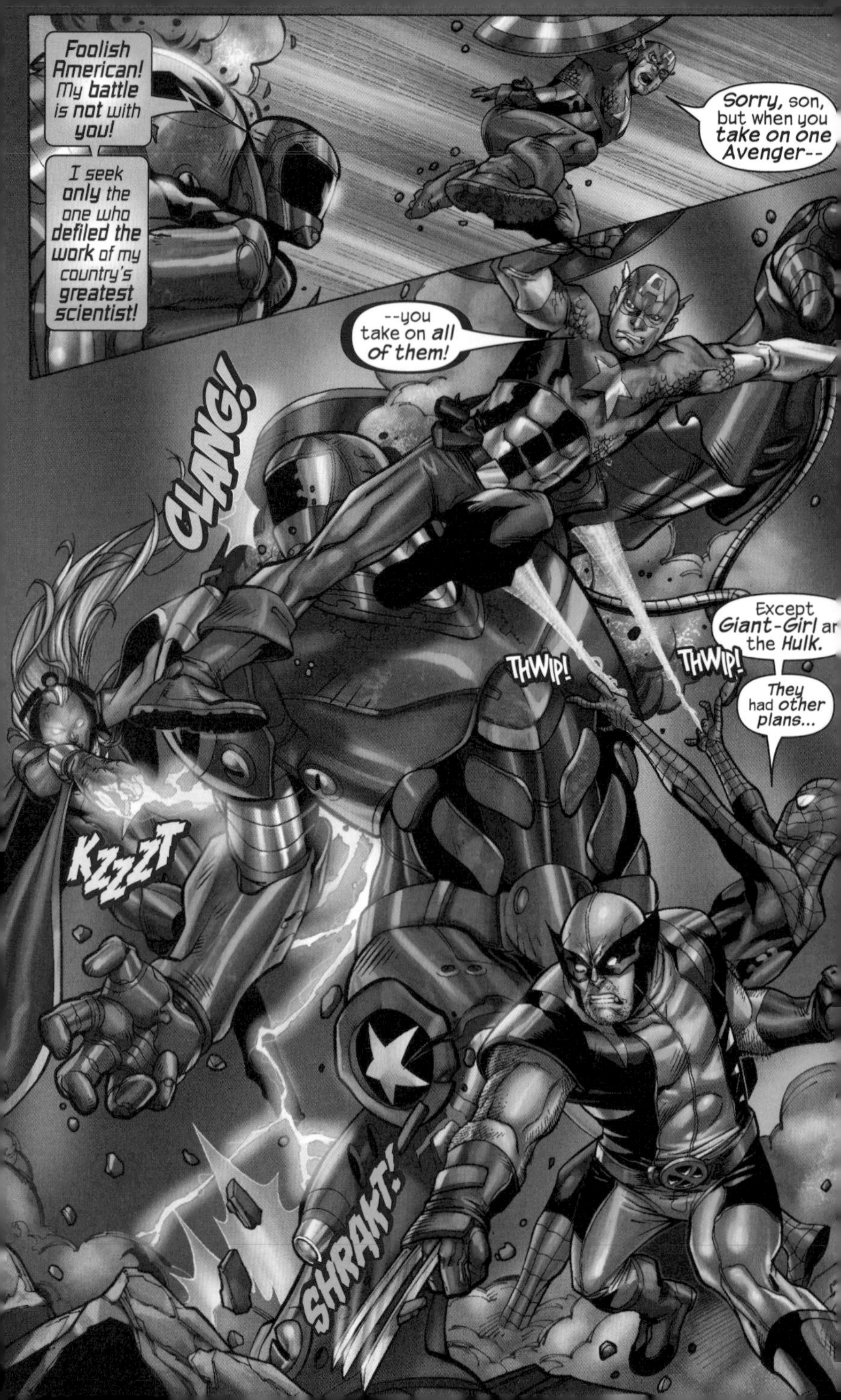

Foolish American! My battle is not with you!
I seek only the one who defiled the work of my country's greatest scientist!
Sorry, son, but when you take on one Avenger--
--you take on all of them!
CLANG!
THWIP!
THWIP!
Except Giant-Girl ar the Hulk.
They had other plans...
KZZZT
SHRAKT!

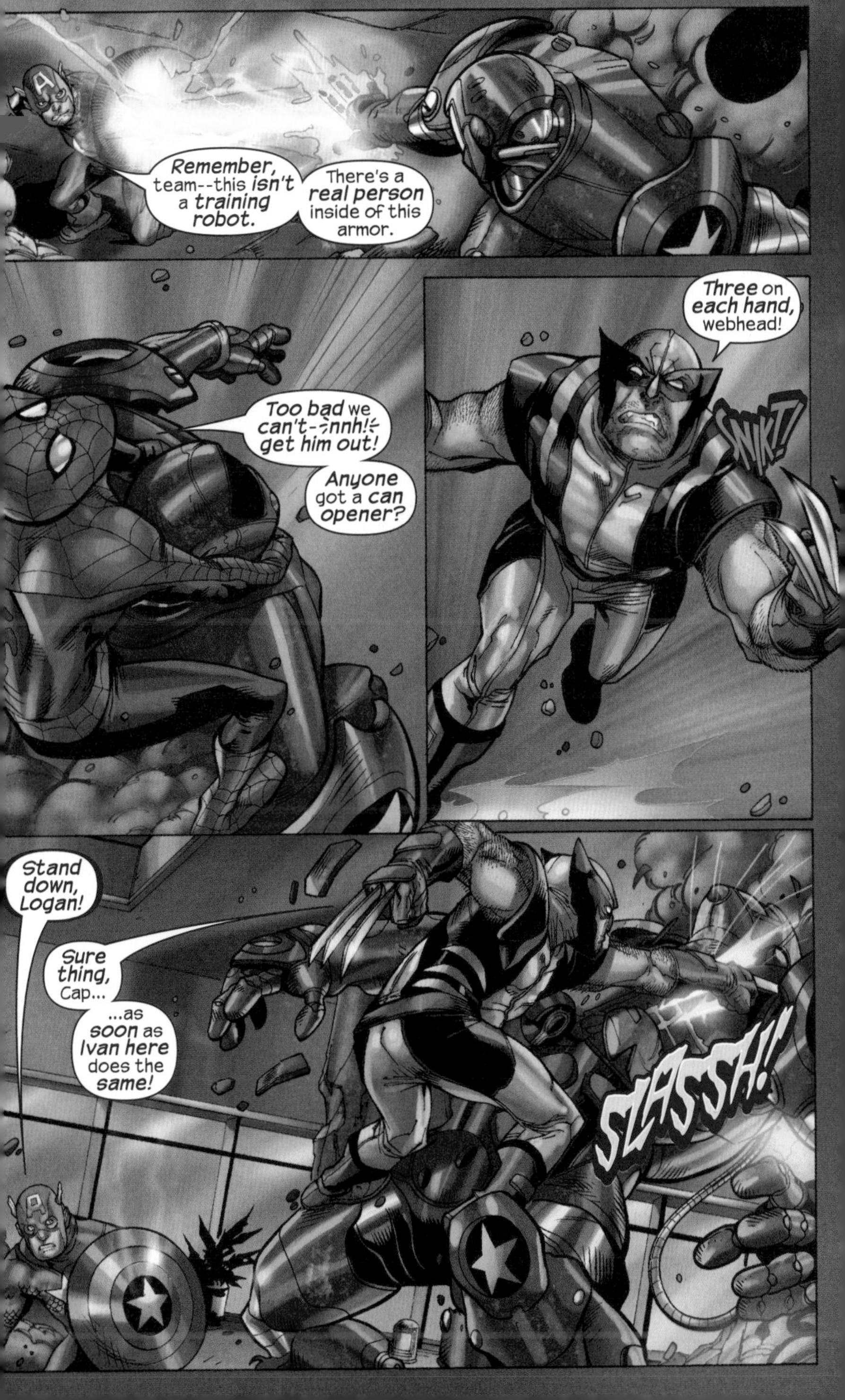
Remember, team--this isn't a training robot.
There's a real person inside of this armor.
Too bad we can't--nnh!-- get him out!
Anyone got a can opener?
Three on each hand, webhead!
SNIKT!
Stand down, Logan!
Sure thing, Cap...
...as soon as Ivan here does the same!
SLASSH!!

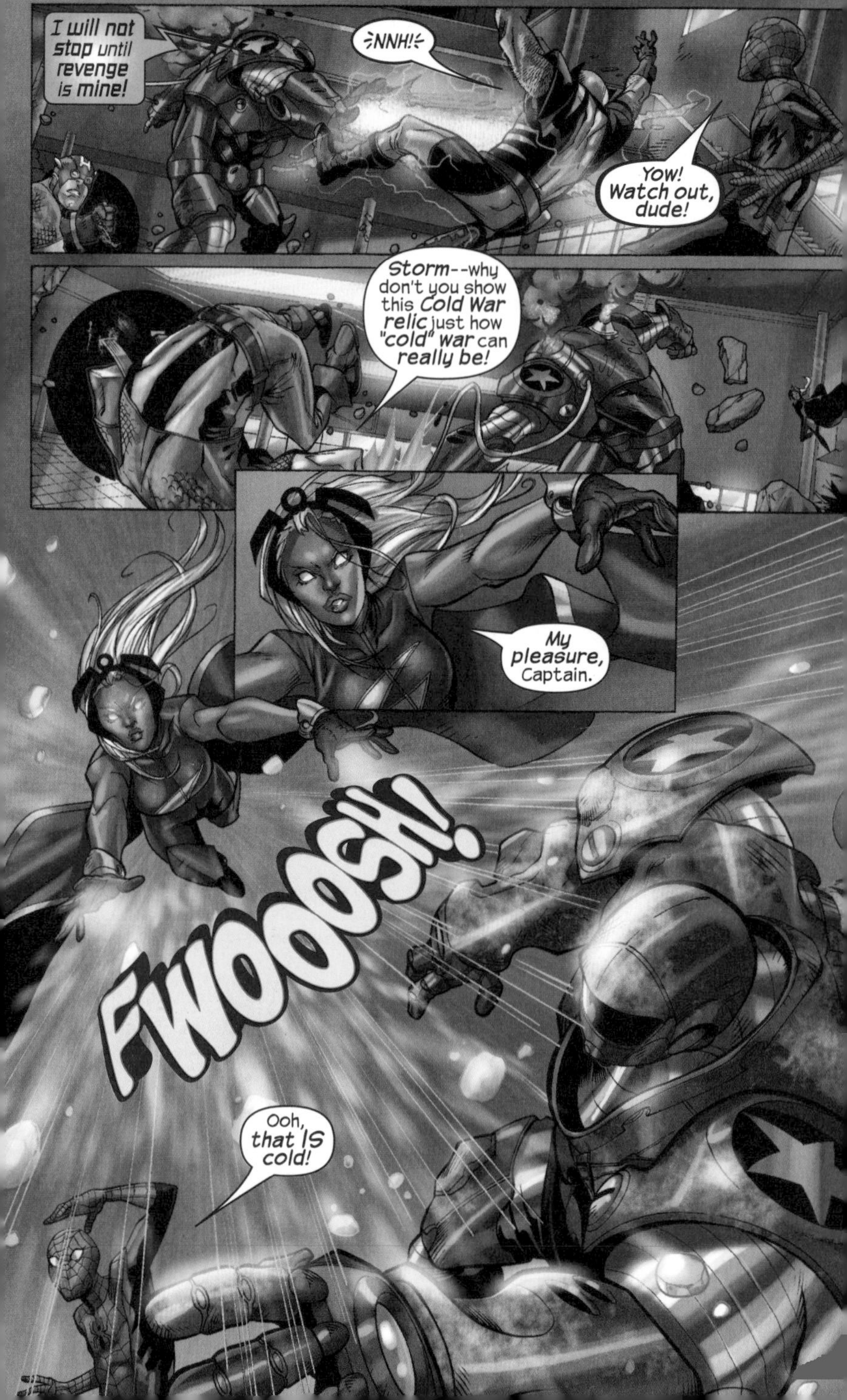
I will not stop until revenge is mine!
NNH!
Yow! Watch out, dude!
Storm--why don't you show this Cold War relic just how "cold" war can really be!
My pleasure, Captain.
FWOOOSH!!
Ooh, that IS cold!

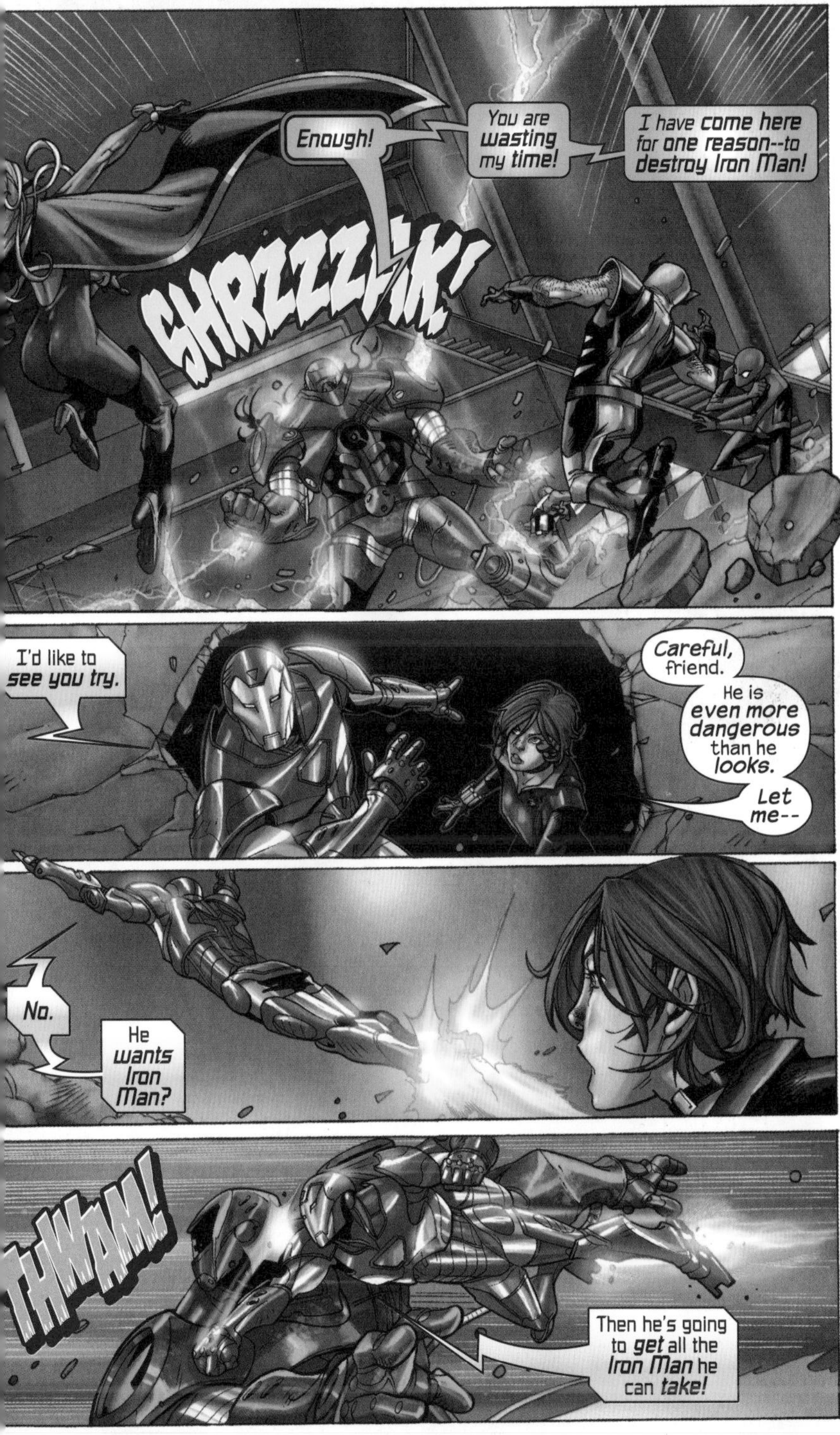
Enough!
You are wasting my time!
I have come here for one reason--to destroy Iron Man!
SHRZZZAK!
I'd like to see you try.
Careful, friend.
He is even more dangerous than he looks.
Let me--
No.
He wants Iron Man?
THWAM!
Then he's going to get all the Iron Man he can take!

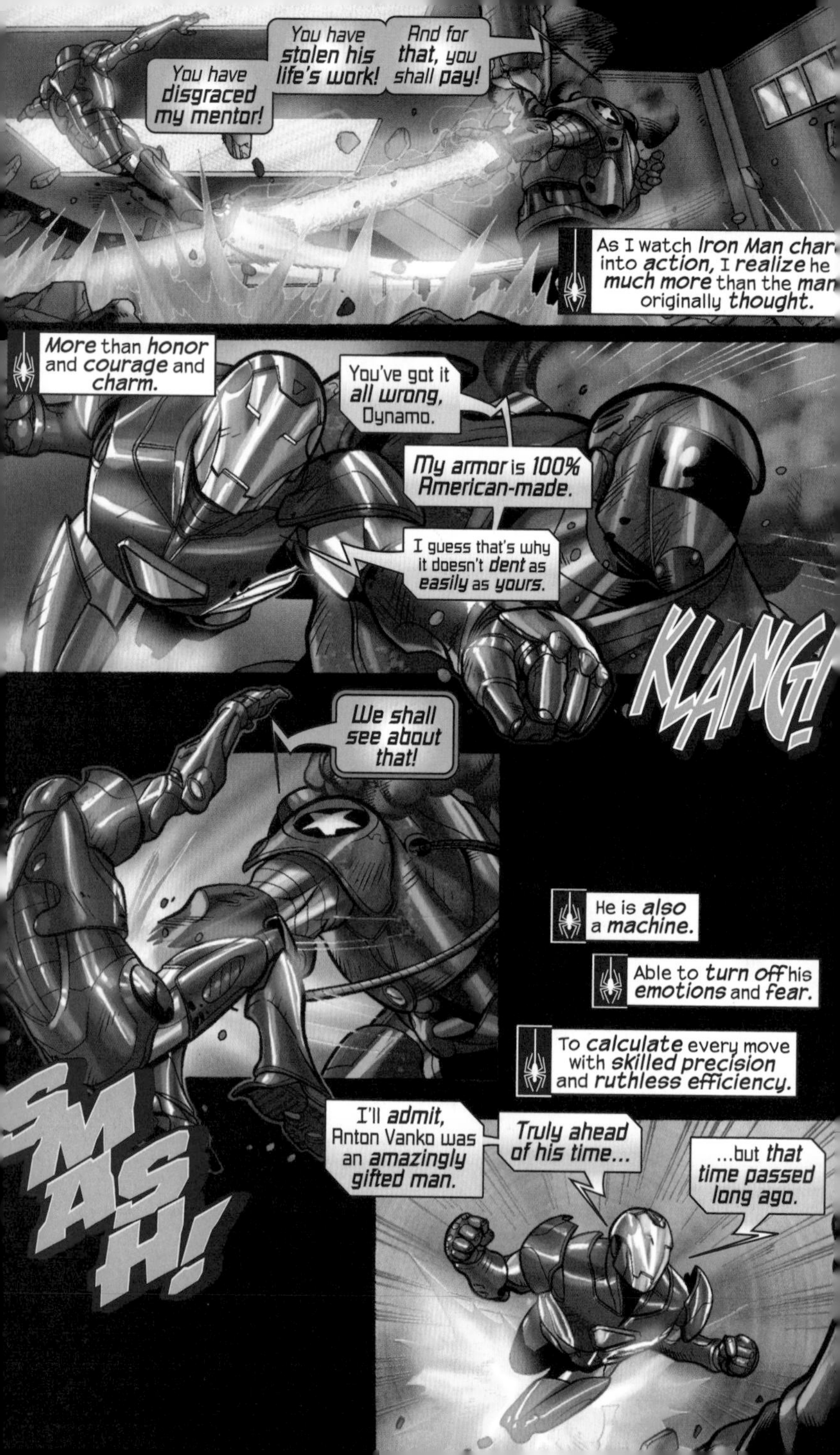

You have disgraced my mentor!
You have stolen his life's work!
And for that, you shall pay!
As I watch Iron Man char
into action, I realize he
much more than the man
originally thought.
More than honor and courage and charm.
You've got it all wrong, Dynamo.
My armor is 100% American-made.
I guess that's why it doesn't dent as easily as yours.
KLANG!
We shall see about that!
He is also a machine.
Able to turn off his emotions and fear.
To calculate every move with skilled precision and ruthless efficiency.
SMASH!
I'll admit, Anton Vanko was an amazingly gifted man.
Truly ahead of his time...
...but that time passed long ago.

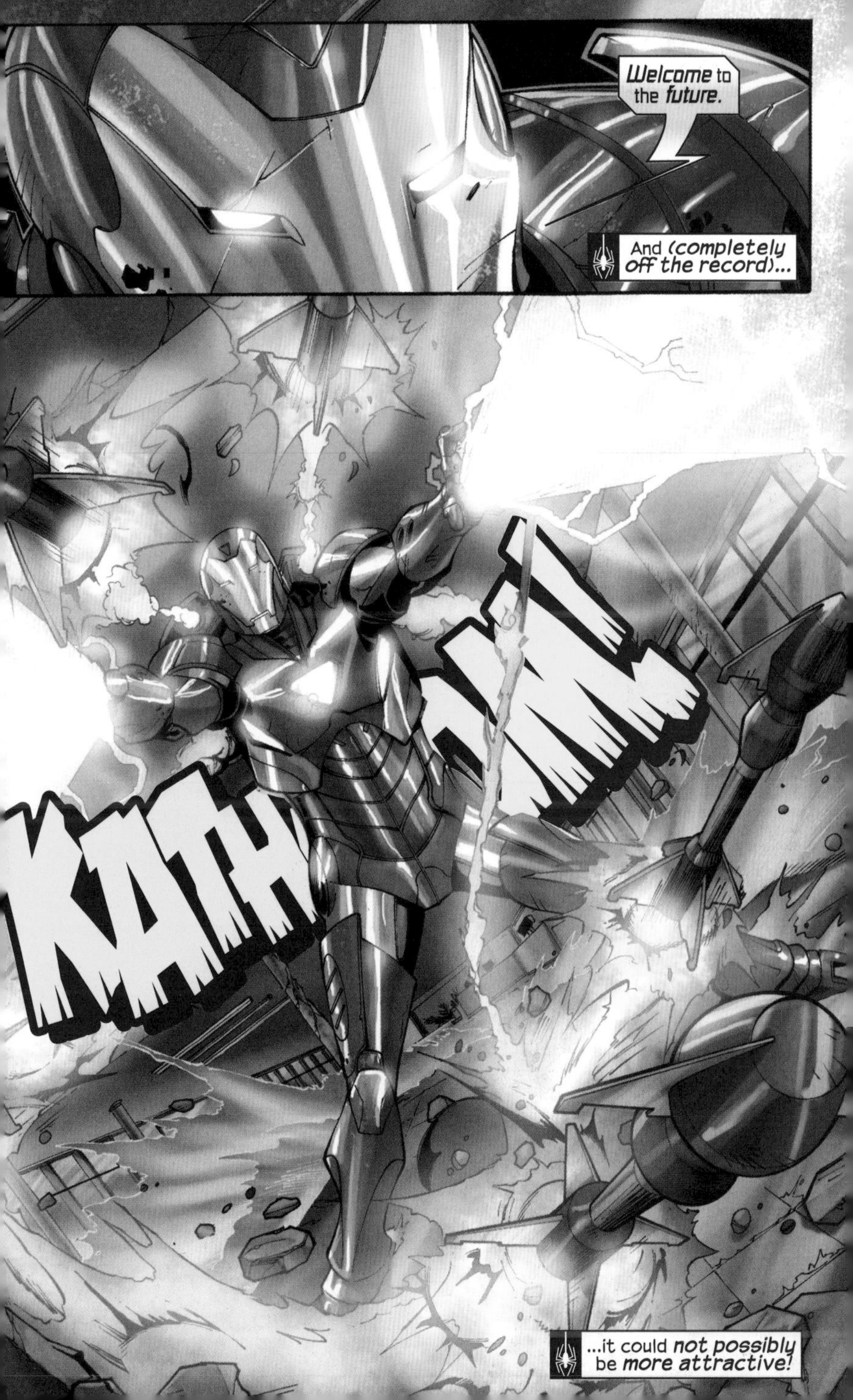
Welcome to the future.
And (completely off the record)...
...it could not possibly be more attractive!

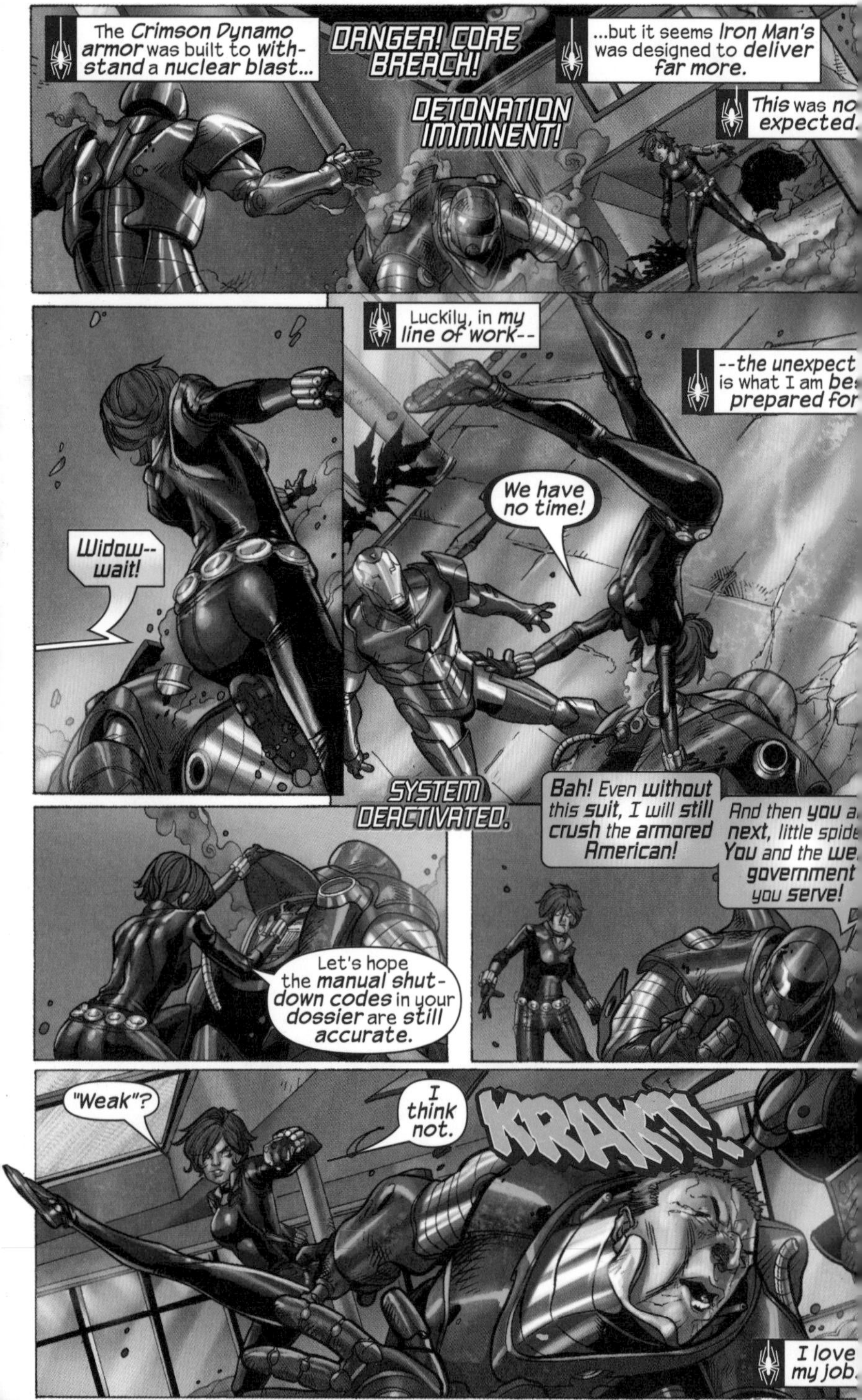

The Crimson Dynamo armor was built to withstand a nuclear blast...
DANGER! CORE BREACH!
DETONATION IMMINENT!
...but it seems Iron Man's was designed to deliver far more.
This was no expected.
Luckily, in my line of work--
--the unexpect is what I am be prepared for
Widow-- wait!
We have no time!
SYSTEM DEACTIVATED.
Let's hope the manual shut-down codes in your dossier are still accurate.
Bah! Even without this suit, I will still crush the armored American!
And then you a next, little spide You and the we government you serve!
"Weak"?
I think not.
KRAKT!
I love my job.

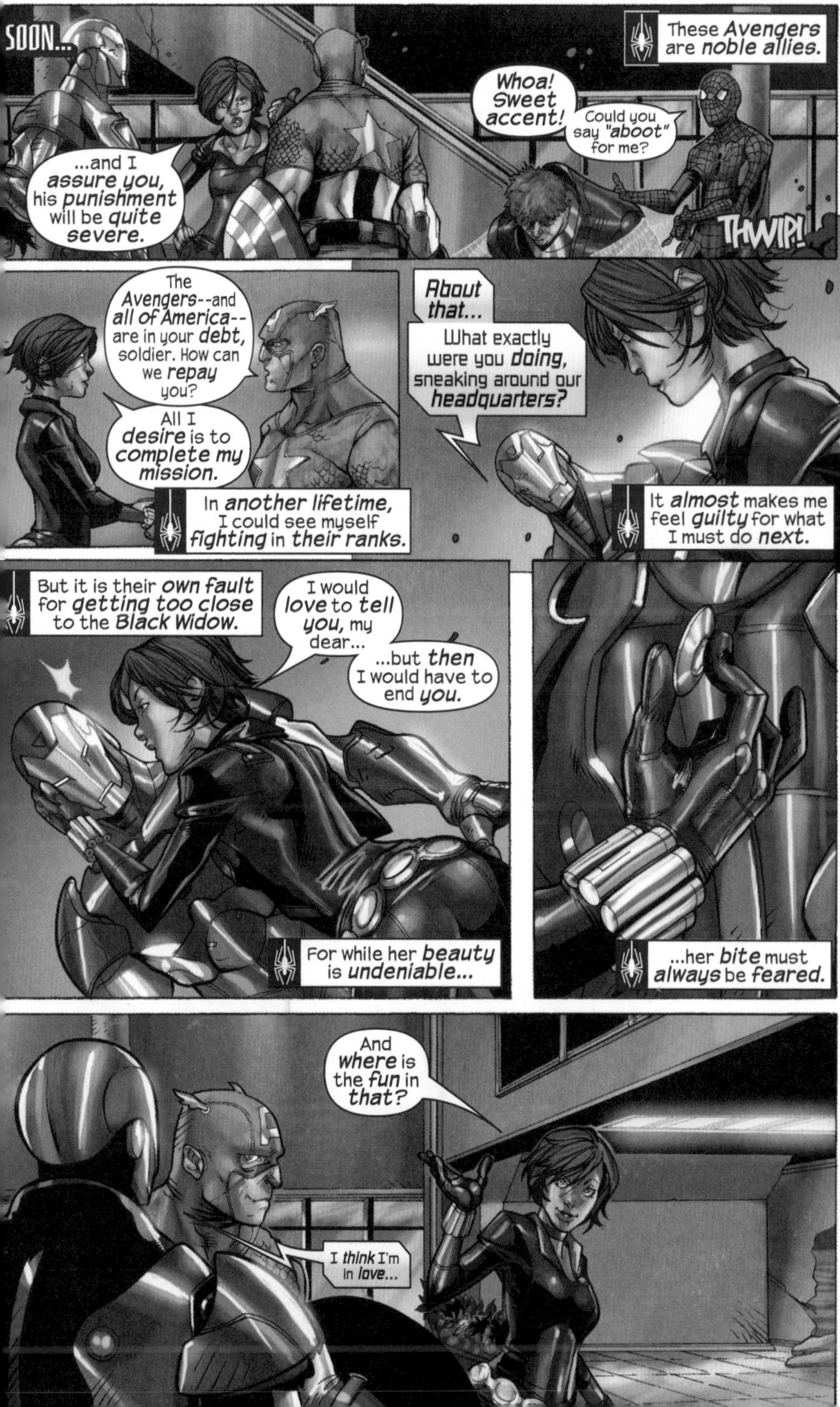
SOON...
These Avengers are noble allies.
Whoa! Sweet accent!
Could you say "aboot" for me?
...and I assure you, his punishment will be quite severe.
THWIP!
The Avengers--and all of America--are in your debt, soldier. How can we repay you?
All I desire is to complete my mission.
In another lifetime, I could see myself fighting in their ranks.
About that...
What exactly were you doing, sneaking around our headquarters?
It almost makes me feel guilty for what I must do next.
But it is their own fault for getting too close to the Black Widow.
I would love to tell you, my dear...
...but then I would have to end you.
For while her beauty is undeniable...
...her bite must always be feared.
And where is the fun in that?
I think I'm in love...

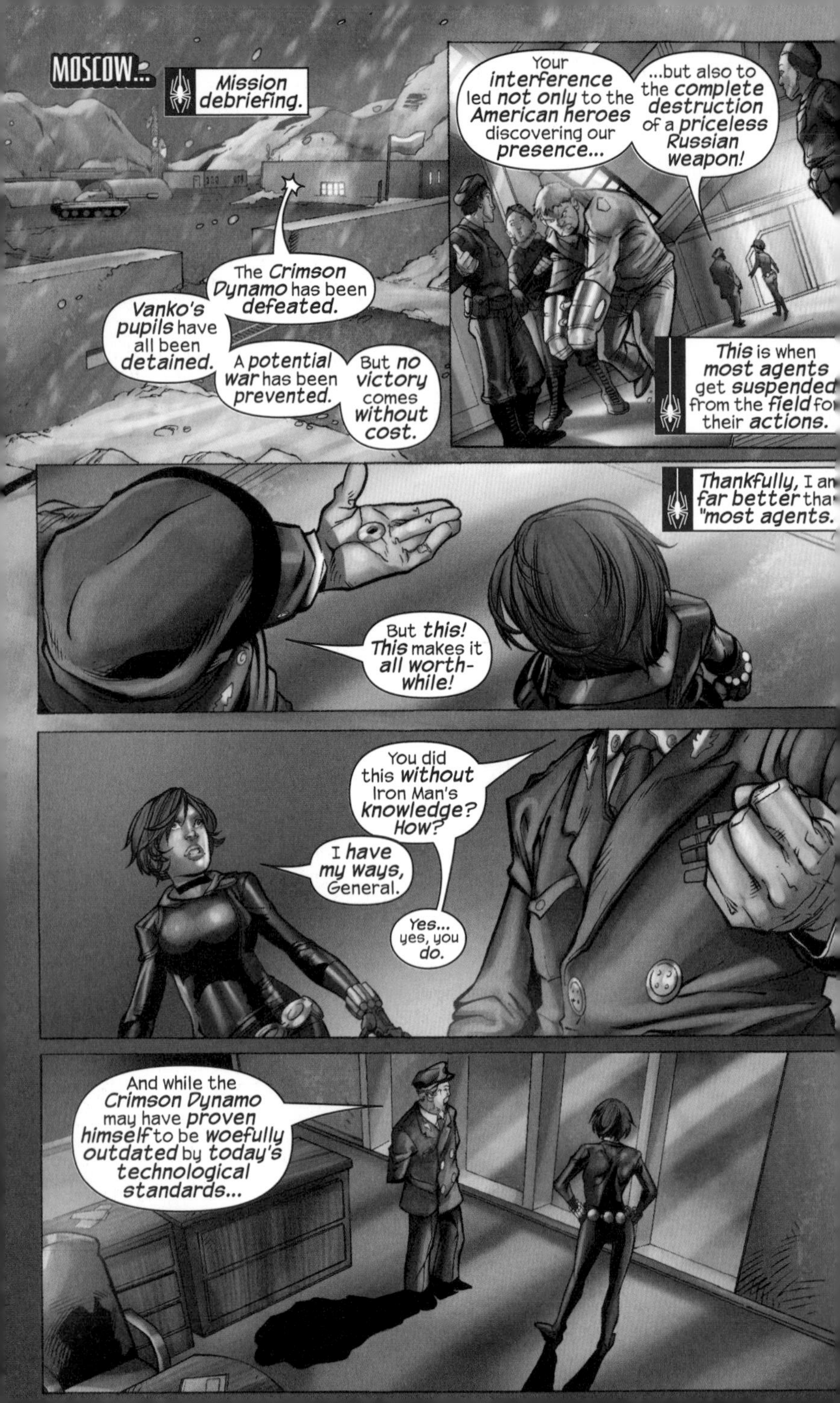
MOSCOW...
Mission debriefing.
The Crimson Dynamo has been defeated.
Vanko's pupils have all been detained.
A potential war has been prevented.
But no victory comes without cost.
Your interference led not only to the American heroes discovering our presence...
...but also to the complete destruction of a priceless Russian weapon!
This is when most agents get suspended from the field fo their actions.
Thankfully, I an far better tha "most agents.
But this! This makes it all worth-while!
You did this without Iron Man's knowledge? How?
I have my ways, General.
Yes... yes, you do.
And while the Crimson Dynamo may have proven himself to be woefully outdated by today's technological standards...

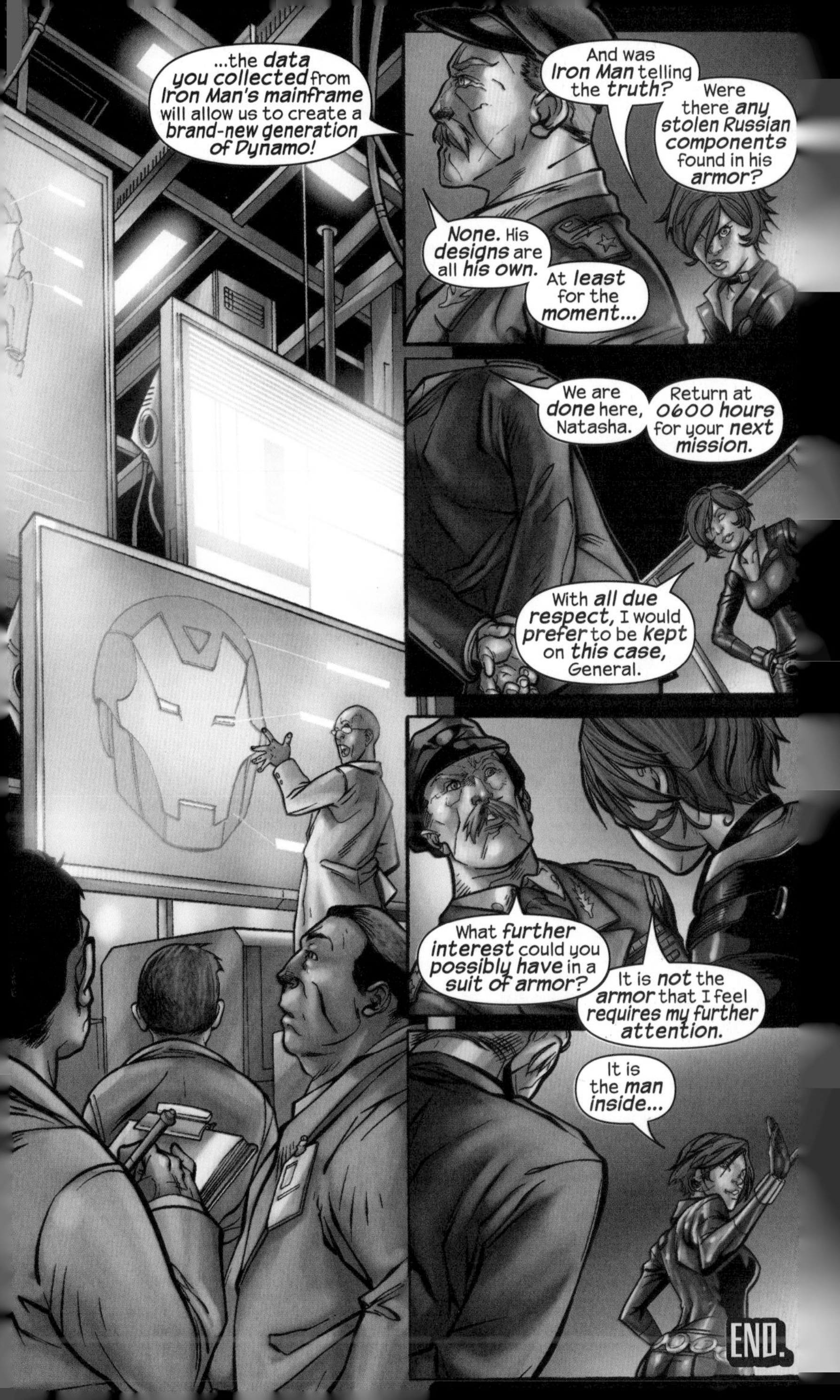
...the data you collected from Iron Man's mainframe will allow us to create a brand-new generation of Dynamo!
And was Iron Man telling the truth?
Were there any stolen Russian components found in his armor?
None. His designs are all his own.
At least for the moment...
We are done here, Natasha.
Return at 0600 hours for your next mission.
With all due respect, I would prefer to be kept on this case, General.
What further interest could you possibly have in a suit of armor?
It is not the armor that I feel requires my further attention.
It is the man inside...
END.

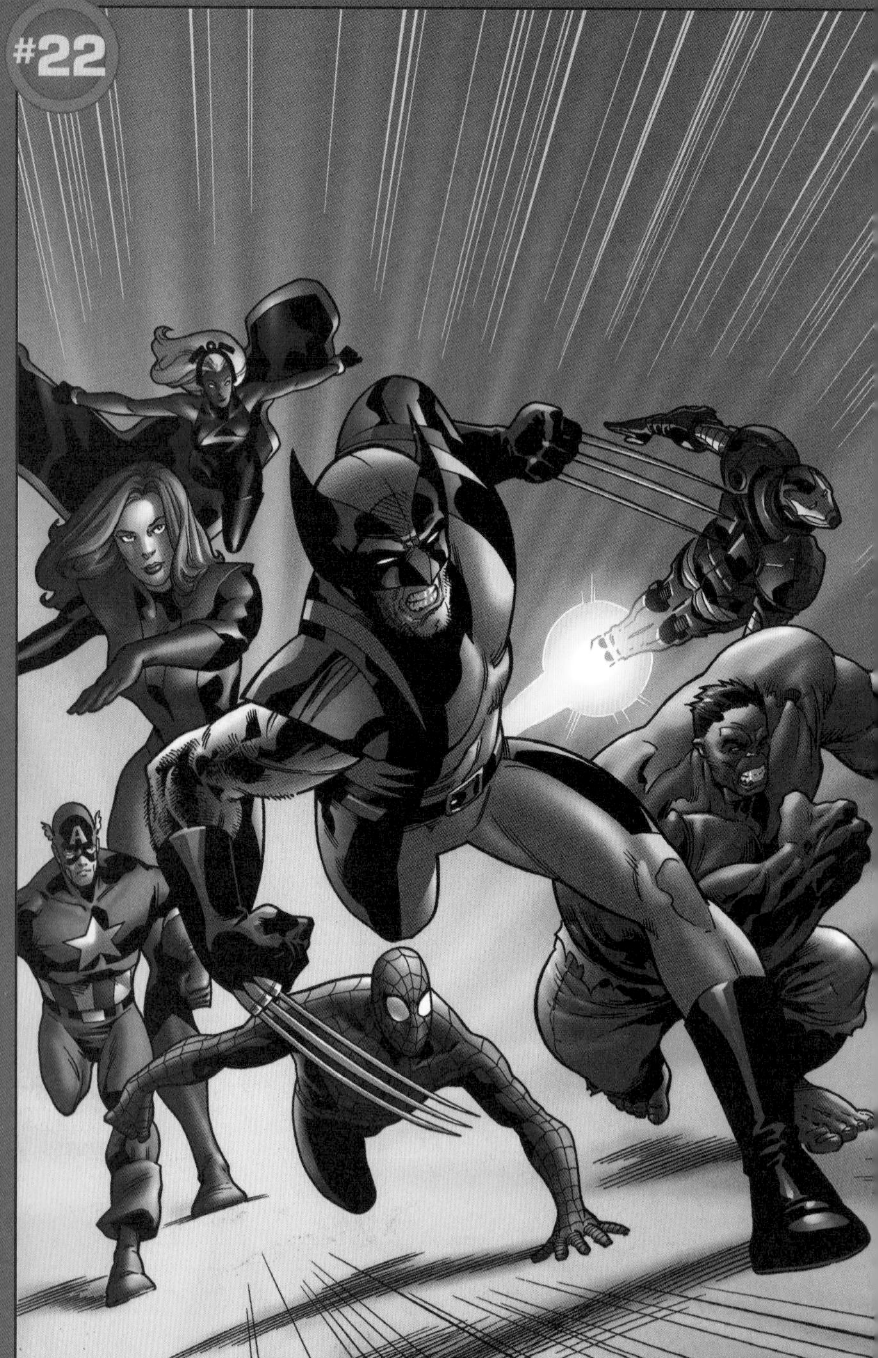
#22
KIRK & FARLOT

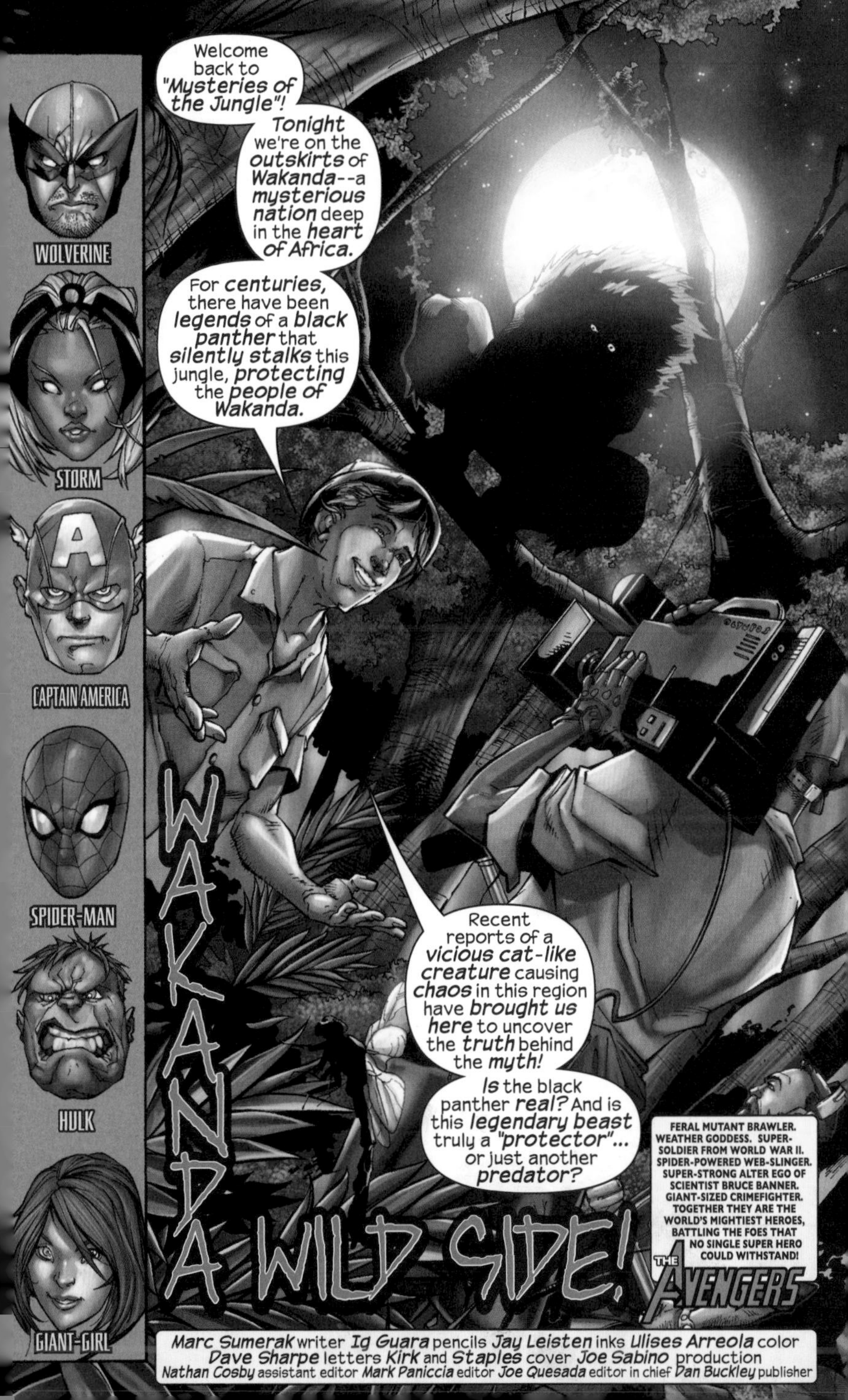

Welcome back to "Mysteries of the Jungle"!
Tonight we're on the outskirts of Wakanda--a mysterious nation deep in the heart of Africa.
For centuries, there have been legends of a black panther that silently stalks this jungle, protecting the people of Wakanda.
Recent reports of a vicious cat-like creature causing chaos in this region have brought us here to uncover the truth behind the myth!
Is the black panther real? And is this legendary beast truly a "protector"... or just another predator?
WOLVERINE
STORM
CAPTAIN AMERICA
SPIDER-MAN
HULK
GIANT-GIRL
WAKANDA A WILD SIDE!
FERAL MUTANT BRAWLER. WEATHER GODDESS. SUPER-SOLDIER FROM WORLD WAR II. SPIDER-POWERED WEB-SLINGER. SUPER-STRONG ALTER EGO OF SCIENTIST BRUCE BANNER. GIANT-SIZED CRIMEFIGHTER. TOGETHER THEY ARE THE WORLD'S MIGHTIEST HEROES, BATTLING THE FOES THAT NO SINGLE SUPER HERO COULD WITHSTAND!
THE AVENGERS
Marc Sumerak writer Ig Guara pencils Jay Leisten inks Ulises Arreola color
Dave Sharpe letters Kirk and Staples cover Joe Sabino production
Nathan Cosby assistant editor Mark Paniccia editor Joe Quesada editor in chief Dan Buckley publisher

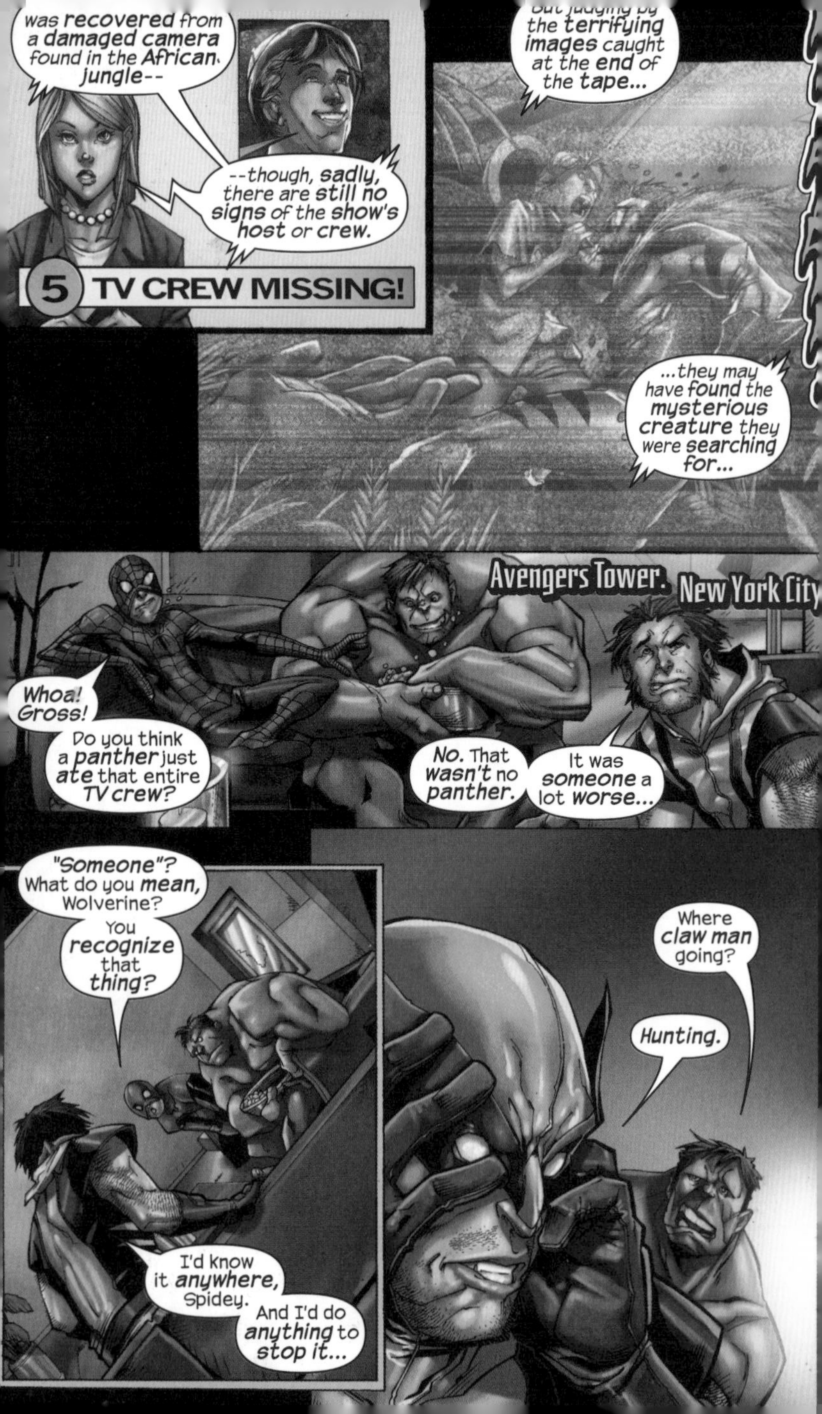

was recovered from a damaged camera found in the African jungle--
--though, sadly, there are still no signs of the show's host or crew.
5 TV CREW MISSING!
the terrifying images caught at the end of the tape...
...they may have found the mysterious creature they were searching for...
Avengers Tower. New York City
Whoa! Gross!
Do you think a panther just ate that entire TV crew?
No. That wasn't no panther.
It was someone a lot worse...
"Someone"? What do you mean, Wolverine?
You recognize that thing?
I'd know it anywhere, Spidey.
And I'd do anything to stop it...
Where claw man going?
Hunting.

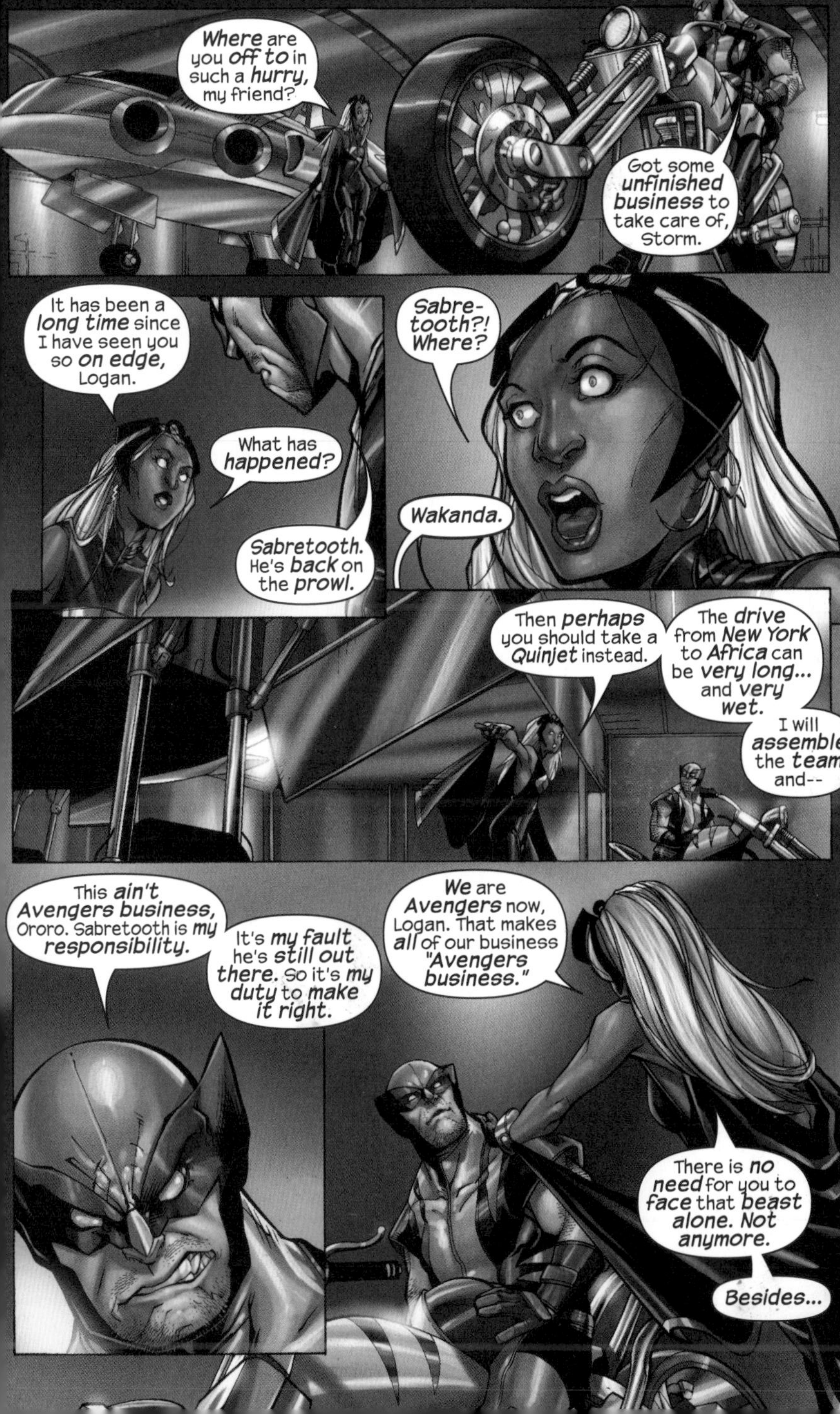
Where are you off to in such a hurry, my friend?
Got some unfinished business to take care of, Storm.
It has been a long time since I have seen you so on edge, Logan.
What has happened?
Sabretooth. He's back on the prowl.
Sabre-tooth?! Where?
Wakanda.
Then perhaps you should take a Quinjet instead.
The drive from New York to Africa can be very long... and very wet.
I will assemble the team and--
This ain't Avengers business, Ororo. Sabretooth is my responsibility.
It's my fault he's still out there. So it's my duty to make it right.
We are Avengers now, Logan. That makes all of our business "Avengers business."
There is no need for you to face that beast alone. Not anymore.
Besides...

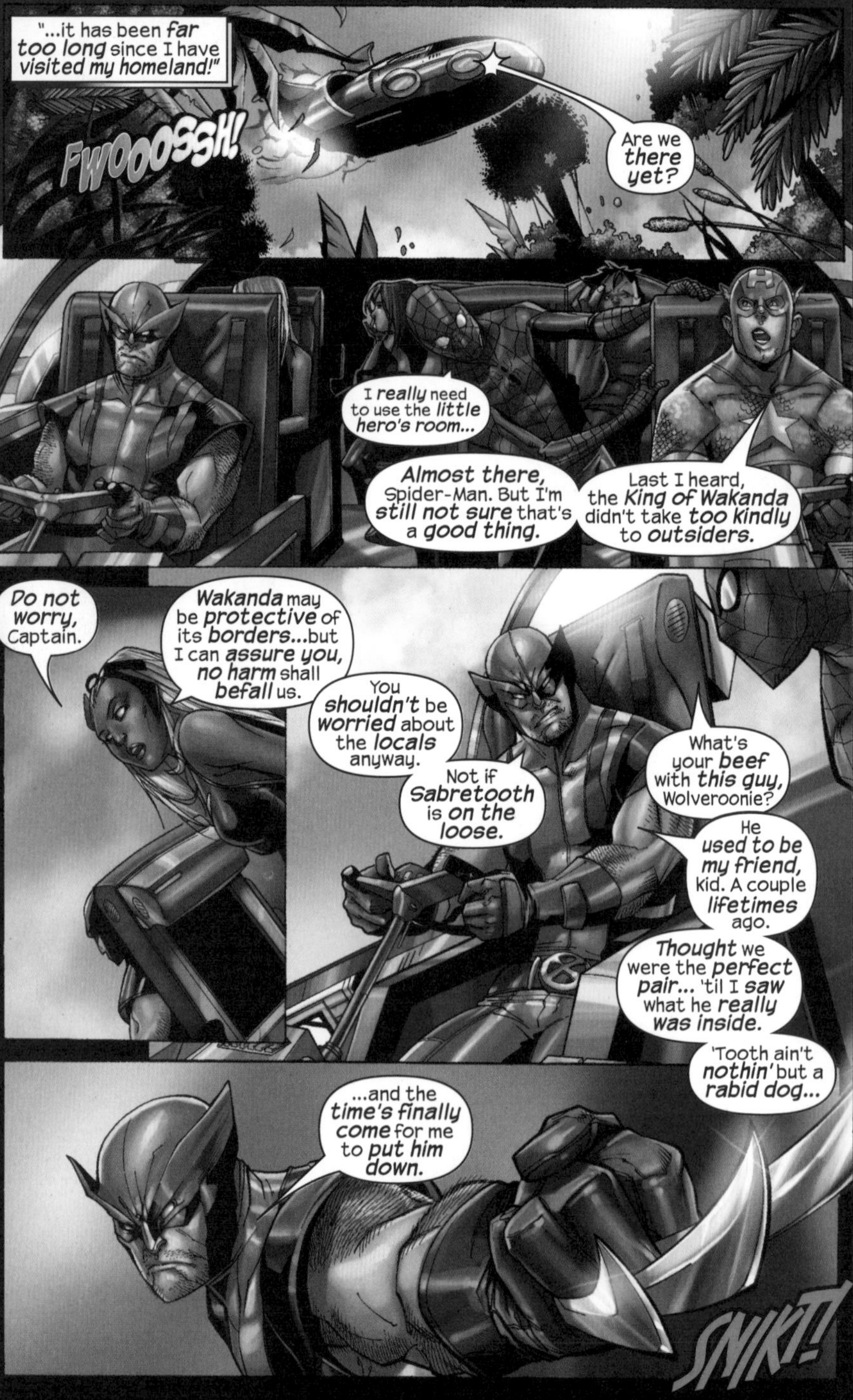
"...it has been far too long since I have visited my homeland!"
FWOOOSSH!
Are we there yet?
I really need to use the little hero's room...
Almost there, Spider-Man. But I'm still not sure that's a good thing.
Last I heard, the King of Wakanda didn't take too kindly to outsiders.
Do not worry, Captain.
Wakanda may be protective of its borders...but I can assure you, no harm shall befall us.
You shouldn't be worried about the locals anyway.
Not if Sabretooth is on the loose.
What's your beef with this guy, Wolveroonie?
He used to be my friend, kid. A couple lifetimes ago.
Thought we were the perfect pair... 'til I saw what he really was inside.
'Tooth ain't nothin' but a rabid dog...
...and the time's finally come for me to put him down.
SNIKT!

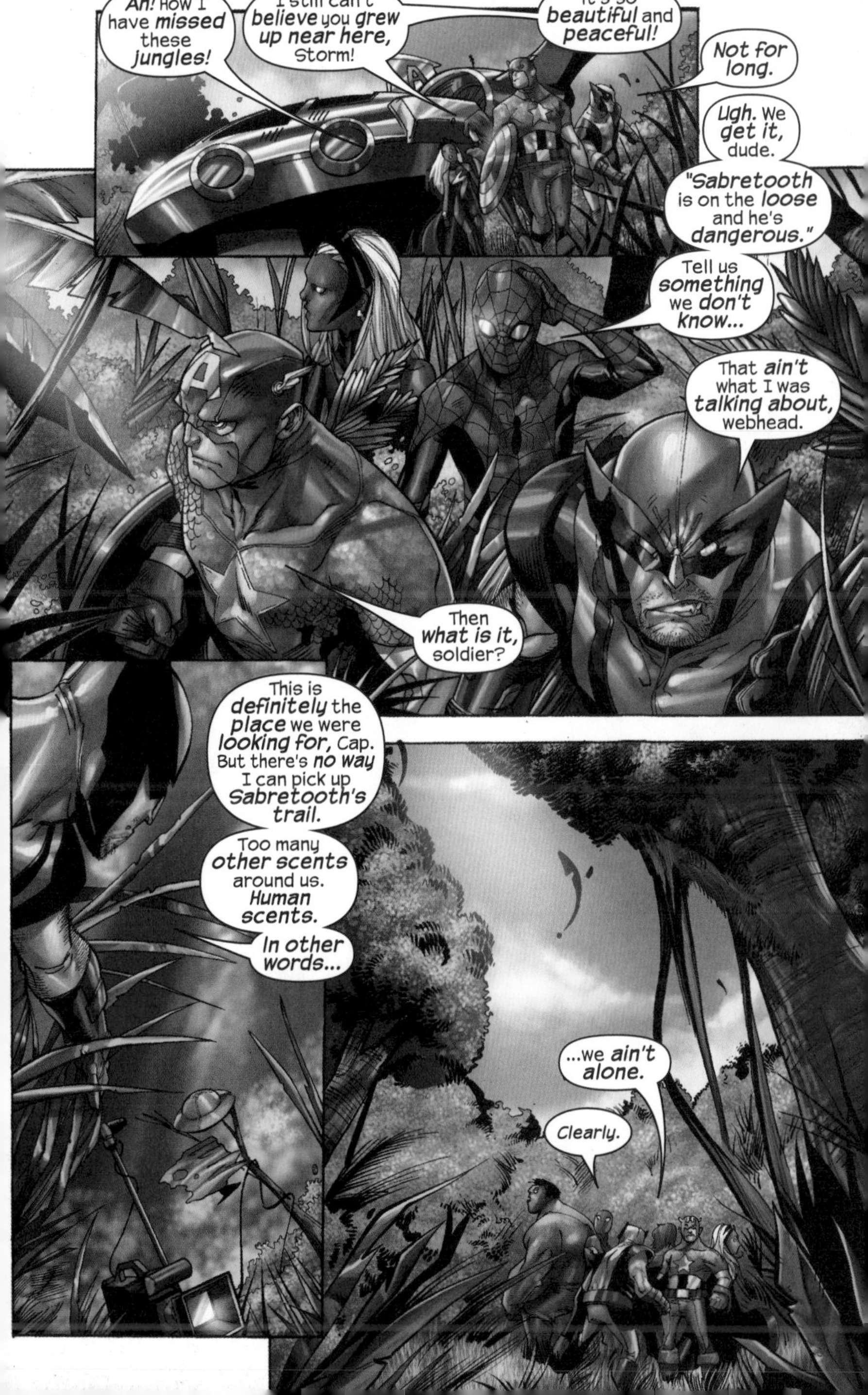

Ah! How I have missed these jungles!
I still can't believe you grew up near here, Storm!
It's so beautiful and peaceful!
Not for long.
Ugh. We get it, dude.
"Sabretooth is on the loose and he's dangerous."
Tell us something we don't know...
That ain't what I was talking about, webhead.
Then what is it, soldier?
This is definitely the place we were looking for, Cap. But there's no way I can pick up Sabretooth's trail.
Too many other scents around us. Human scents.
In other words...
...we ain't alone.
Clearly.

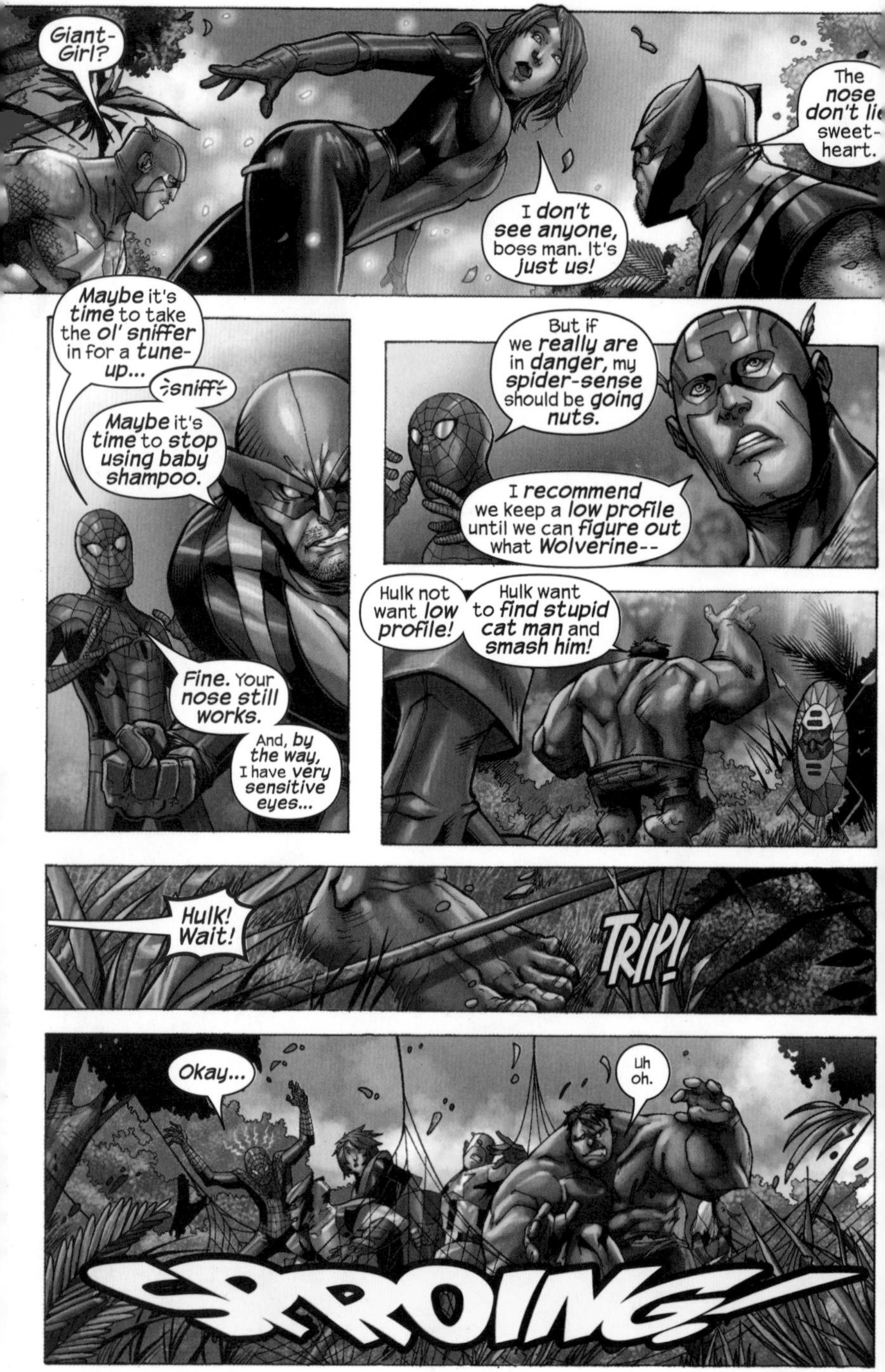

Giant-Girl?
I don't see anyone, boss man. It's just us!
The nose don't lie sweetheart.
Maybe it's time to take the ol' sniffer in for a tune-up...
sniff
Maybe it's time to stop using baby shampoo.
Fine. Your nose still works.
And, by the way, I have very sensitive eyes...
But if we really are in danger, my spider-sense should be going nuts.
I recommend we keep a low profile until we can figure out what Wolverine--
Hulk not want low profile!
Hulk want to find stupid cat man and smash him!
Hulk! Wait!
TRIP!
Okay...
Uh oh.
SPROING!

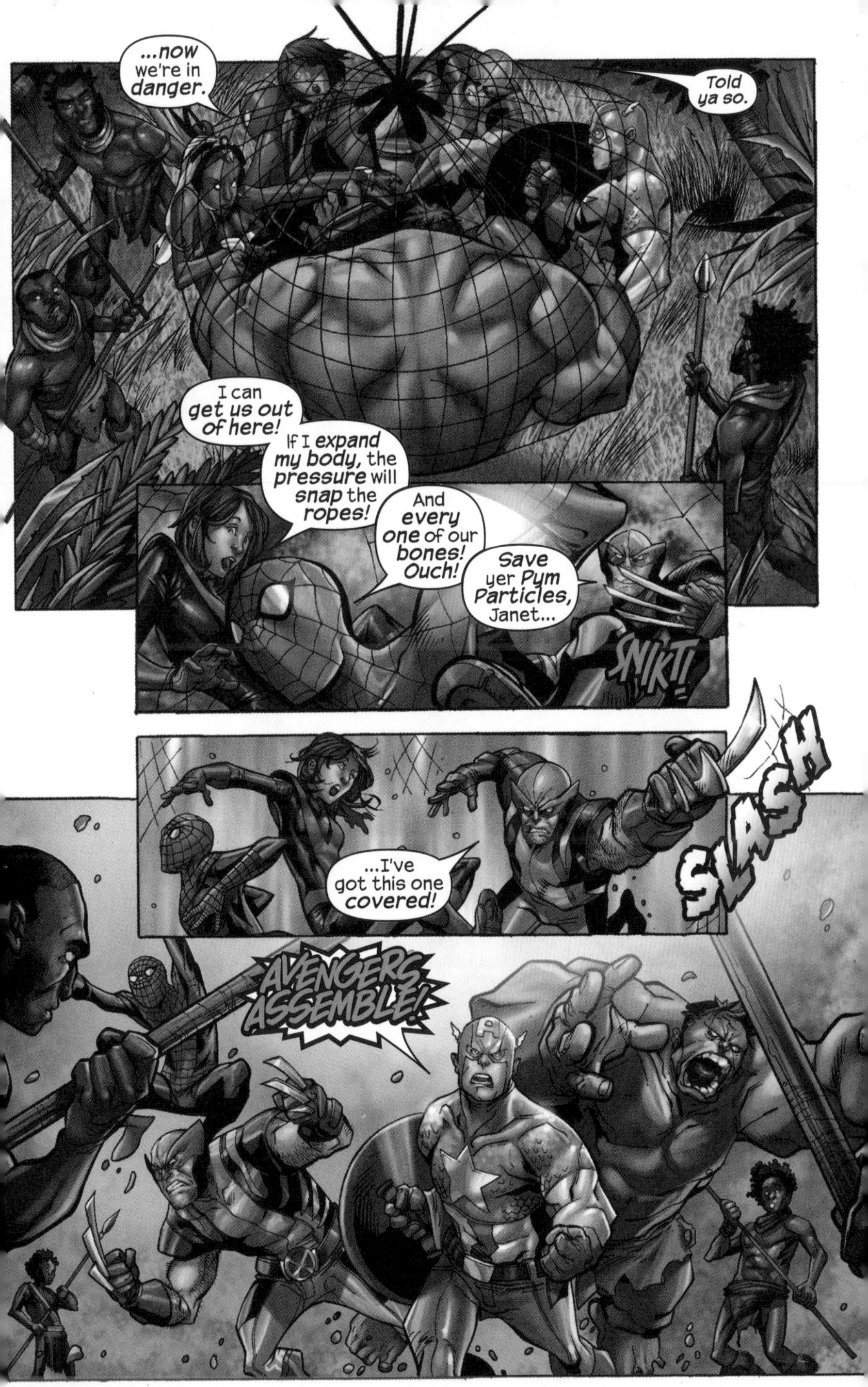

...now we're in danger.
Told ya so.
I can get us out of here!
If I expand my body, the pressure will snap the ropes!
And every one of our bones! Ouch!
Save yer Pym Particles, Janet...
SNIKT!
SLASH
...I've got this one covered!
AVENGERS ASSEMBLE!

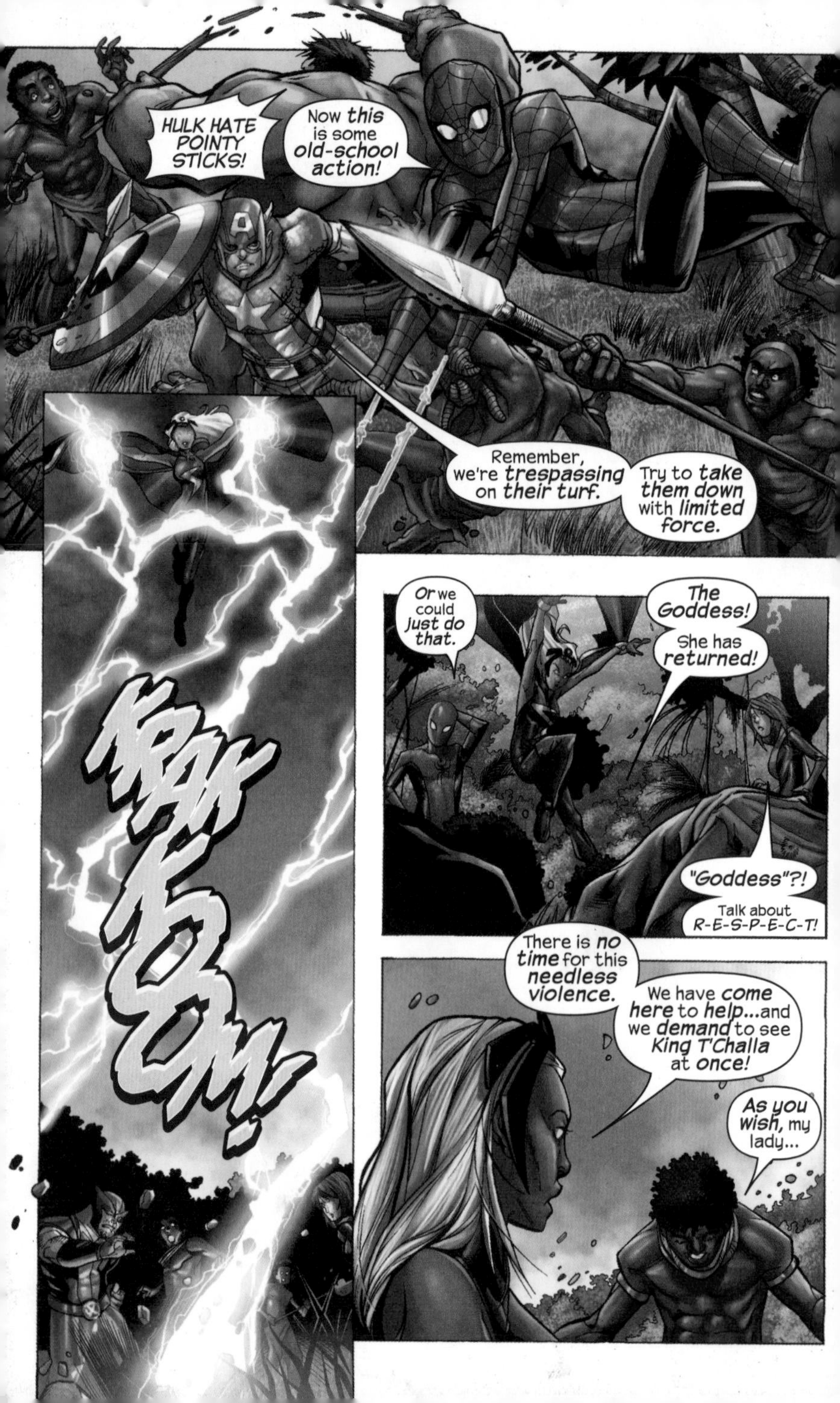

HULK HATE POINTY STICKS!
Now this is some old-school action!
Remember, we're trespassing on their turf.
Try to take them down with limited force.
Or we could just do that.
The Goddess!
She has returned!
"Goddess"?!
Talk about R-E-S-P-E-C-T!
There is no time for this needless violence.
We have come here to help...and we demand to see King T'Challa at once!
As you wish, my lady...

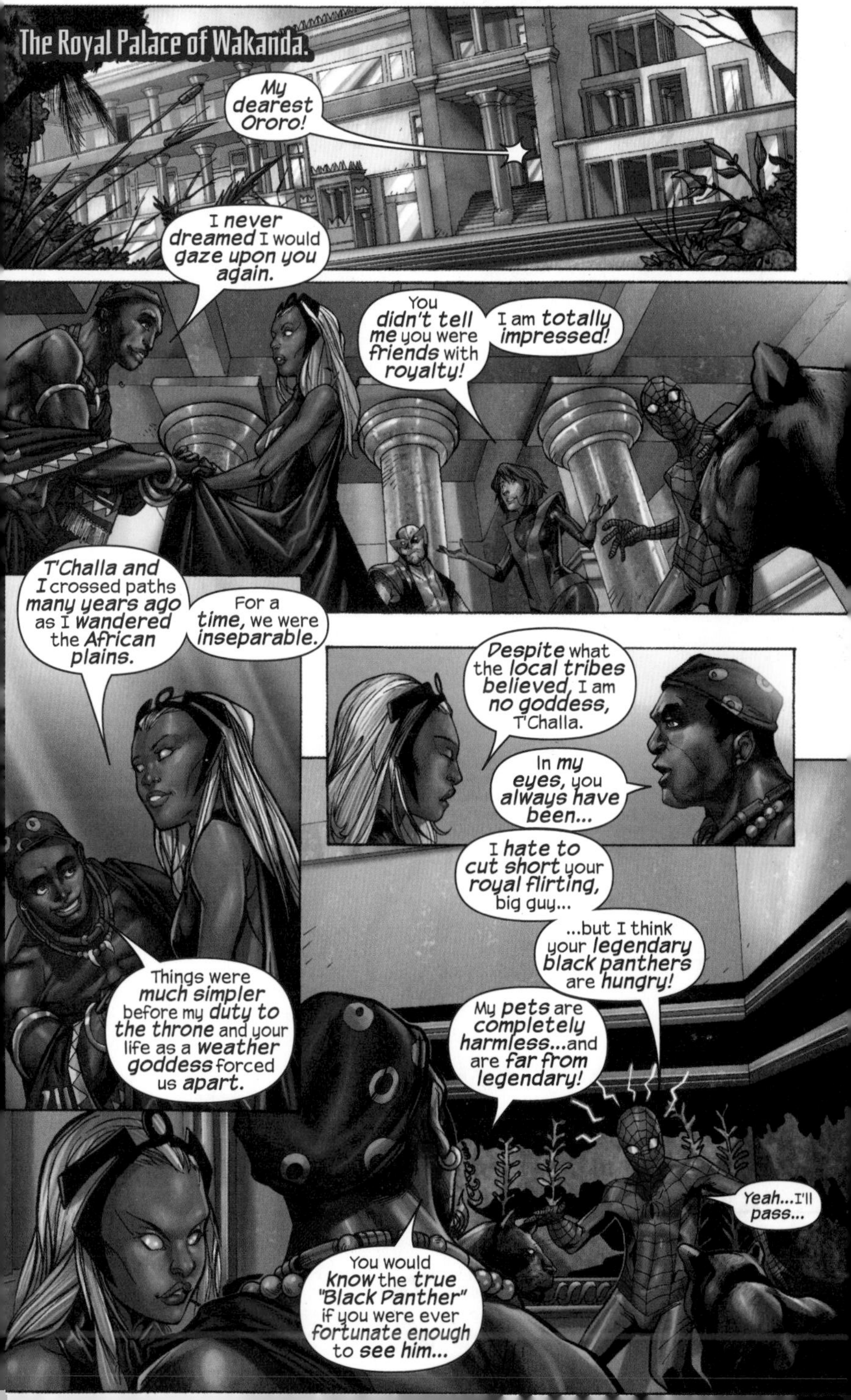

The Royal Palace of Wakanda.
My dearest Ororo!
I never dreamed I would gaze upon you again.
You didn't tell me you were friends with royalty!
I am totally impressed!
T'Challa and I crossed paths many years ago as I wandered the African plains.
For a time, we were inseparable.
Things were much simpler before my duty to the throne and your life as a weather goddess forced us apart.
Despite what the local tribes believed, I am no goddess, T'Challa.
In my eyes, you always have been...
I hate to cut short your royal flirting, big guy...
...but I think your legendary black panthers are hungry!
My pets are completely harmless...and are far from legendary!
Yeah...I'll pass...
You would know the true "Black Panther" if you were ever fortunate enough to see him...

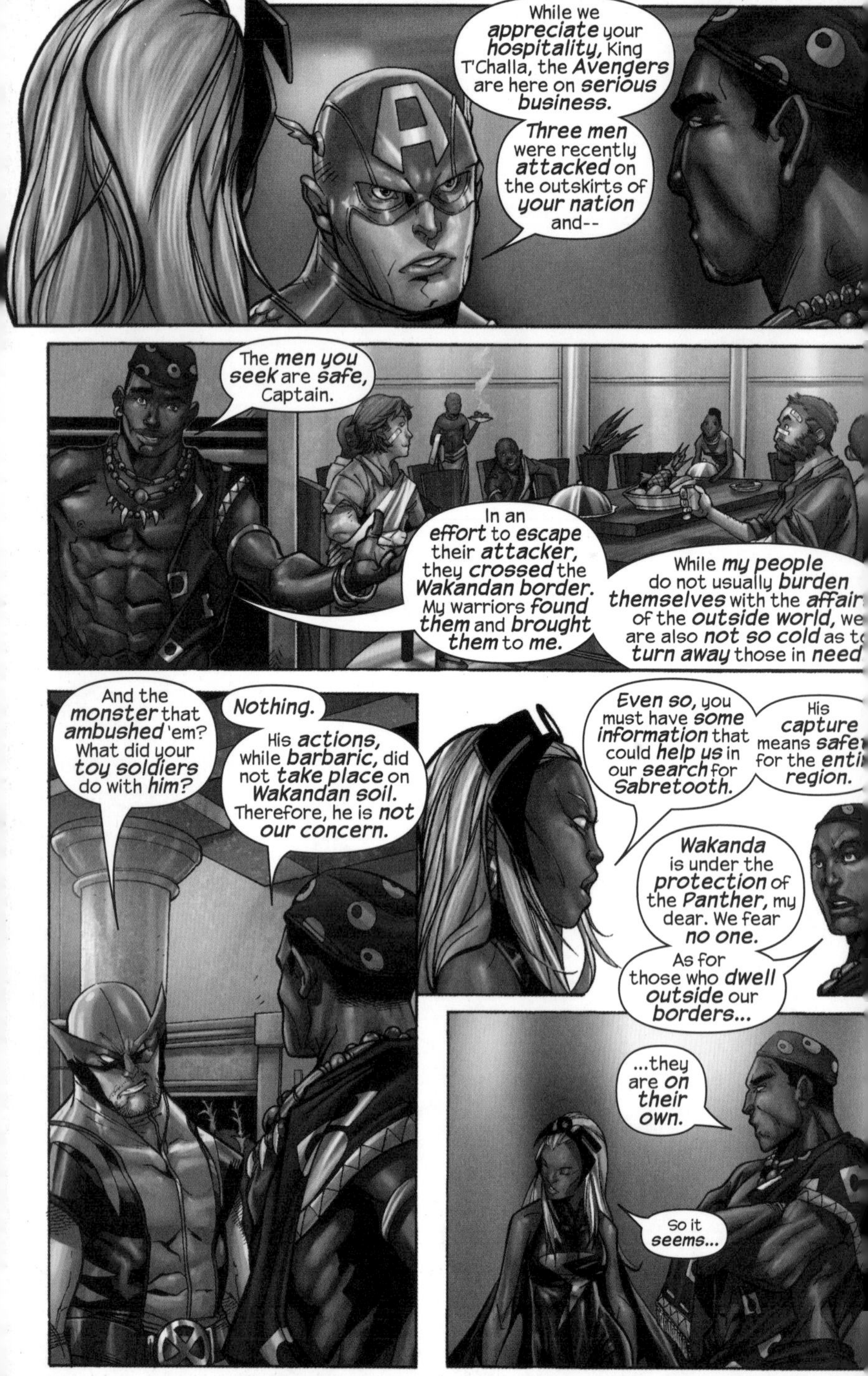
While we appreciate your hospitality, King T'Challa, the Avengers are here on serious business.
Three men were recently attacked on the outskirts of your nation and--
The men you seek are safe, Captain.
In an effort to escape their attacker, they crossed the Wakandan border. My warriors found them and brought them to me.
While my people do not usually burden themselves with the affair of the outside world, we are also not so cold as t turn away those in need
And the monster that ambushed 'em? What did your toy soldiers do with him?
Nothing.
His actions, while barbaric, did not take place on Wakandan soil. Therefore, he is not our concern.
Even so, you must have some information that could help us in our search for Sabretooth.
His capture means safe for the enti region.
Wakanda is under the protection of the Panther, my dear. We fear no one.
As for those who dwell outside our borders...
...they are on their own.
So it seems...

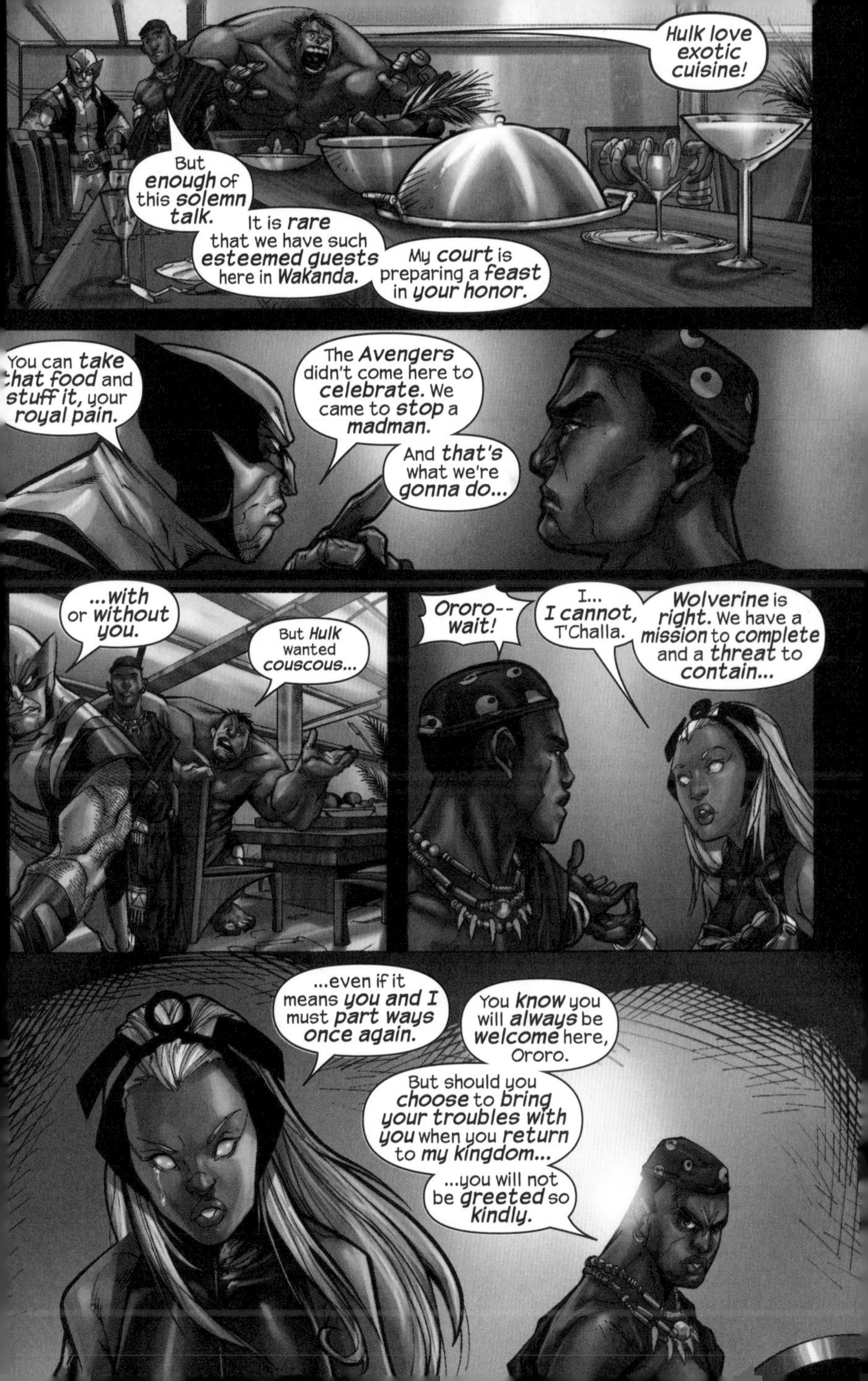
Hulk love exotic cuisine!
But enough of this solemn talk.
It is rare that we have such esteemed guests here in Wakanda.
My court is preparing a feast in your honor.
You can take that food and stuff it, your royal pain.
The Avengers didn't come here to celebrate. We came to stop a madman.
And that's what we're gonna do...
...with or without you.
But Hulk wanted couscous...
Ororo-- wait!
I... I cannot, T'Challa.
Wolverine is right. We have a mission to complete and a threat to contain...
...even if it means you and I must part ways once again.
You know you will always be welcome here, Ororo.
But should you choose to bring your troubles with you when you return to my kingdom...
...you will not be greeted so kindly.

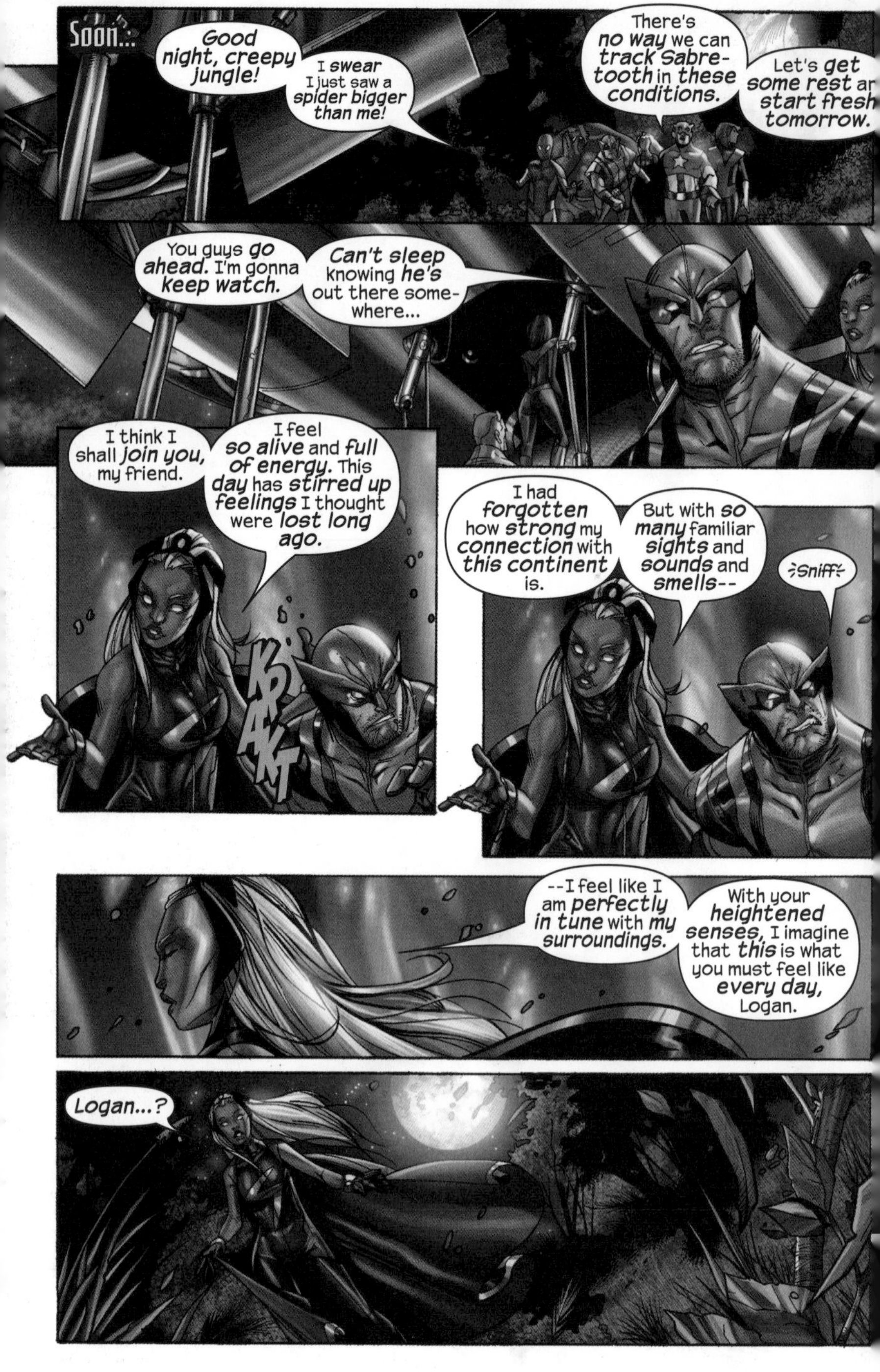
Soon...
Good night, creepy jungle!
I swear I just saw a spider bigger than me!
There's no way we can track Sabre-tooth in these conditions.
Let's get some rest an start fresh tomorrow.
You guys go ahead. I'm gonna keep watch.
Can't sleep knowing he's out there some-where...
I think I shall join you, my friend.
I feel so alive and full of energy. This day has stirred up feelings I thought were lost long ago.
KRAKT
I had forgotten how strong my connection with this continent is.
But with so many familiar sights and sounds and smells--
Sniff
--I feel like I am perfectly in tune with my surroundings.
With your heightened senses, I imagine that this is what you must feel like every day, Logan.
Logan...?

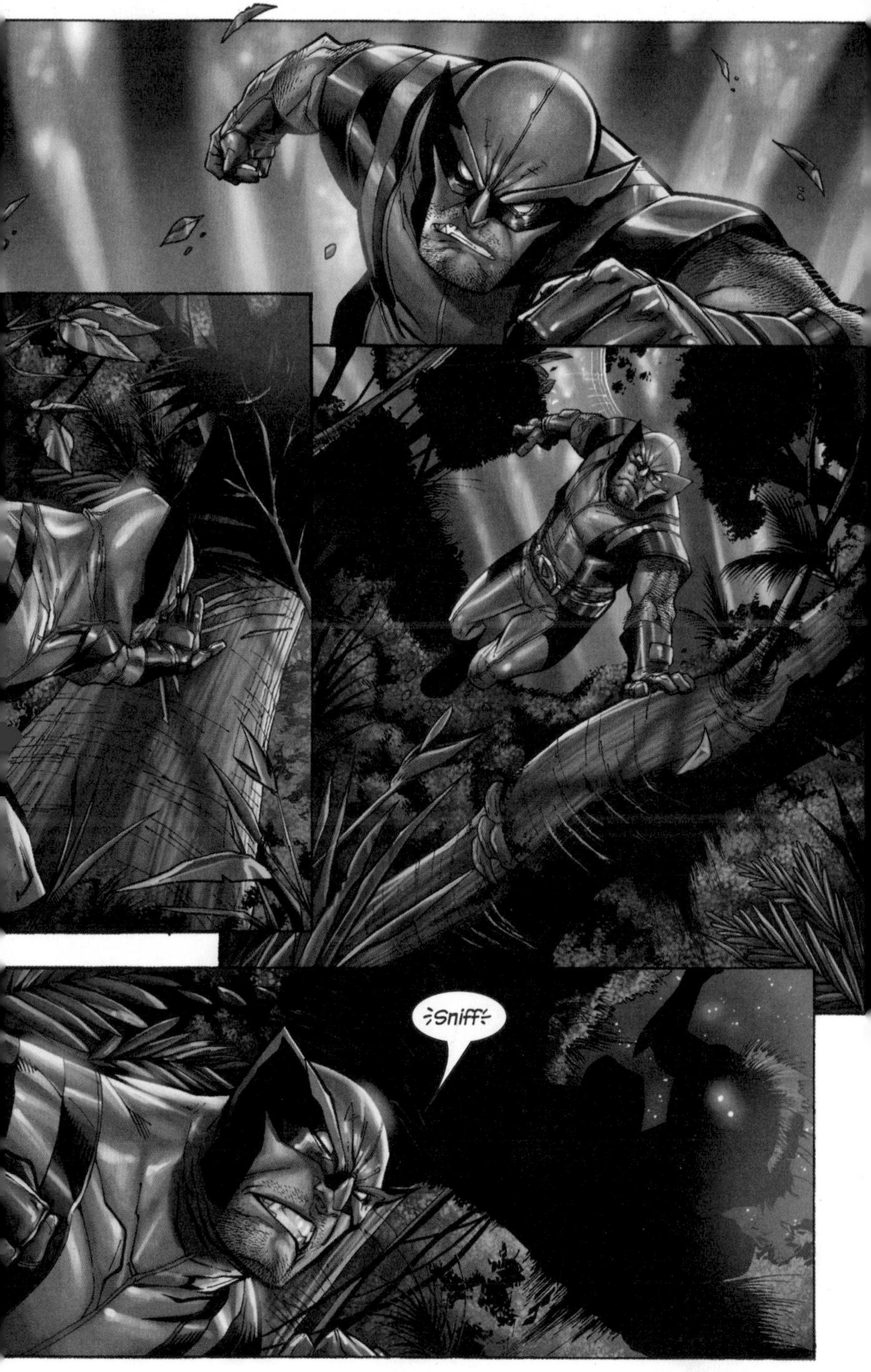

Sniff

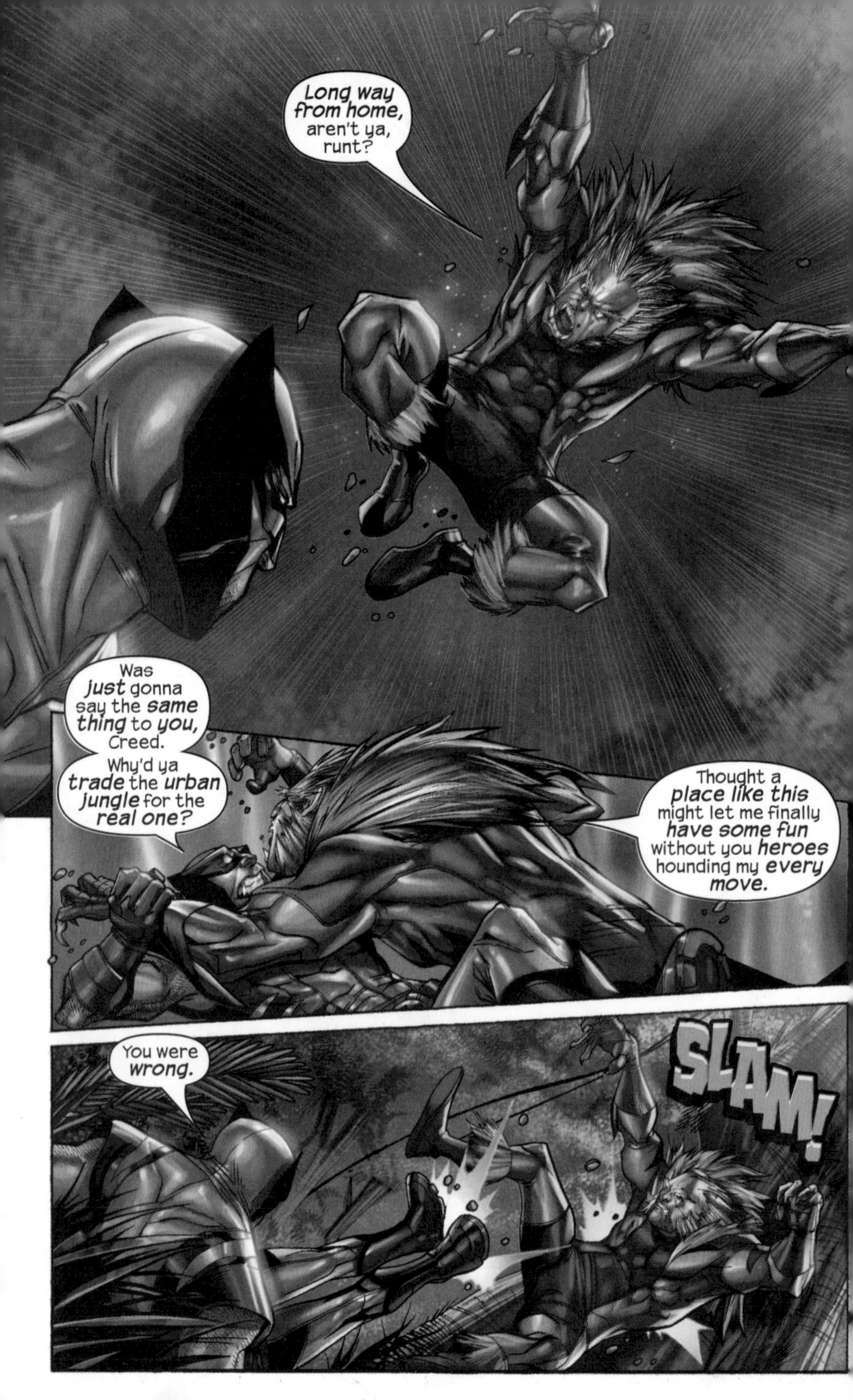
Long way from home, aren't ya, runt?
Was just gonna say the same thing to you, Creed.
Why'd ya trade the urban jungle for the real one?
Thought a place like this might let me finally have some fun without you heroes hounding my every move.
You were wrong.
SLAM!

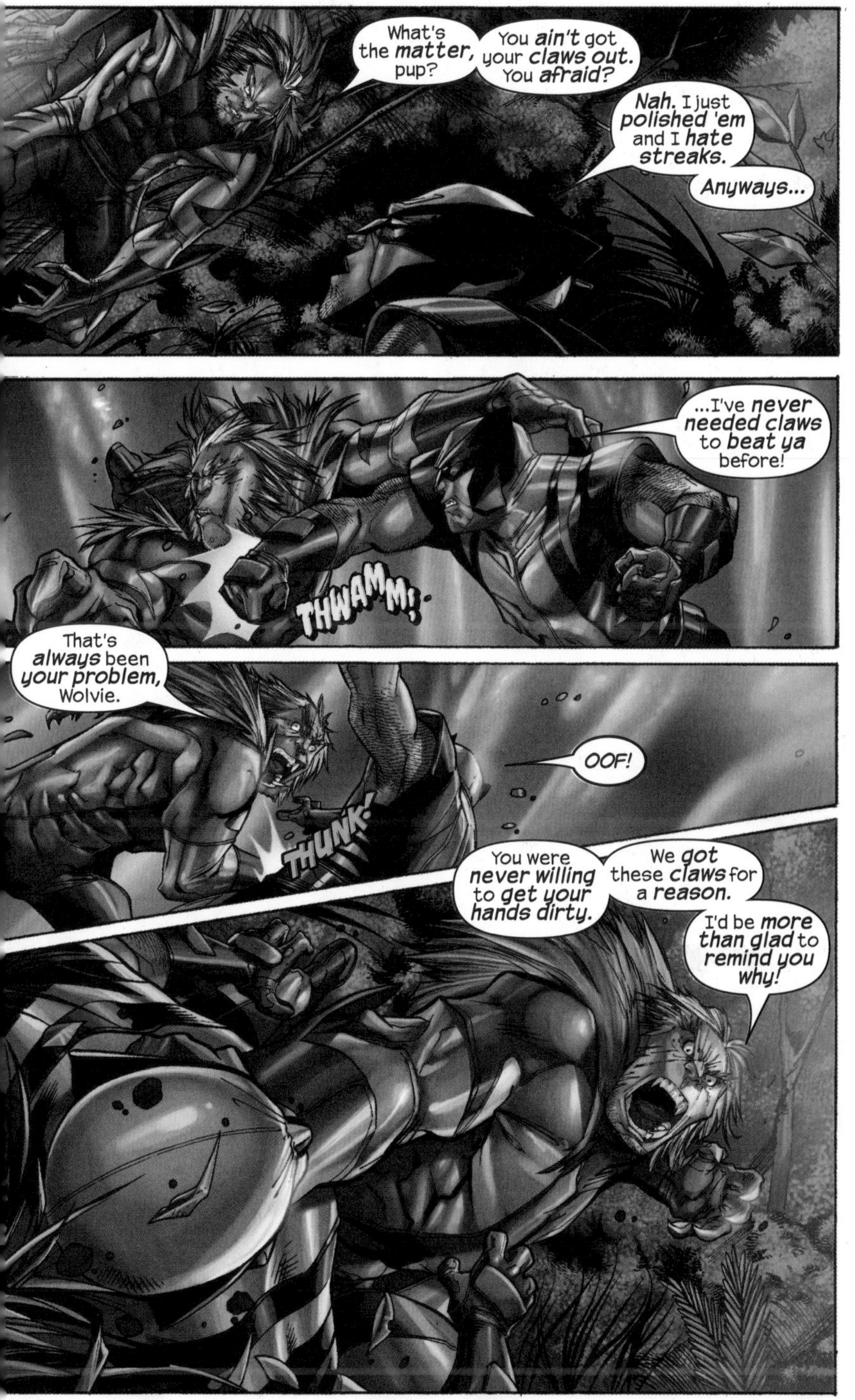
What's the matter, pup?
You ain't got your claws out. You afraid?
Nah. I just polished 'em and I hate streaks.
Anyways...
...I've never needed claws to beat ya before!
THWAMM!
That's always been your problem, Wolvie.
OOF!
THUNK!
You were never willing to get your hands dirty.
We got these claws for a reason.
I'd be more than glad to remind you why!

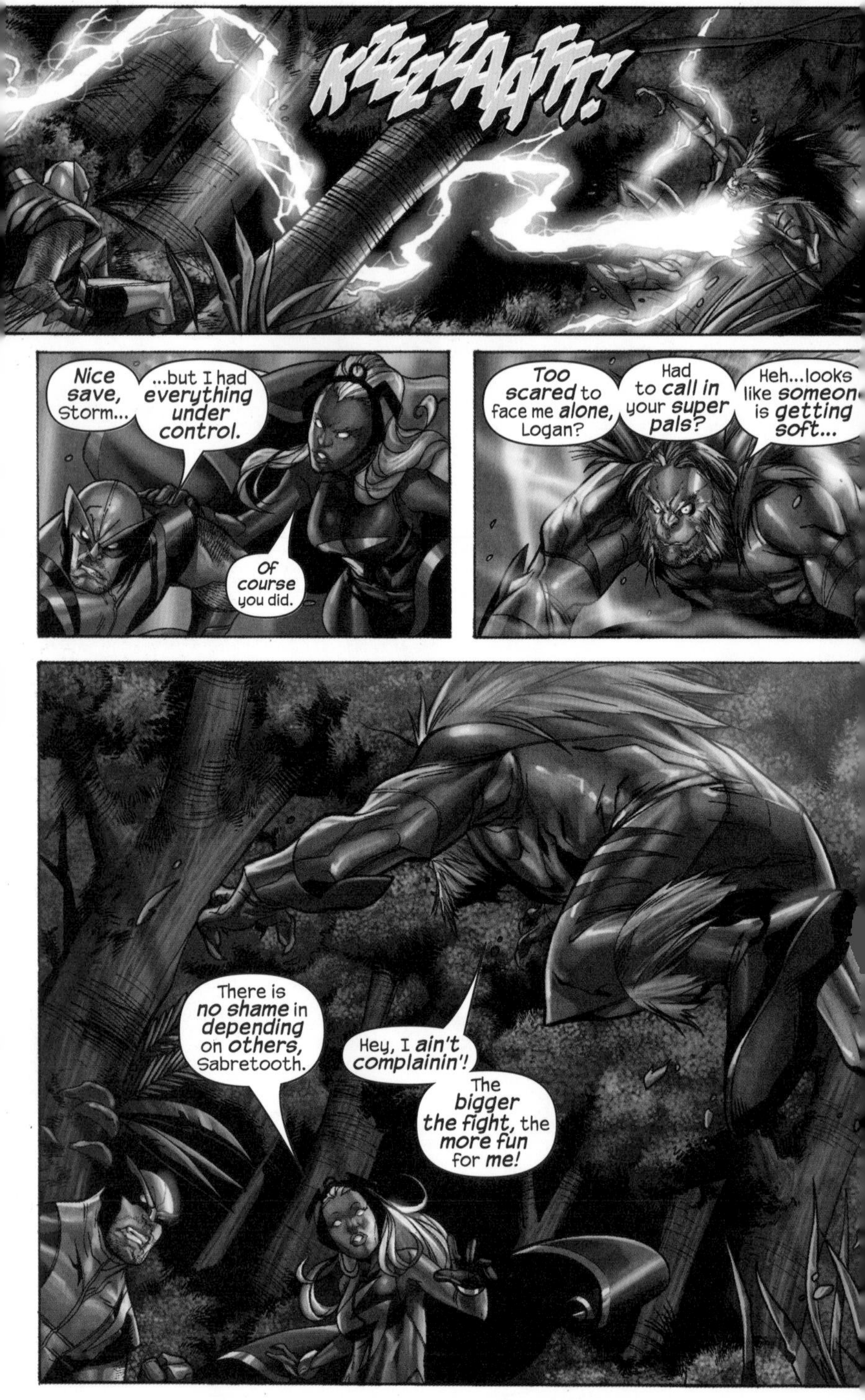
KZZZZAAFFT!
Nice save, Storm...
...but I had everything under control.
Of course you did.
Too scared to face me alone, Logan?
Had to call in your super pals?
Heh...looks like someon is getting soft...
There is no shame in depending on others, Sabretooth.
Hey, I ain't complainin'!
The bigger the fight, the more fun for me!

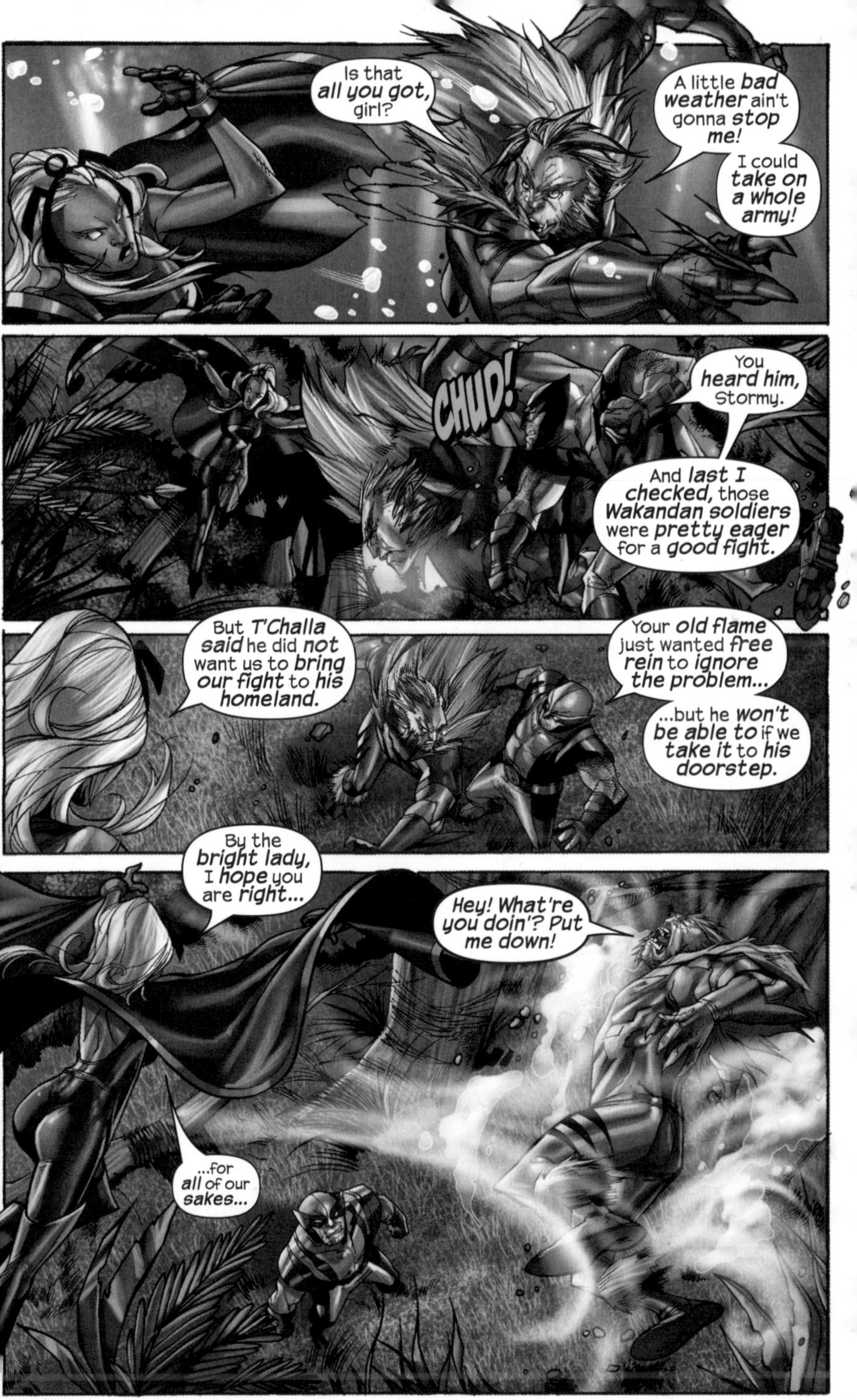

Is that all you got, girl?
A little bad weather ain't gonna stop me!
I could take on a whole army!
CHUD!
You heard him, Stormy.
And last I checked, those Wakandan soldiers were pretty eager for a good fight.
But T'Challa said he did not want us to bring our fight to his homeland.
Your old flame just wanted free rein to ignore the problem...
...but he won't be able to if we take it to his doorstep.
By the bright lady, I hope you are right...
Hey! What're you doin'? Put me down!
...for all of our sakes...

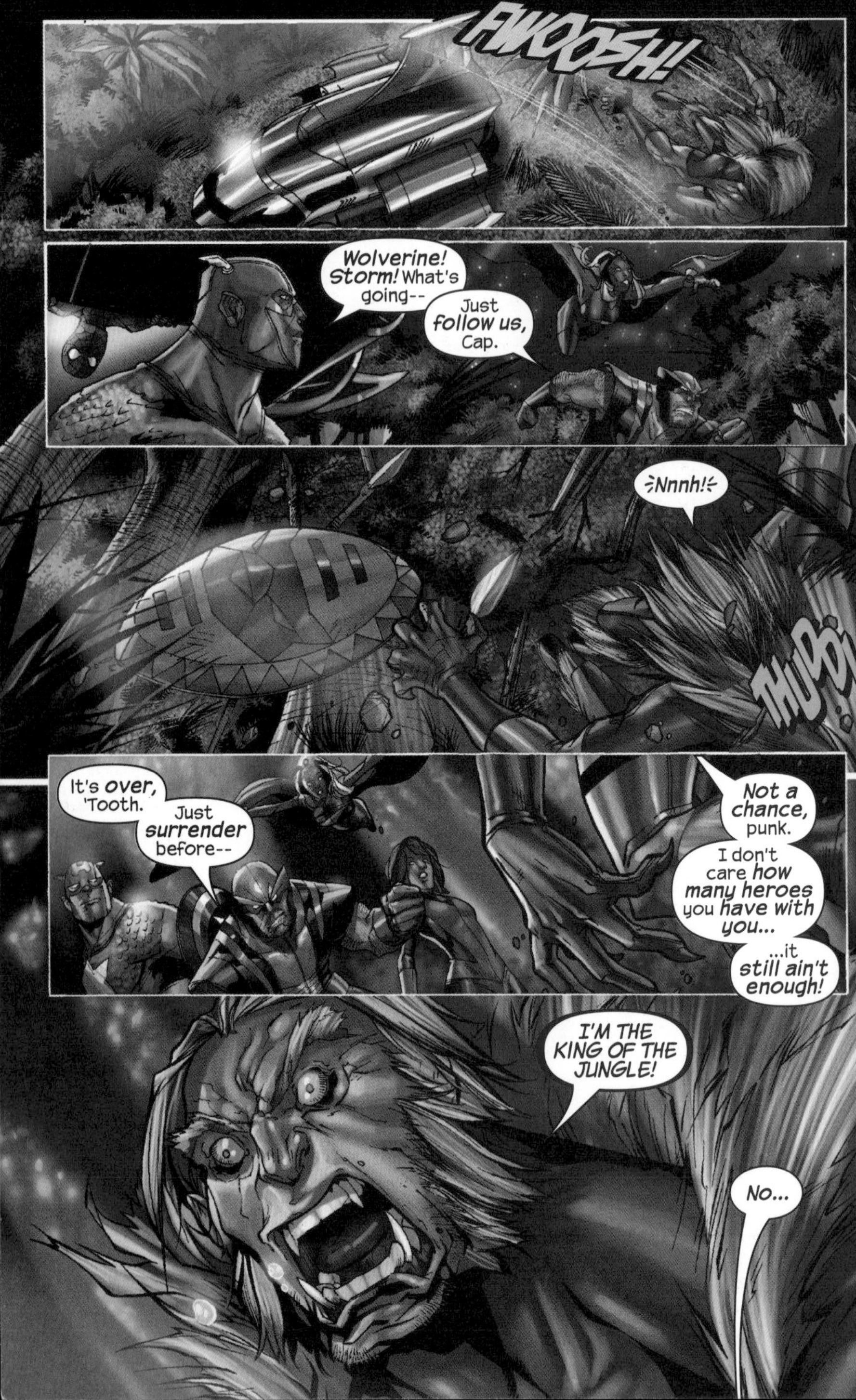
FWOOSH!
Wolverine! Storm! What's going--
Just follow us, Cap.
Nnnh!
THUD
It's over, 'Tooth.
Just surrender before--
Not a chance, punk.
I don't care how many heroes you have with you...
...it still ain't enough!
I'M THE KING OF THE JUNGLE!
No...

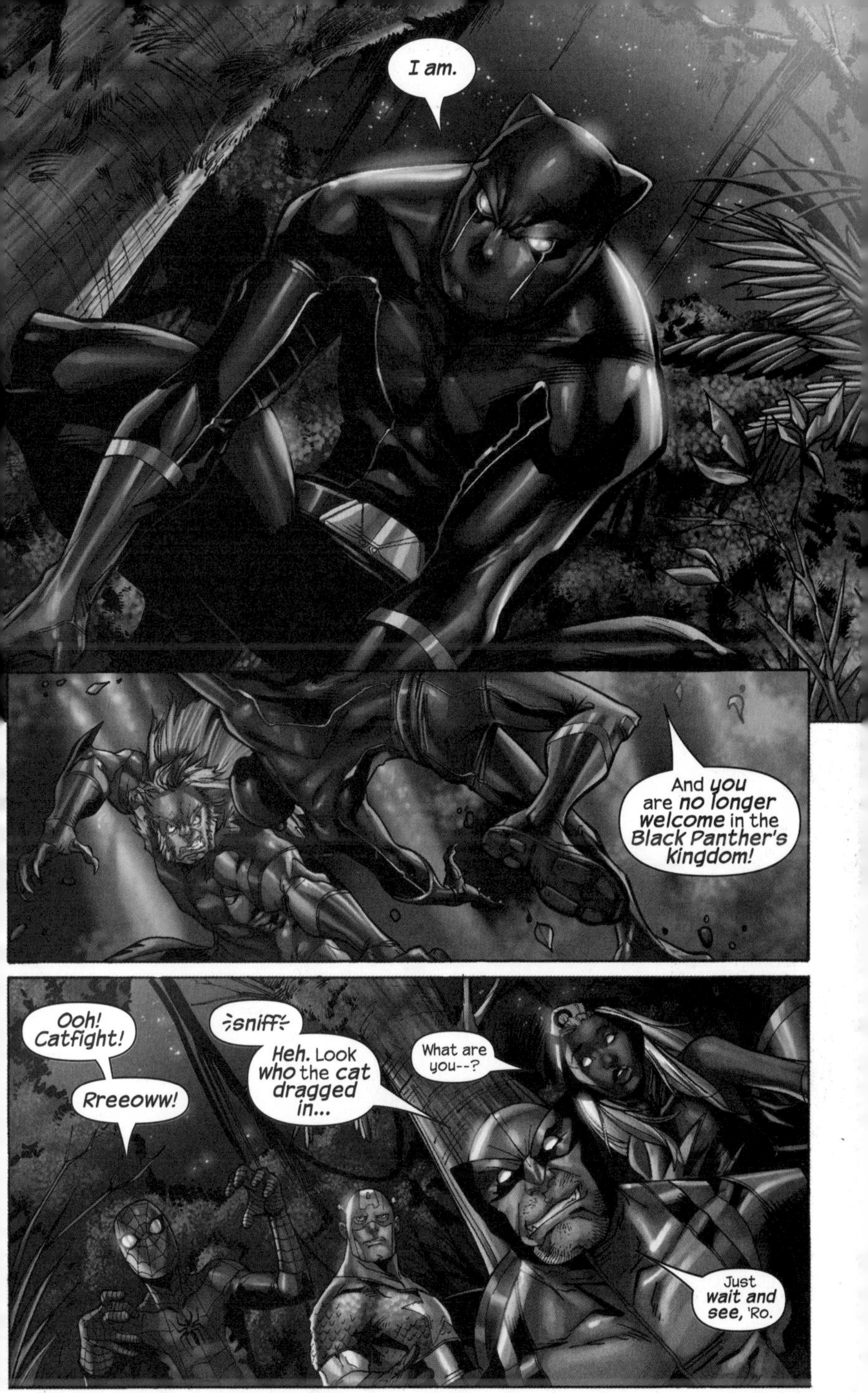

I am.
And you are no longer welcome in the Black Panther's kingdom!
Ooh! Catfight!
Rreeoww!
sniff
Heh. Look who the cat dragged in...
What are you--?
Just wait and see, 'Ro.

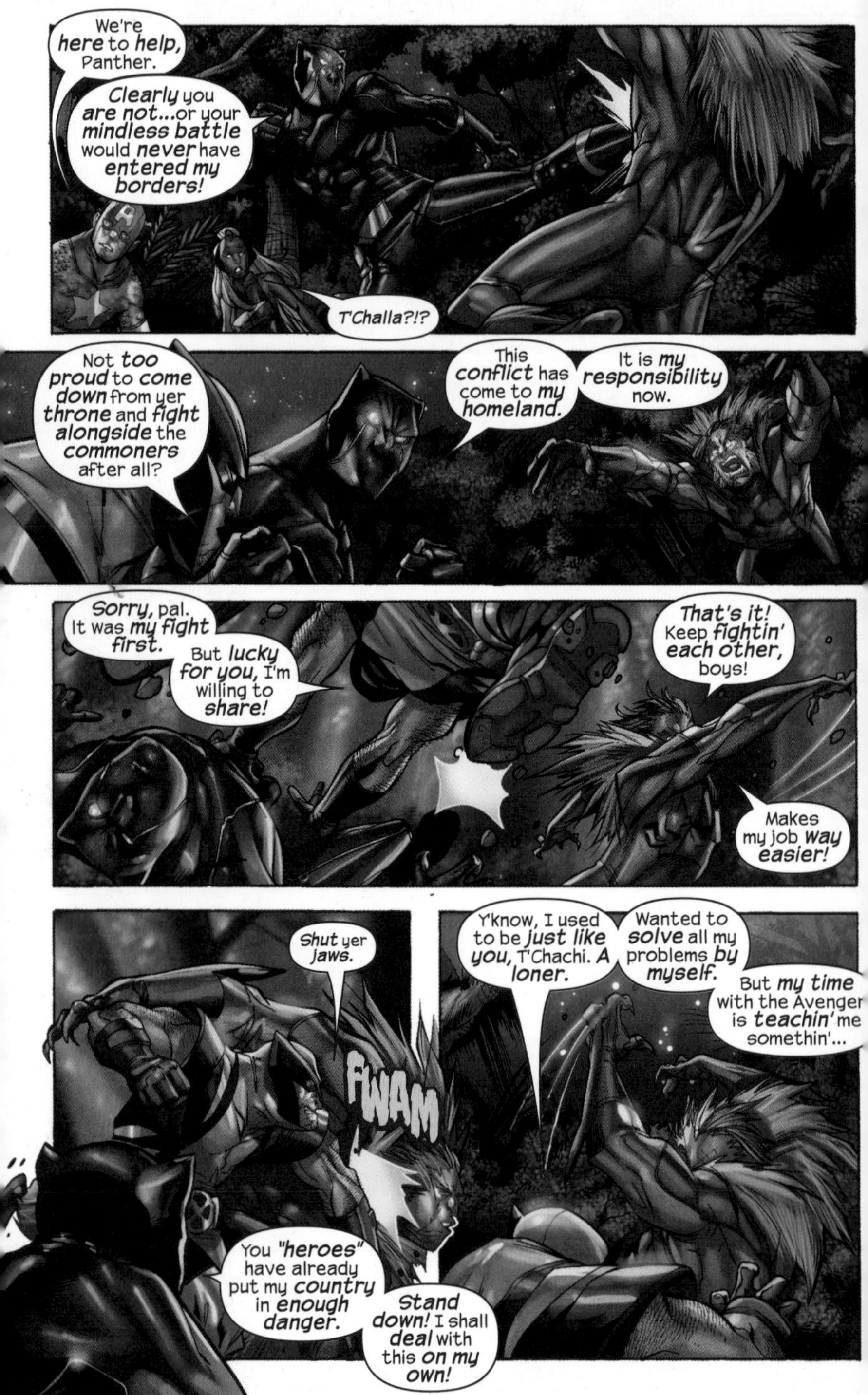
We're here to help, Panther.
Clearly you are not...or your mindless battle would never have entered my borders!
T'Challa?!?
Not too proud to come down from yer throne and fight alongside the commoners after all?
This conflict has come to my homeland.
It is my responsibility now.
Sorry, pal. It was my fight first.
But lucky for you, I'm willing to share!
That's it! Keep fightin' each other, boys!
Makes my job way easier!
Shut yer jaws.
FWAM
You "heroes" have already put my country in enough danger.
Stand down! I shall deal with this on my own!
Y'know, I used to be just like you, T'Chachi. A loner.
Wanted to solve all my problems by myself.
But my time with the Avenger is teachin' me somethin'...

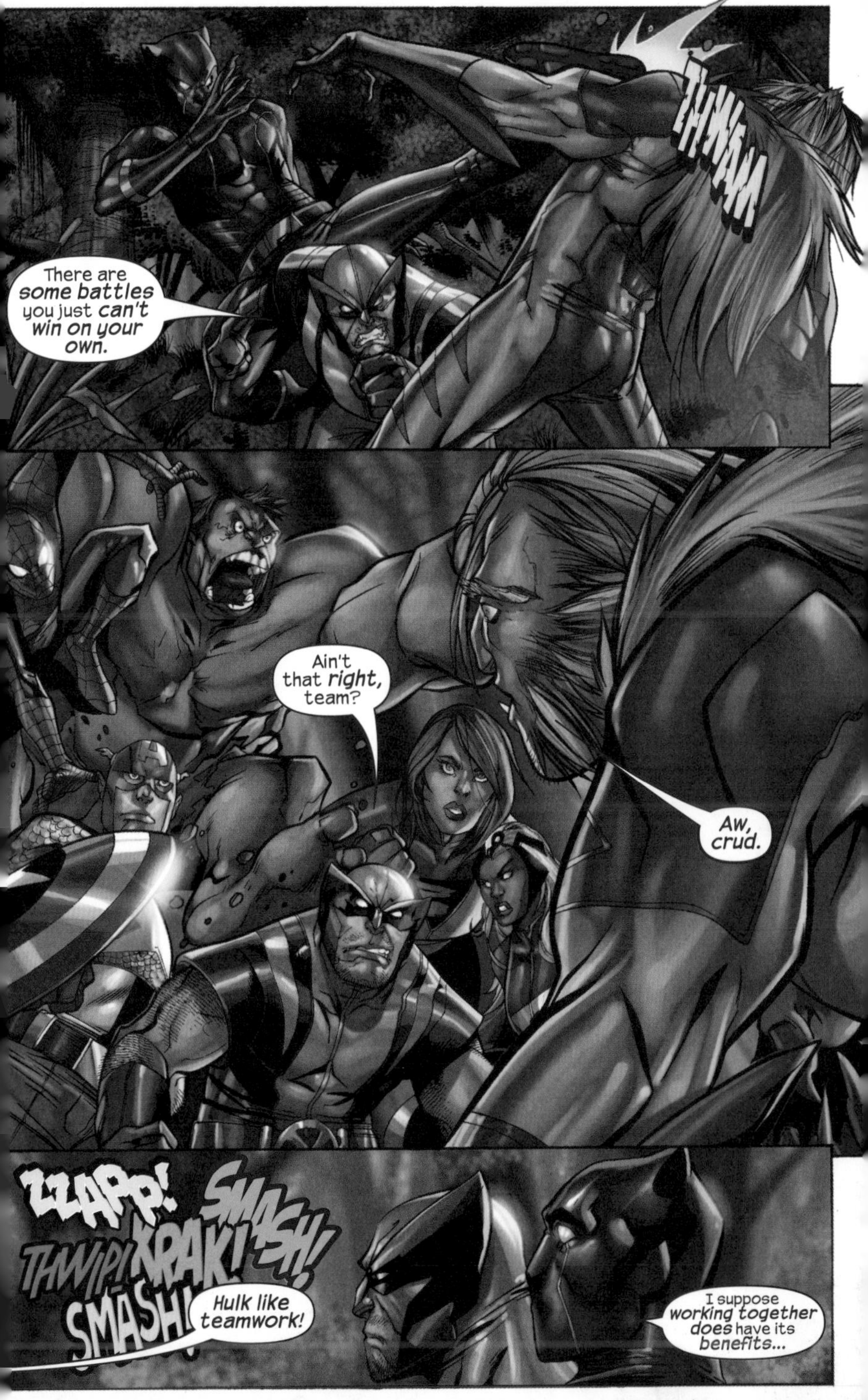
THWAKK
There are some battles you just can't win on your own.
Ain't that right, team?
Aw, crud.
ZZAPP!
SMASH!
THWIP!
KRAK!
SMASH!
Hulk like teamwork!
I suppose working together does have its benefits...

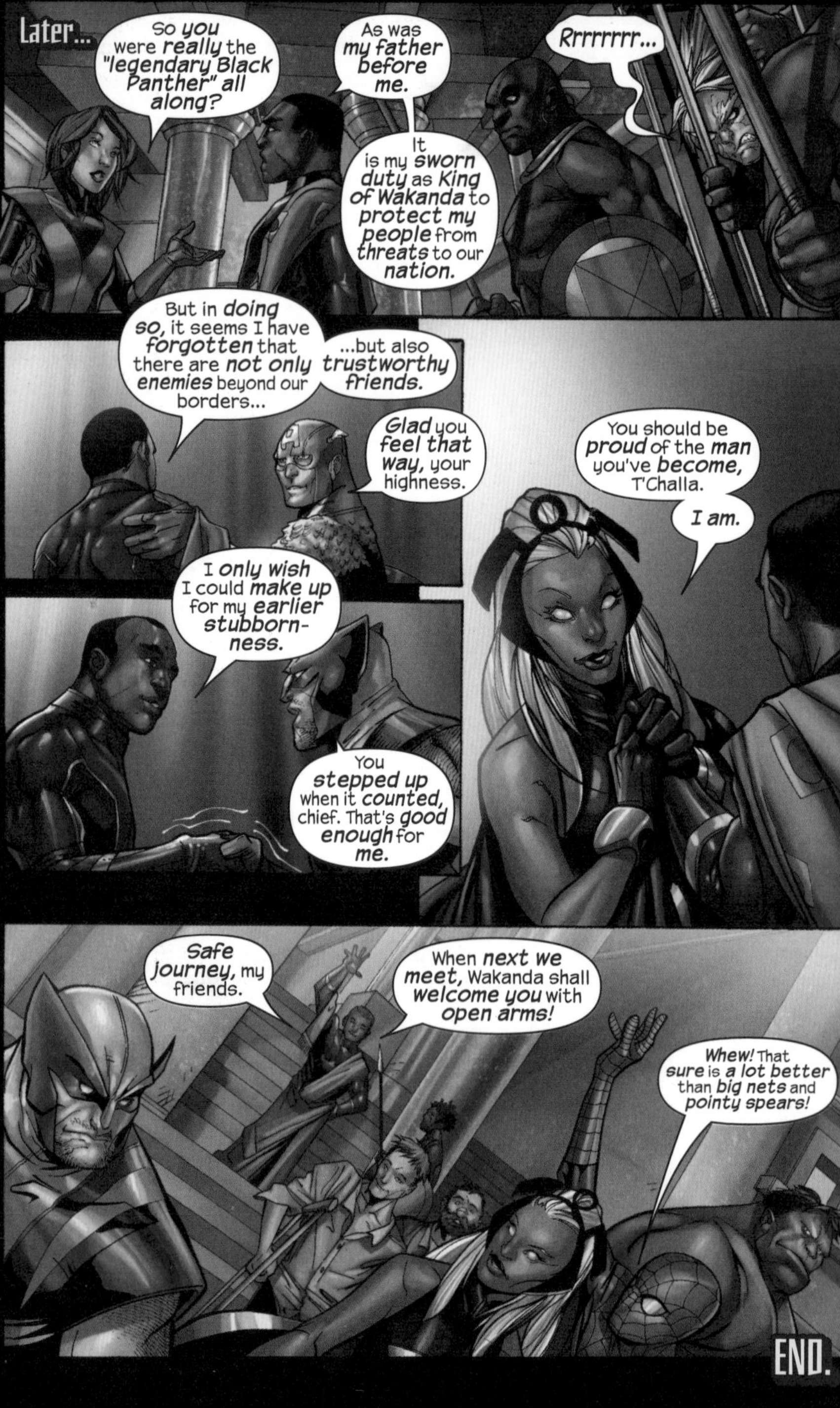

Later...
So you were really the "legendary Black Panther" all along?
As was my father before me.
It is my sworn duty as King of Wakanda to protect my people from threats to our nation.
Rrrrrrrr...
But in doing so, it seems I have forgotten that there are not only enemies beyond our borders...
...but also trustworthy friends.
Glad you feel that way, your highness.
I only wish I could make up for my earlier stubborn-ness.
You stepped up when it counted, chief. That's good enough for me.
You should be proud of the man you've become, T'Challa.
I am.
Safe journey, my friends.
When next we meet, Wakanda shall welcome you with open arms!
Whew! That sure is a lot better than big nets and pointy spears!
END.

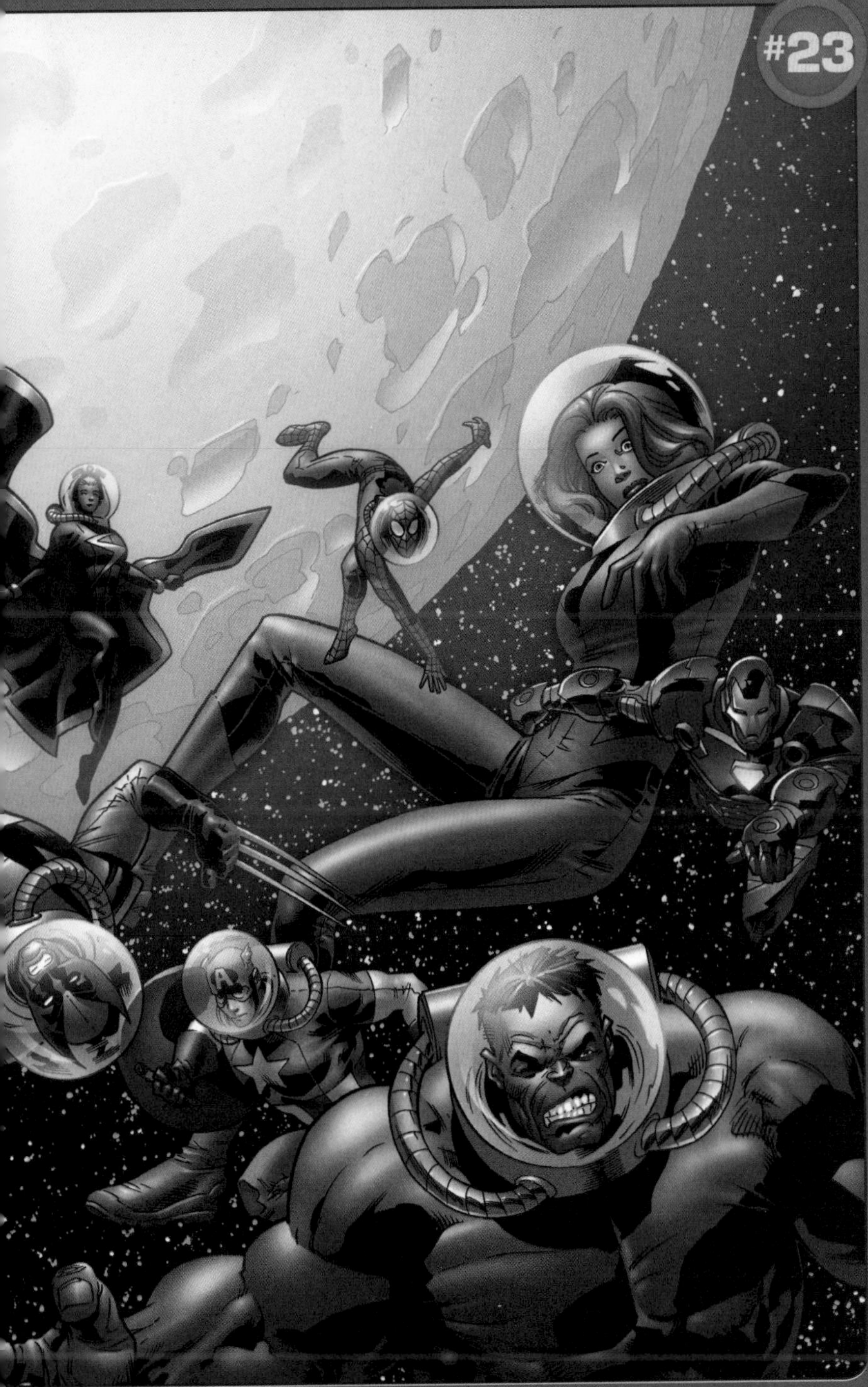
#23

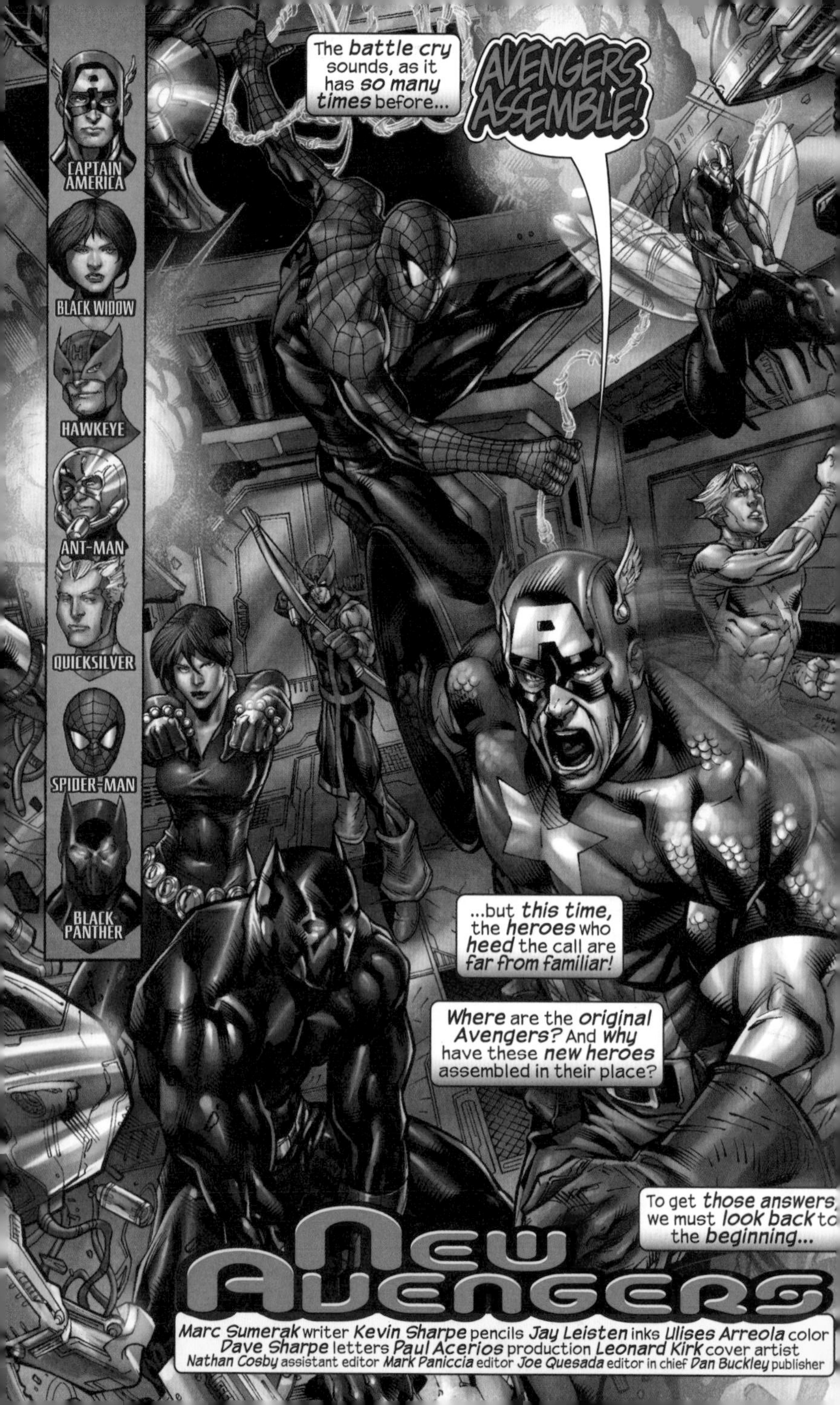
CAPTAIN AMERICA
BLACK WIDOW
HAWKEYE
ANT-MAN
QUICKSILVER
SPIDER-MAN
BLACK PANTHER
The battle cry sounds, as it has so many times before...
AVENGERS ASSEMBLE!
...but this time, the heroes who heed the call are far from familiar!
Where are the original Avengers? And why have these new heroes assembled in their place?
To get those answers, we must look back to the beginning...
NEW AVENGERS
Marc Sumerak writer Kevin Sharpe pencils Jay Leisten inks Ulises Arreola color
Dave Sharpe letters Paul Acerios production Leonard Kirk cover artist
Nathan Cosby assistant editor Mark Paniccia editor Joe Quesada editor in chief Dan Buckley publisher

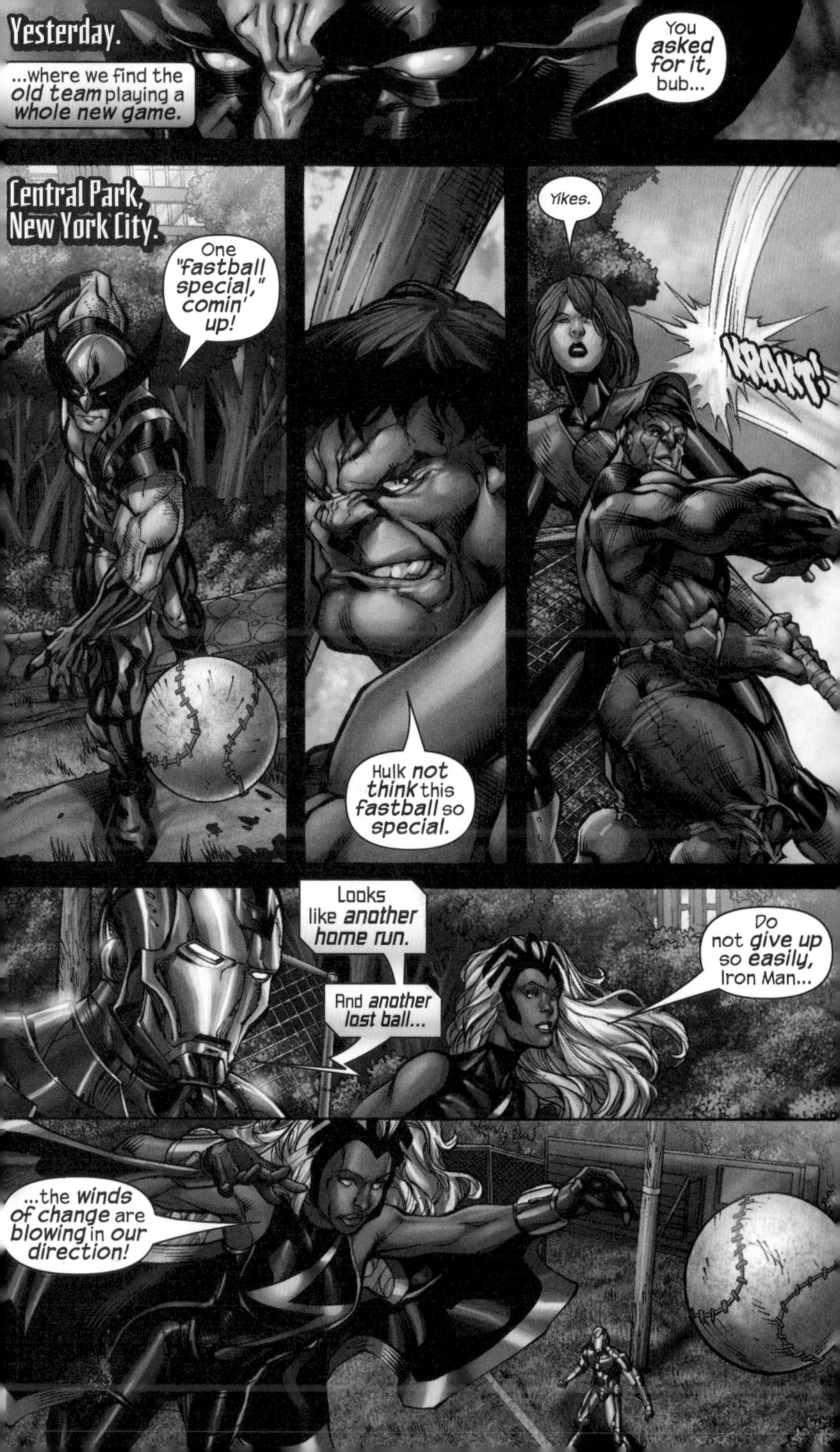

Yesterday.
...where we find the old team playing a whole new game.
You asked for it, bub...
Central Park, New York City.
One "fastball special," comin' up!
Hulk not think this fastball so special.
Yikes.
KRAKT!
Looks like another home run.
And another lost ball...
Do not give up so easily, Iron Man...
...the winds of change are blowing in our direction!

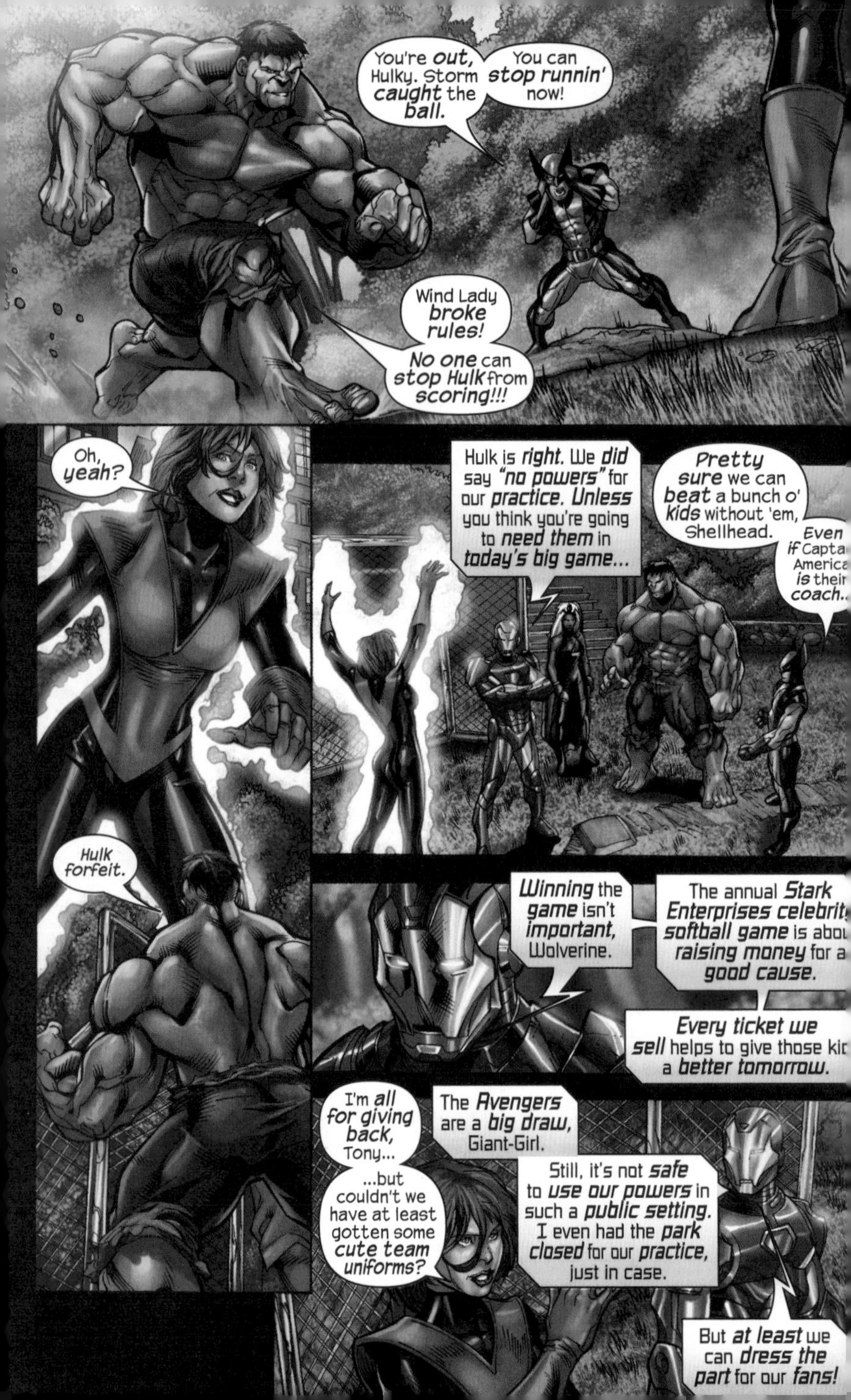

You're out, Hulky. Storm caught the ball.
You can stop runnin' now!
Wind Lady broke rules!
No one can stop Hulk from scoring!!!
Oh, yeah?
Hulk forfeit.
Hulk is right. We did say "no powers" for our practice. Unless you think you're going to need them in today's big game...
Pretty sure we can beat a bunch o' kids without 'em, Shellhead.
Winning the game isn't important, Wolverine.
Every ticket we sell helps to give those kid a better tomorrow.
I'm all for giving back, Tony...
...but couldn't we have at least gotten some cute team uniforms?
The Avengers are a big draw, Giant-Girl.
Still, it's not safe to use our powers in such a public setting. I even had the park closed for our practice, just in case.
But at least we can dress the part for our fans!

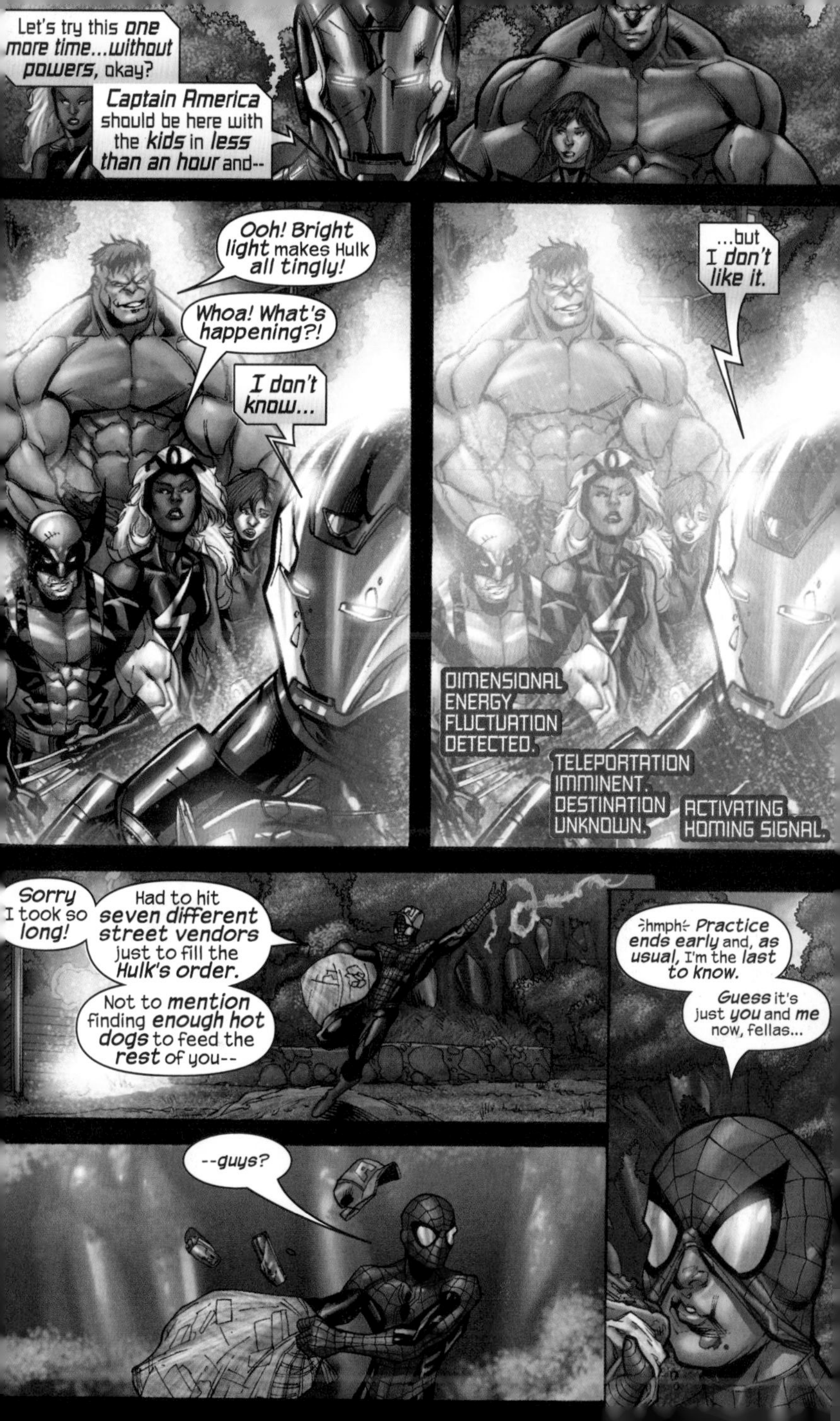

Let's try this one more time...without powers, okay?
Captain America should be here with the kids in less than an hour and--
Ooh! Bright light makes Hulk all tingly!
Whoa! What's happening?!
I don't know...
...but I don't like it.
DIMENSIONAL ENERGY FLUCTUATION DETECTED.
TELEPORTATION IMMINENT. DESTINATION UNKNOWN.
ACTIVATING HOMING SIGNAL.
Sorry I took so long!
Had to hit seven different street vendors just to fill the Hulk's order.
Not to mention finding enough hot dogs to feed the rest of you--
--guys?
hmph Practice ends early and, as usual, I'm the last to know.
Guess it's just you and me now, fellas...

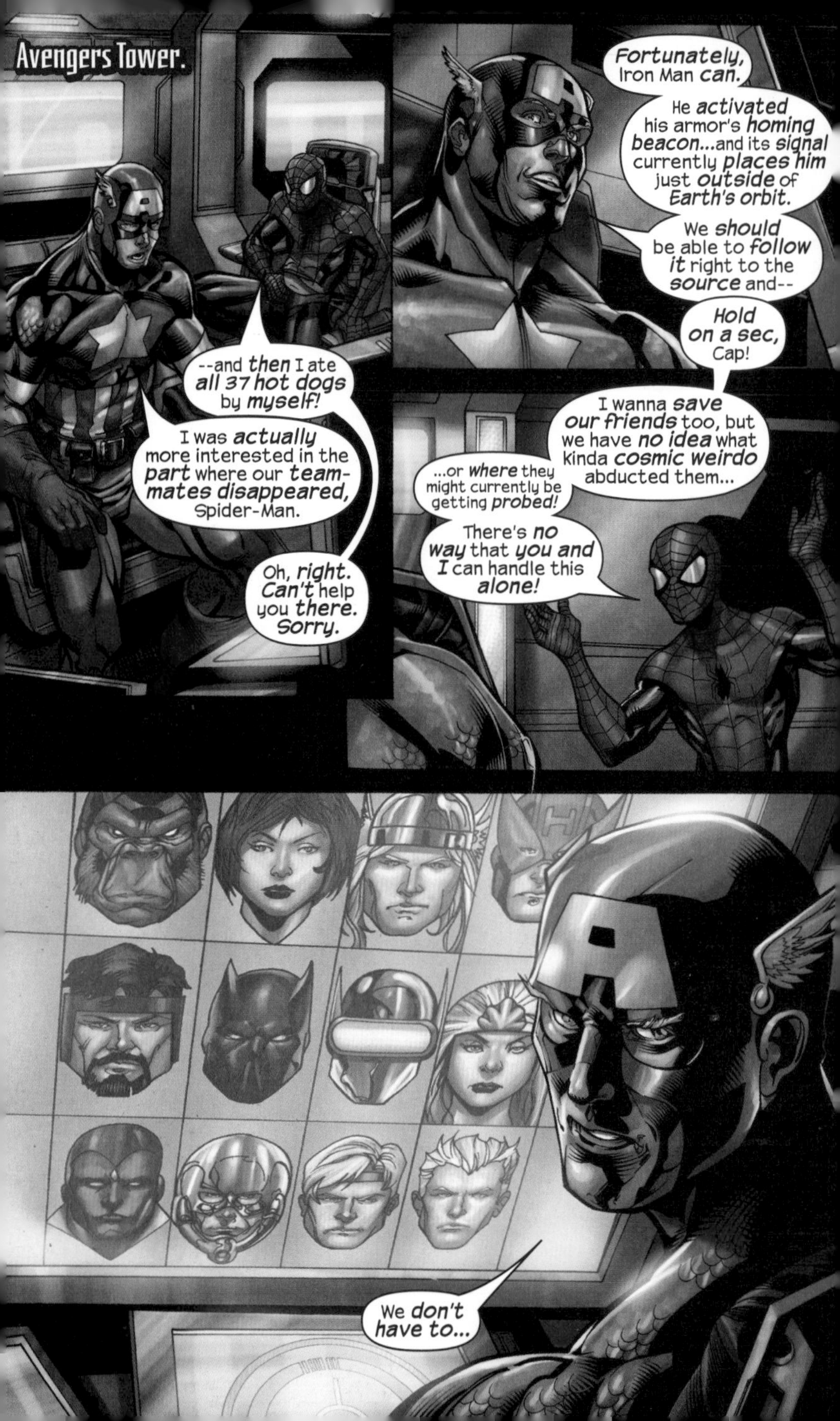

Avengers Tower.
--and then I ate all 37 hot dogs by myself!
I was actually more interested in the part where our team-mates disappeared, Spider-Man.
Oh, right. Can't help you there. Sorry.
Fortunately, Iron Man can.
He activated his armor's homing beacon...and its signal currently places him just outside of Earth's orbit.
We should be able to follow it right to the source and--
Hold on a sec, Cap!
I wanna save our friends too, but we have no idea what kinda cosmic weirdo abducted them...
...or where they might currently be getting probed!
There's no way that you and I can handle this alone!
We don't have to...

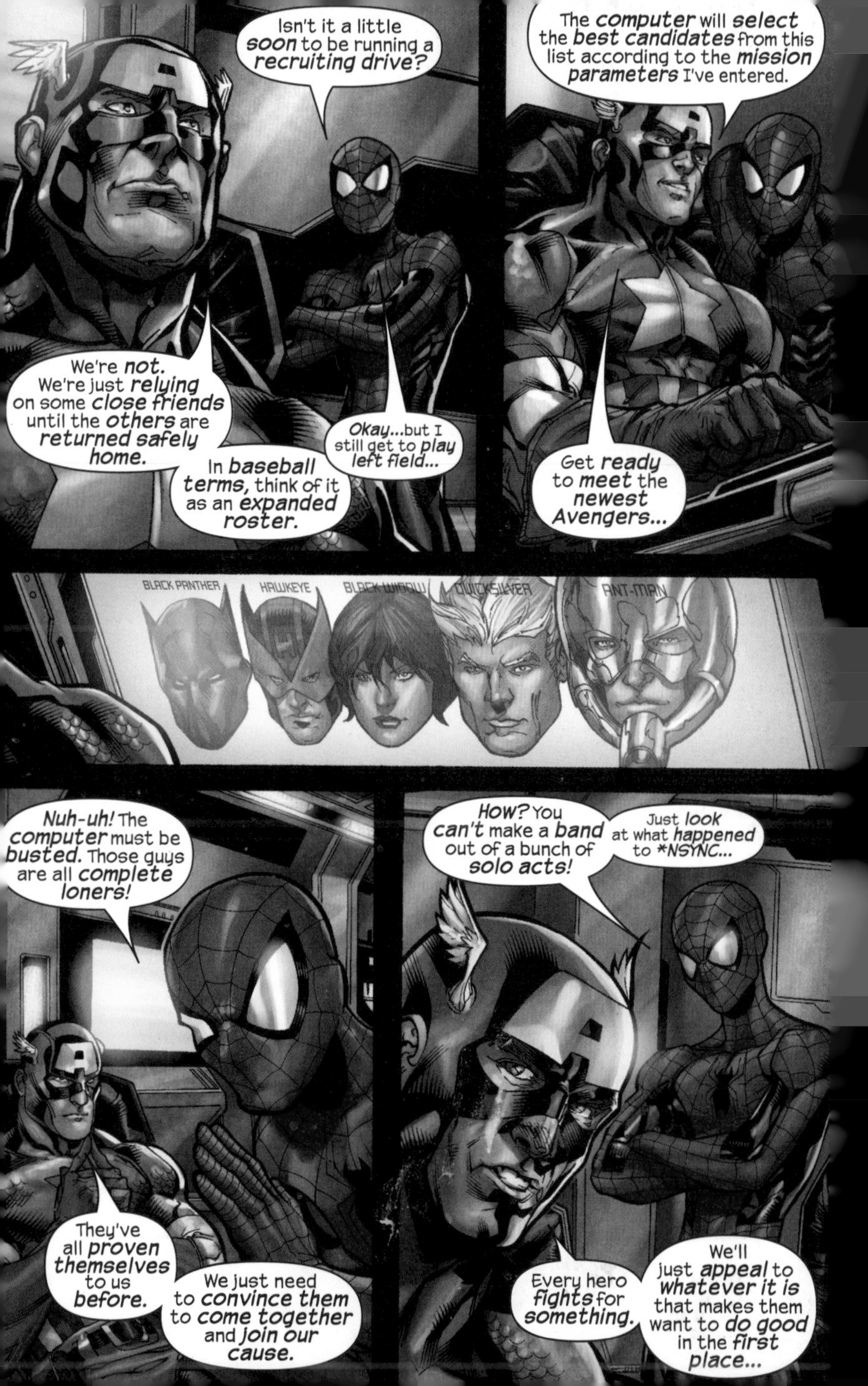
Isn't it a little soon to be running a recruiting drive?
We're not. We're just relying on some close friends until the others are returned safely home.
In baseball terms, think of it as an expanded roster.
Okay...but I still get to play left field...
The computer will select the best candidates from this list according to the mission parameters I've entered.
Get ready to meet the newest Avengers...
BLACK PANTHER
HAWKEYE
BLACK WIDOW
QUICKSILVER
ANT-MAN
Nuh-uh! The computer must be busted. Those guys are all complete loners!
They've all proven themselves to us before.
We just need to convince them to come together and join our cause.
HOW? You can't make a band out of a bunch of solo acts!
Just look at what happened to *NSYNC...
Every hero fights for something.
We'll just appeal to whatever it is that makes them want to do good in the first place...

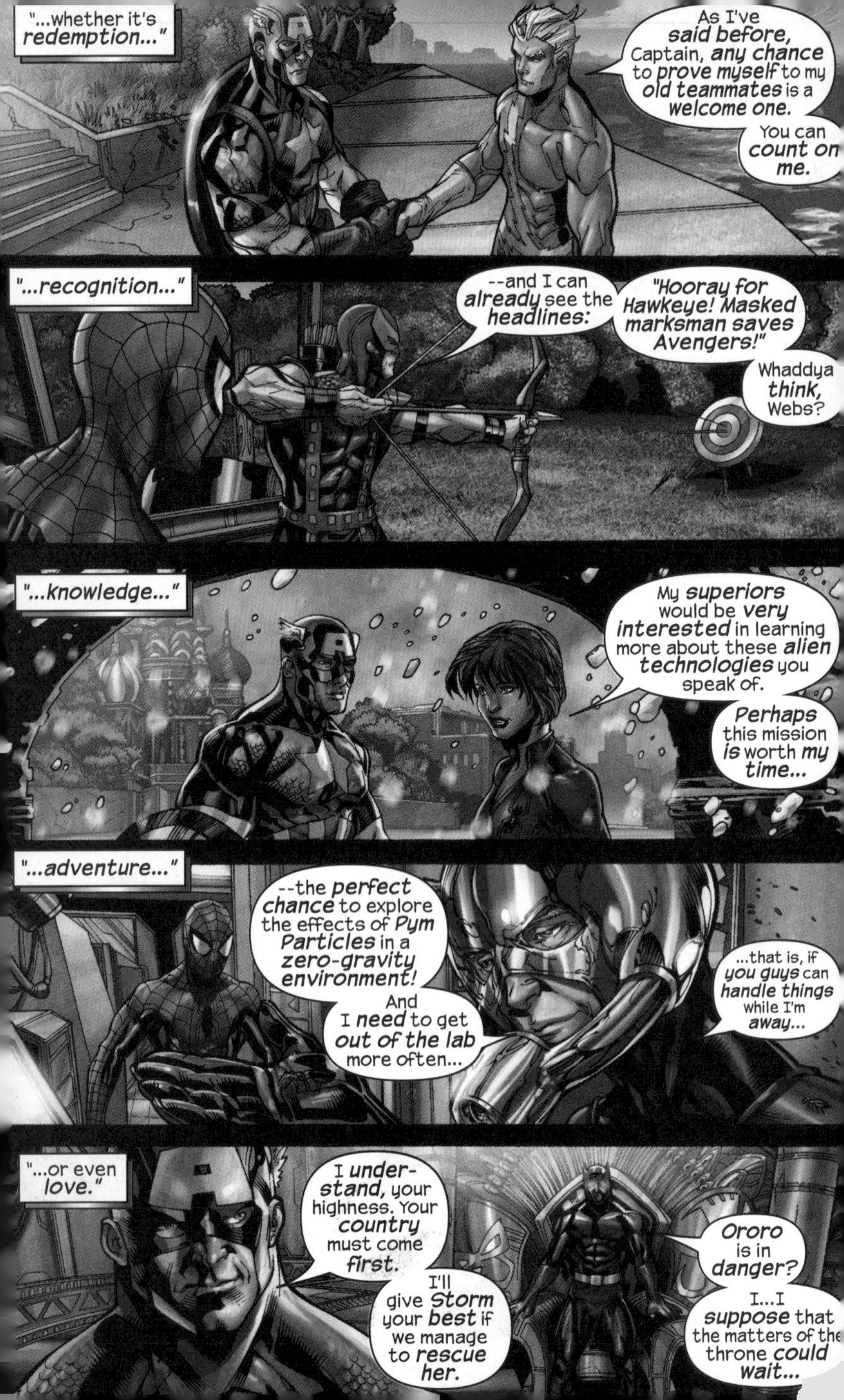
"...whether it's redemption..."
As I've said before, Captain, any chance to prove myself to my old teammates is a welcome one.
You can count on me.
"...recognition..."
--and I can already see the headlines:
"Hooray for Hawkeye! Masked marksman saves Avengers!"
Whaddya think, Webs?
"...knowledge..."
My superiors would be very interested in learning more about these alien technologies you speak of.
Perhaps this mission is worth my time...
"...adventure..."
--the perfect chance to explore the effects of Pym Particles in a zero-gravity environment!
And I need to get out of the lab more often...
...that is, if you guys can handle things while I'm away...
"...or even love."
I under-stand, your highness. Your country must come first.
I'll give Storm your best if we manage to rescue her.
Ororo is in danger?
I...I suppose that the matters of the throne could wait...

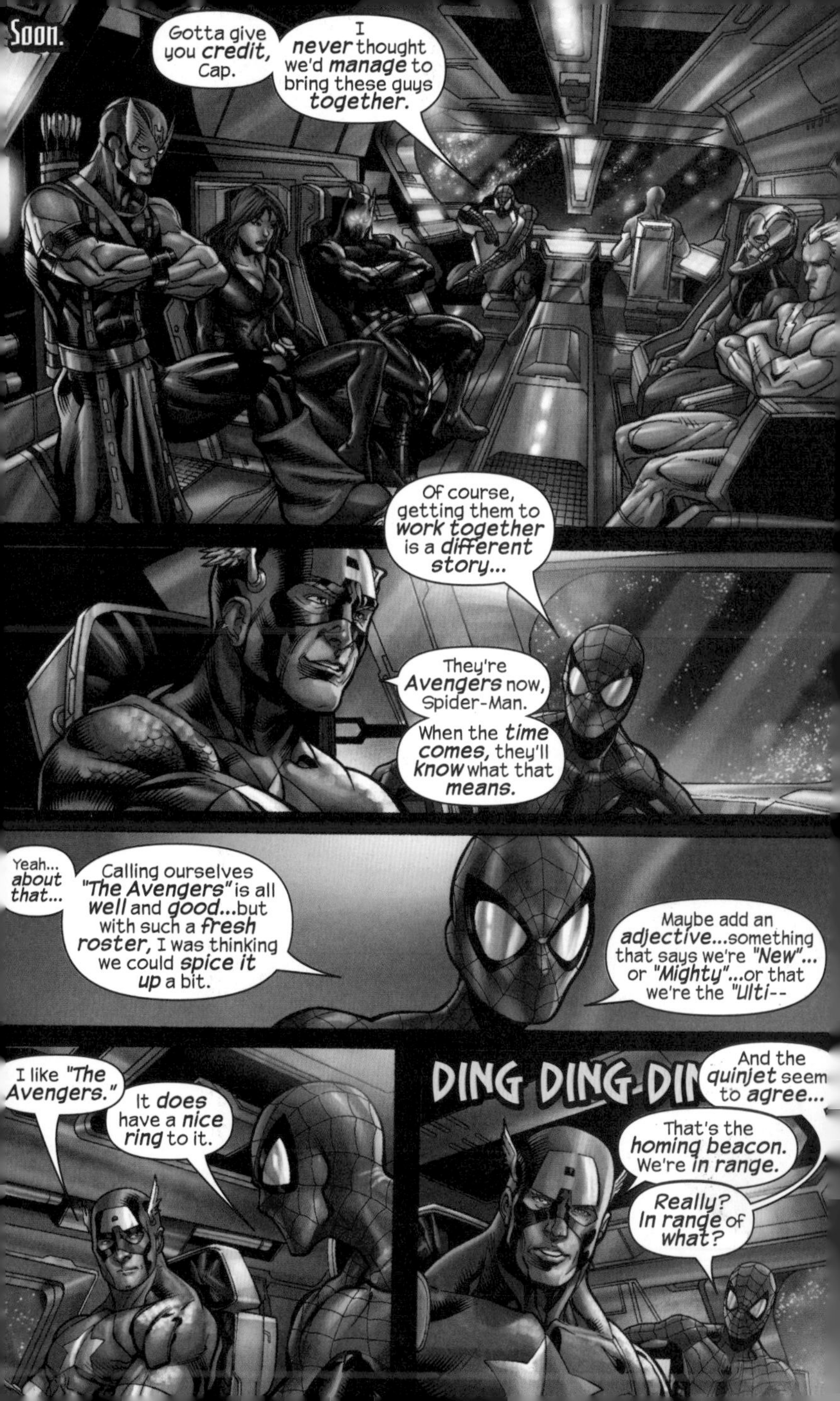
Soon.
Gotta give you credit, Cap.
I never thought we'd manage to bring these guys together.
Of course, getting them to work together is a different story...
They're Avengers now, Spider-Man.
When the time comes, they'll know what that means.
Yeah... about that...
Calling ourselves "The Avengers" is all well and good...but with such a fresh roster, I was thinking we could spice it up a bit.
Maybe add an adjective...something that says we're "New"... or "Mighty"...or that we're the "Ulti--
I like "The Avengers."
It does have a nice ring to it.
DING DING DIN
And the quinjet seem to agree...
That's the homing beacon. We're in range.
Really? In range of what?

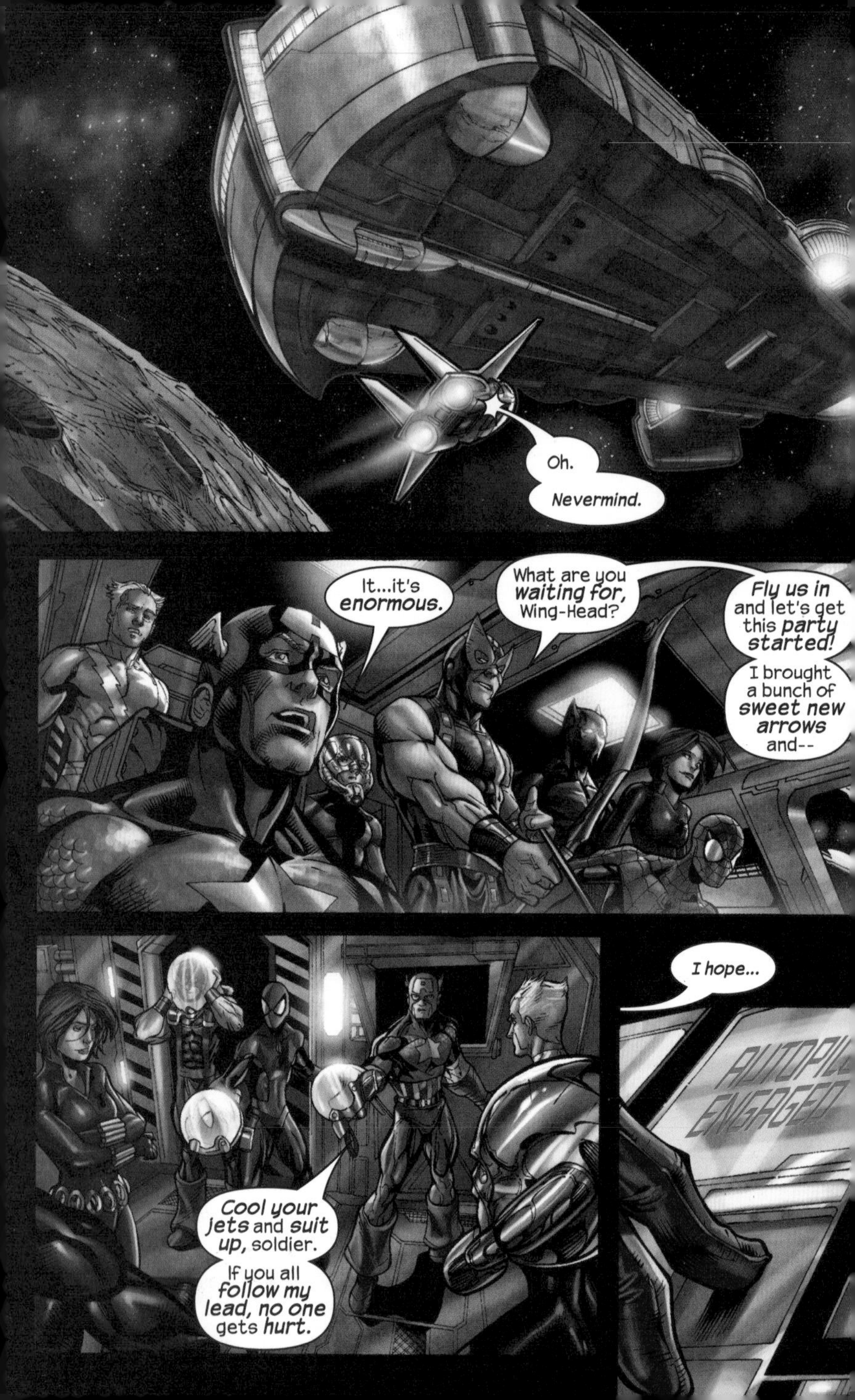
Oh.
Nevermind.
It...it's enormous.
What are you waiting for, Wing-Head?
Fly us in and let's get this party started!
I brought a bunch of sweet new arrows and--
Cool your jets and suit up, soldier.
If you all follow my lead, no one gets hurt.
I hope...
AUTOPILO
ENGAGED

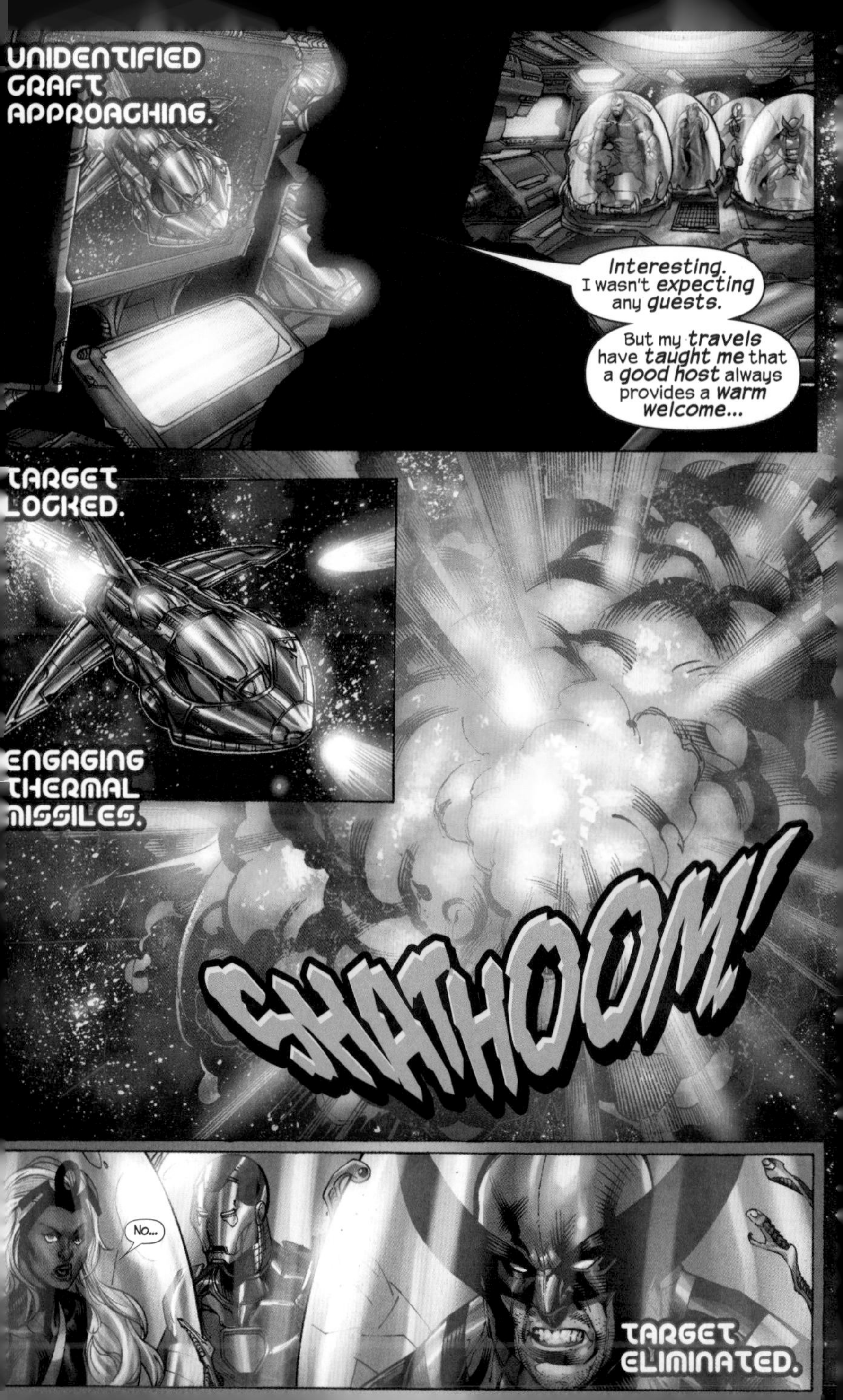
UNIDENTIFIED CRAFT APPROACHING.
Interesting. I wasn't expecting any guests.
But my travels have taught me that a good host always provides a warm welcome...
TARGET LOCKED.
ENGAGING THERMAL MISSILES.
SHATHOOM!
No...
TARGET ELIMINATED.

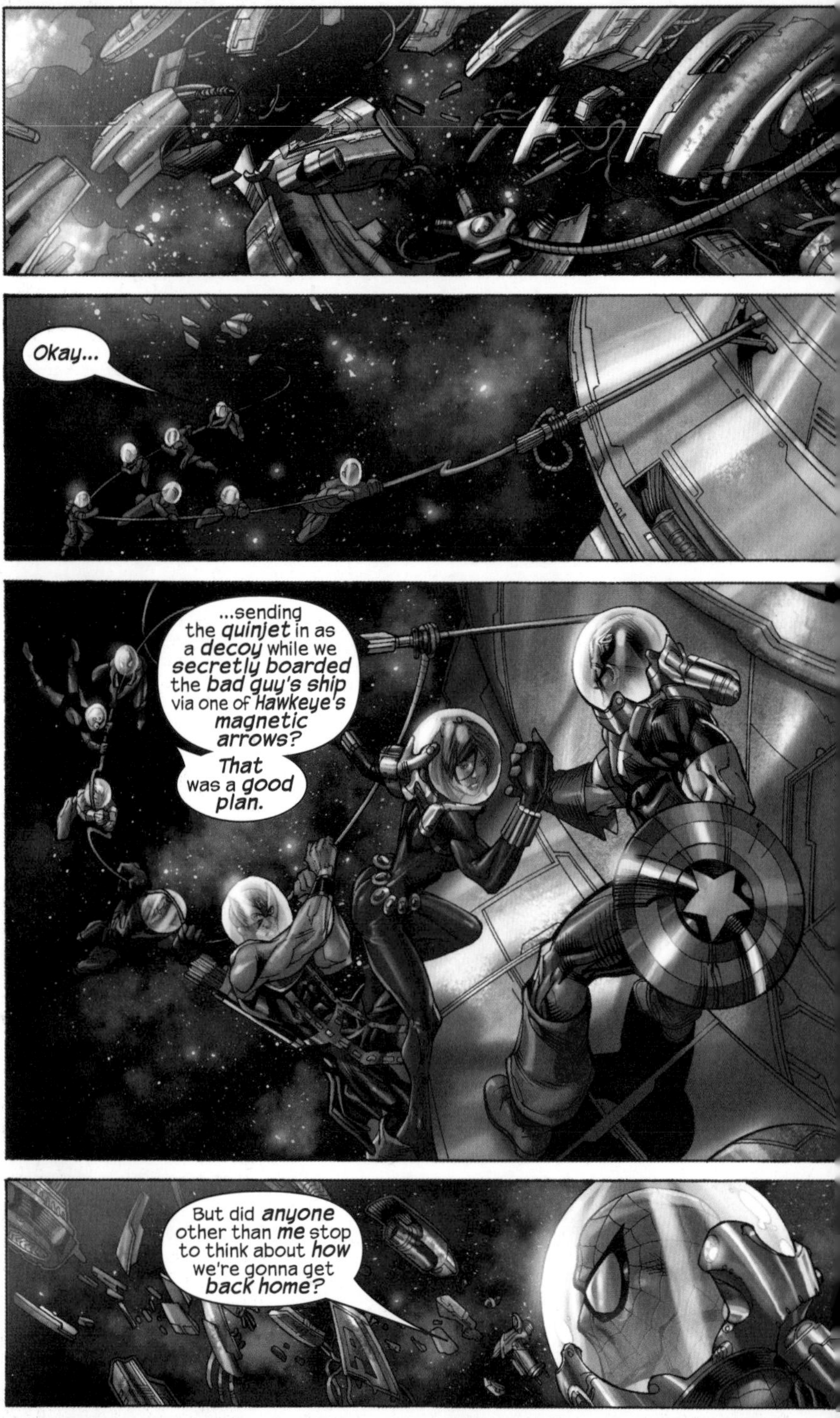
Okay...
...sending the quinjet in as a decoy while we secretly boarded the bad guy's ship via one of Hawkeye's magnetic arrows?
That was a good plan.
But did anyone other than me stop to think about how we're gonna get back home?

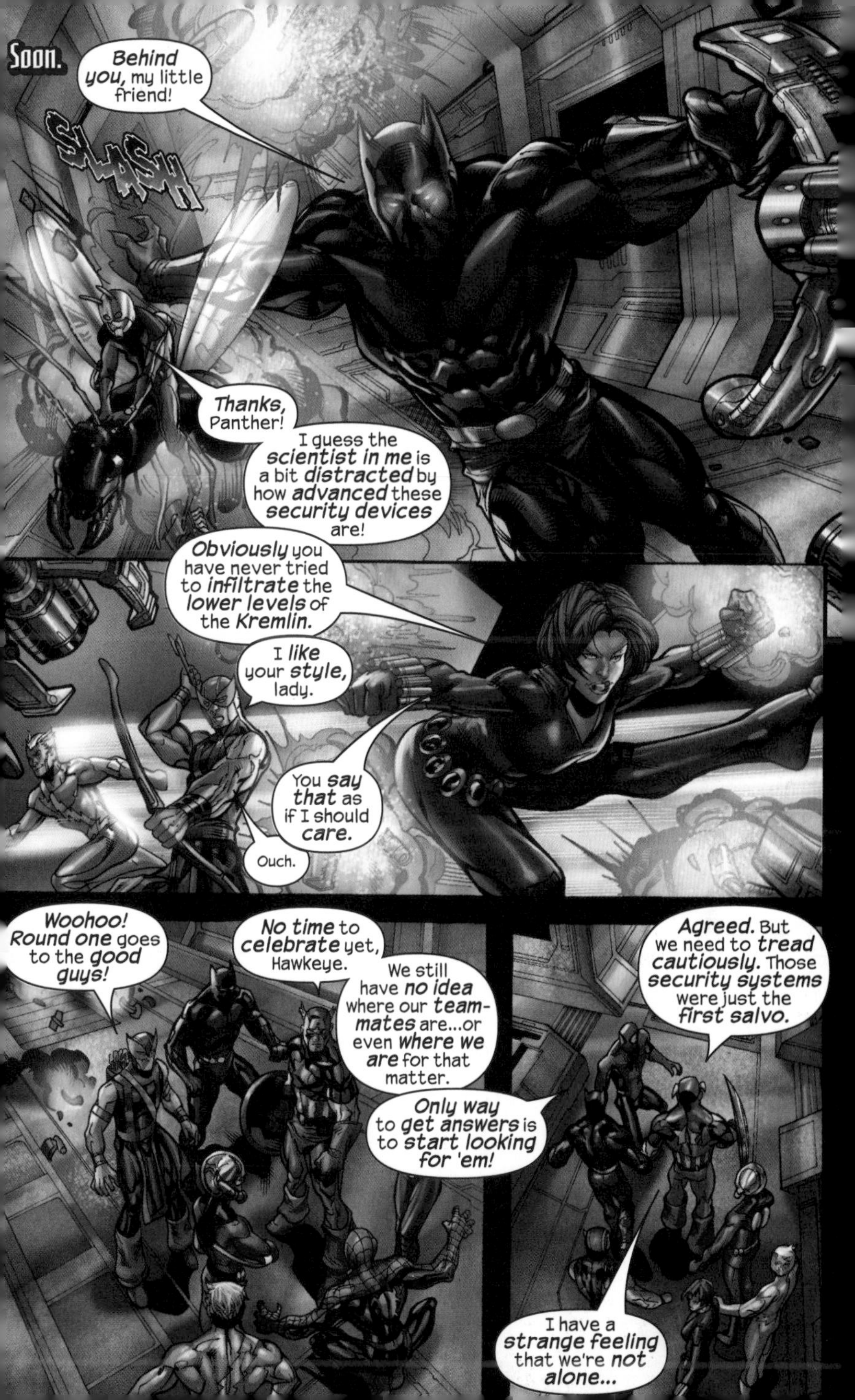
Soon.
Behind you, my little friend!
SLASH
Thanks, Panther!
I guess the scientist in me is a bit distracted by how advanced these security devices are!
Obviously you have never tried to infiltrate the lower levels of the Kremlin.
I like your style, lady.
You say that as if I should care.
Ouch.
Woohoo! Round one goes to the good guys!
No time to celebrate yet, Hawkeye.
We still have no idea where our teammates are...or even where we are for that matter.
Only way to get answers is to start looking for 'em!
Agreed. But we need to tread cautiously. Those security systems were just the first salvo.
I have a strange feeling that we're not alone...

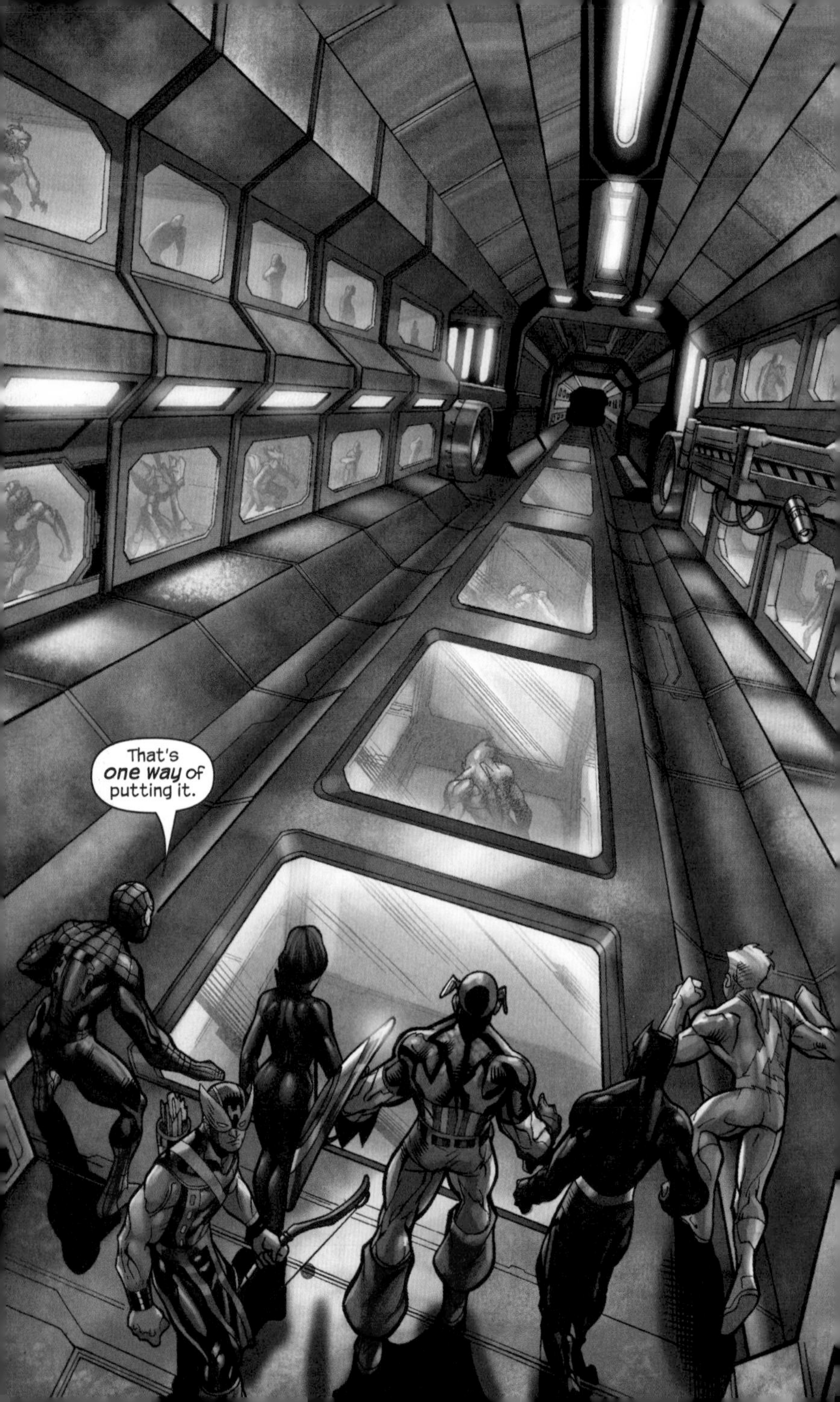
That's one way of putting it.

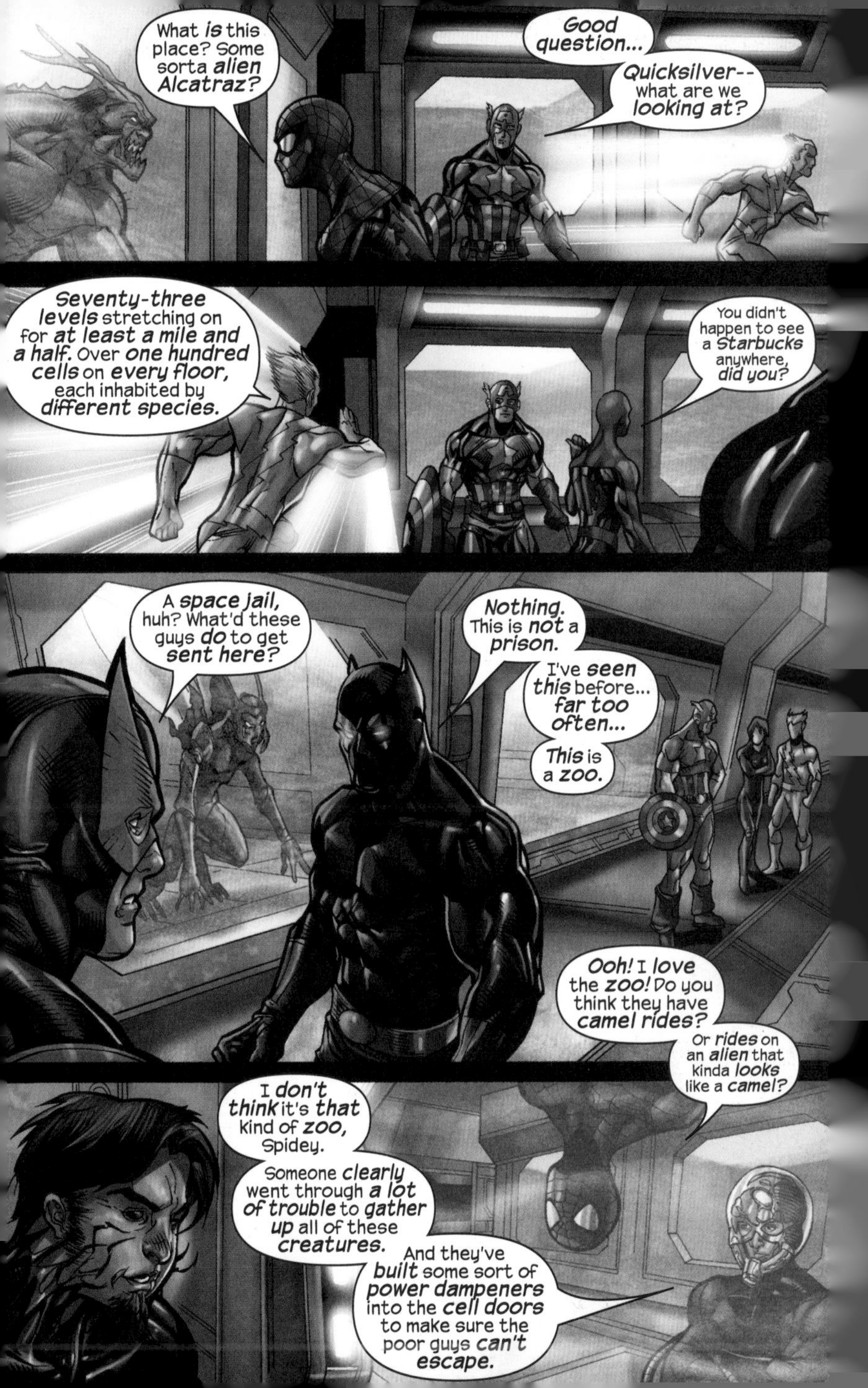
What is this place? Some sorta alien Alcatraz?
Good question...
Quicksilver-- what are we looking at?
Seventy-three levels stretching on for at least a mile and a half. Over one hundred cells on every floor, each inhabited by different species.
You didn't happen to see a Starbucks anywhere, did you?
A space jail, huh? What'd these guys do to get sent here?
Nothing. This is not a prison.
I've seen this before... far too often...
This is a zoo.
Ooh! I love the zoo! Do you think they have camel rides?
Or rides on an alien that kinda looks like a camel?
I don't think it's that kind of zoo, Spidey.
Someone clearly went through a lot of trouble to gather up all of these creatures.
And they've built some sort of power dampeners into the cell doors to make sure the poor guys can't escape.

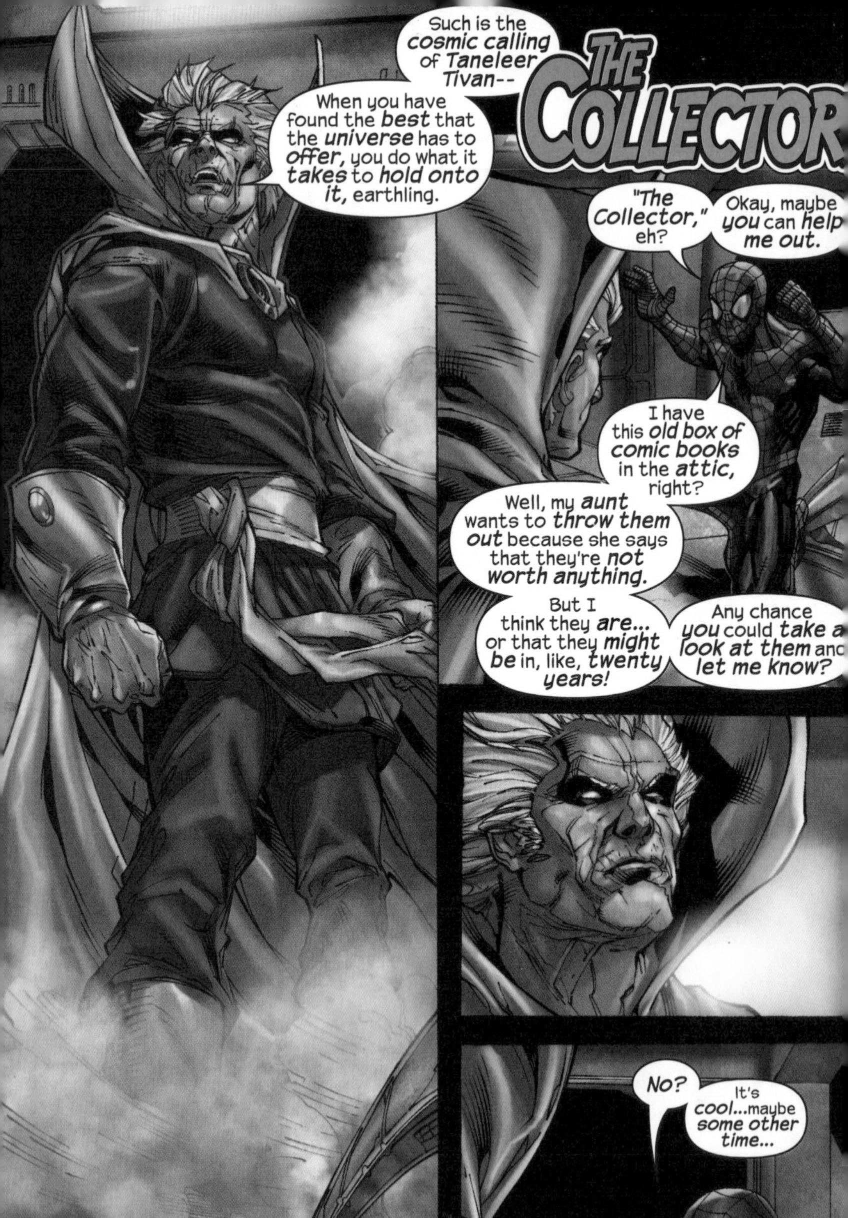
Such is the cosmic calling of Taneleer Tivan--
When you have found the best that the universe has to offer, you do what it takes to hold onto it, earthling.
THE COLLECTOR
"The Collector," eh?
Okay, maybe you can help me out.
I have this old box of comic books in the attic, right?
Well, my aunt wants to throw them out because she says that they're not worth anything.
But I think they are... or that they might be in, like, twenty years!
Any chance you could take a look at them and let me know?
No?
It's cool...maybe some other time...

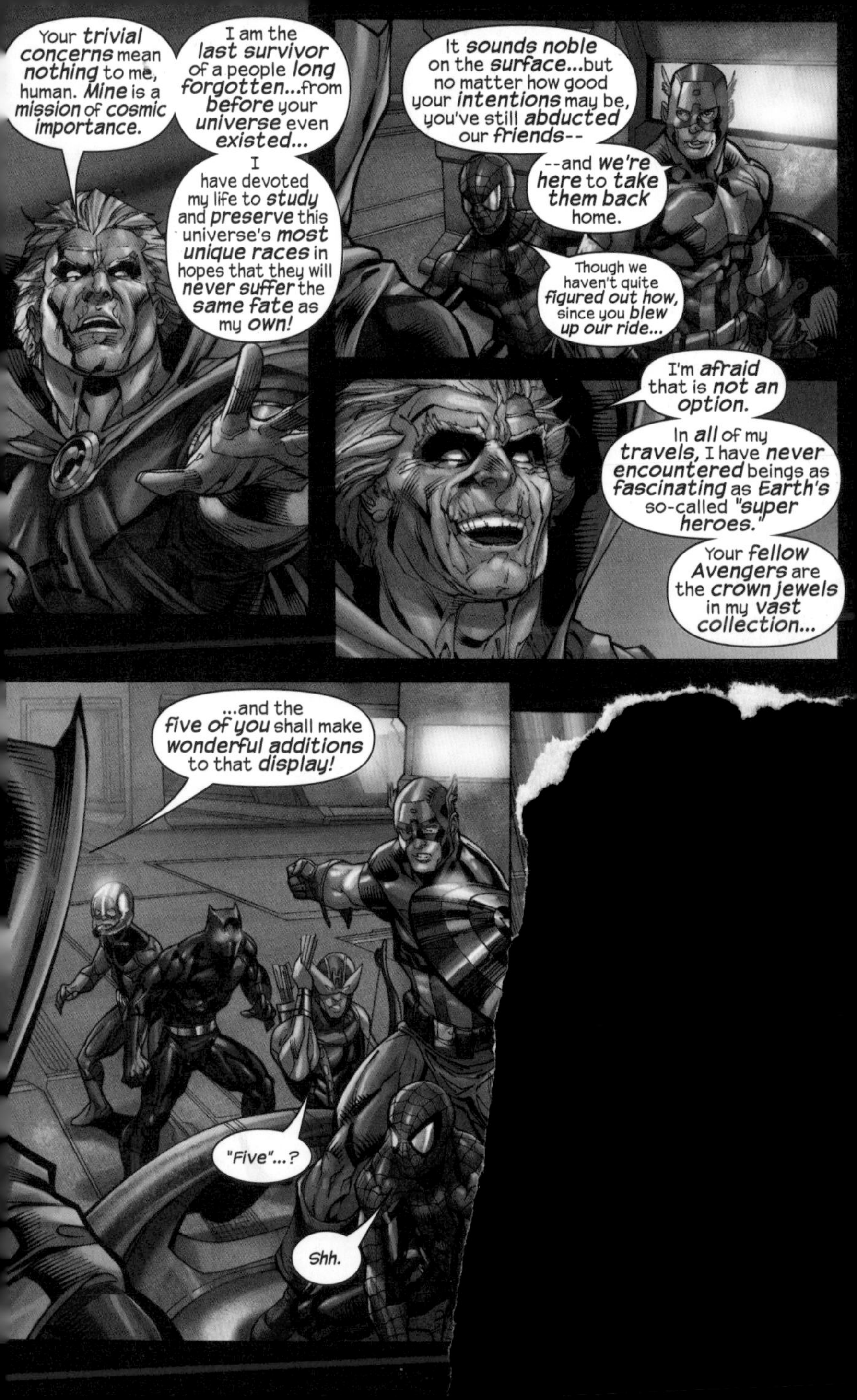
Your trivial concerns mean nothing to me, human. Mine is a mission of cosmic importance.
I am the last survivor of a people long forgotten...from before your universe even existed...
I have devoted my life to study and preserve this universe's most unique races in hopes that they will never suffer the same fate as my own!
It sounds noble on the surface...but no matter how good your intentions may be, you've still abducted our friends--
--and we're here to take them back home.
Though we haven't quite figured out how, since you blew up our ride...
I'm afraid that is not an option.
In all of my travels, I have never encountered beings as fascinating as Earth's so-called "super heroes."
Your fellow Avengers are the crown jewels in my vast collection...
...and the five of you shall make wonderful additions to that display!
"Five"...?
Shh.

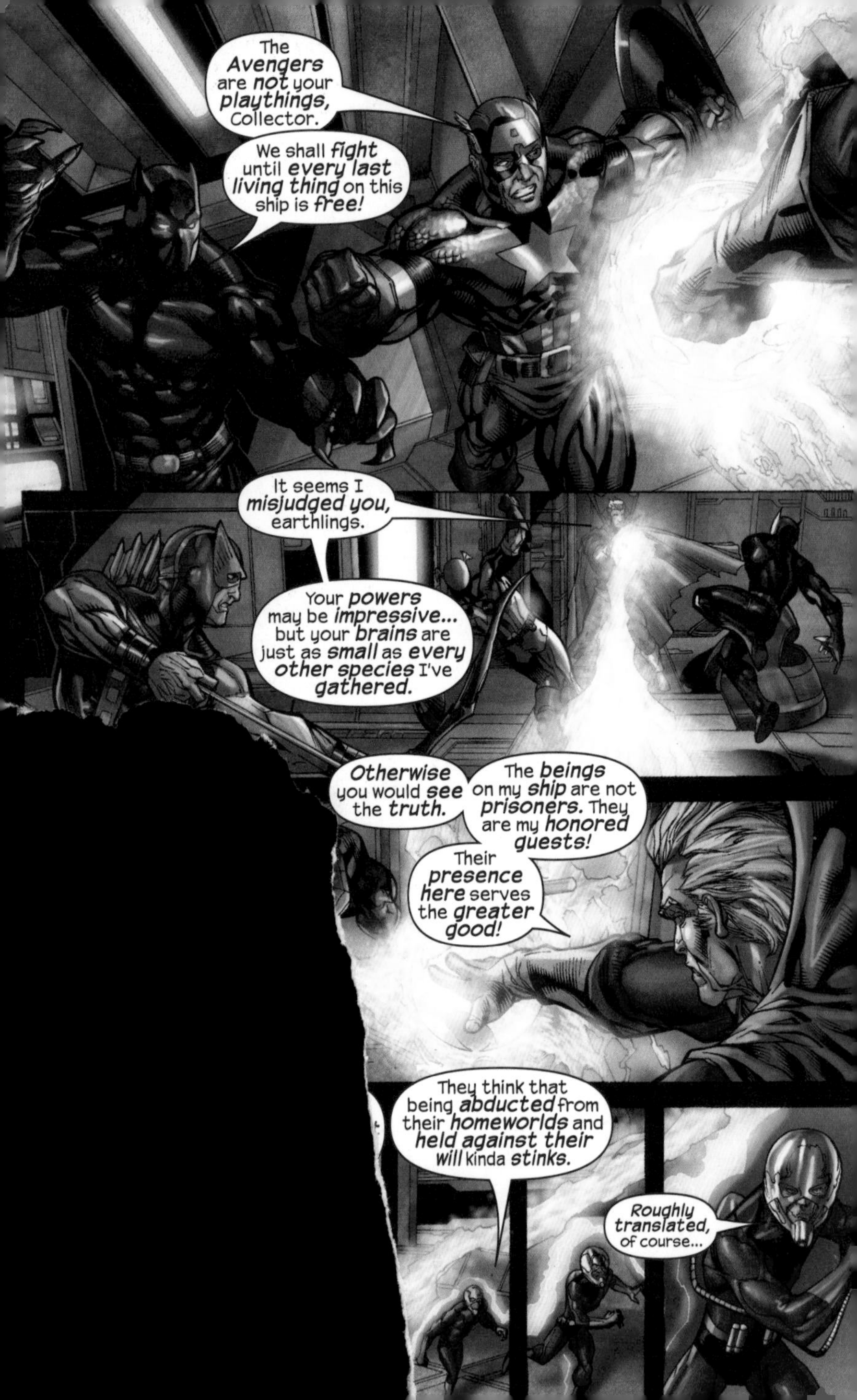
The Avengers are not your playthings, Collector.
We shall fight until every last living thing on this ship is free!
It seems I misjudged you, earthlings.
Your powers may be impressive... but your brains are just as small as every other species I've gathered.
Otherwise you would see the truth.
The beings on my ship are not prisoners. They are my honored guests!
Their presence here serves the greater good!
They think that being abducted from their homeworlds and held against their will kinda stinks.
Roughly translated, of course...

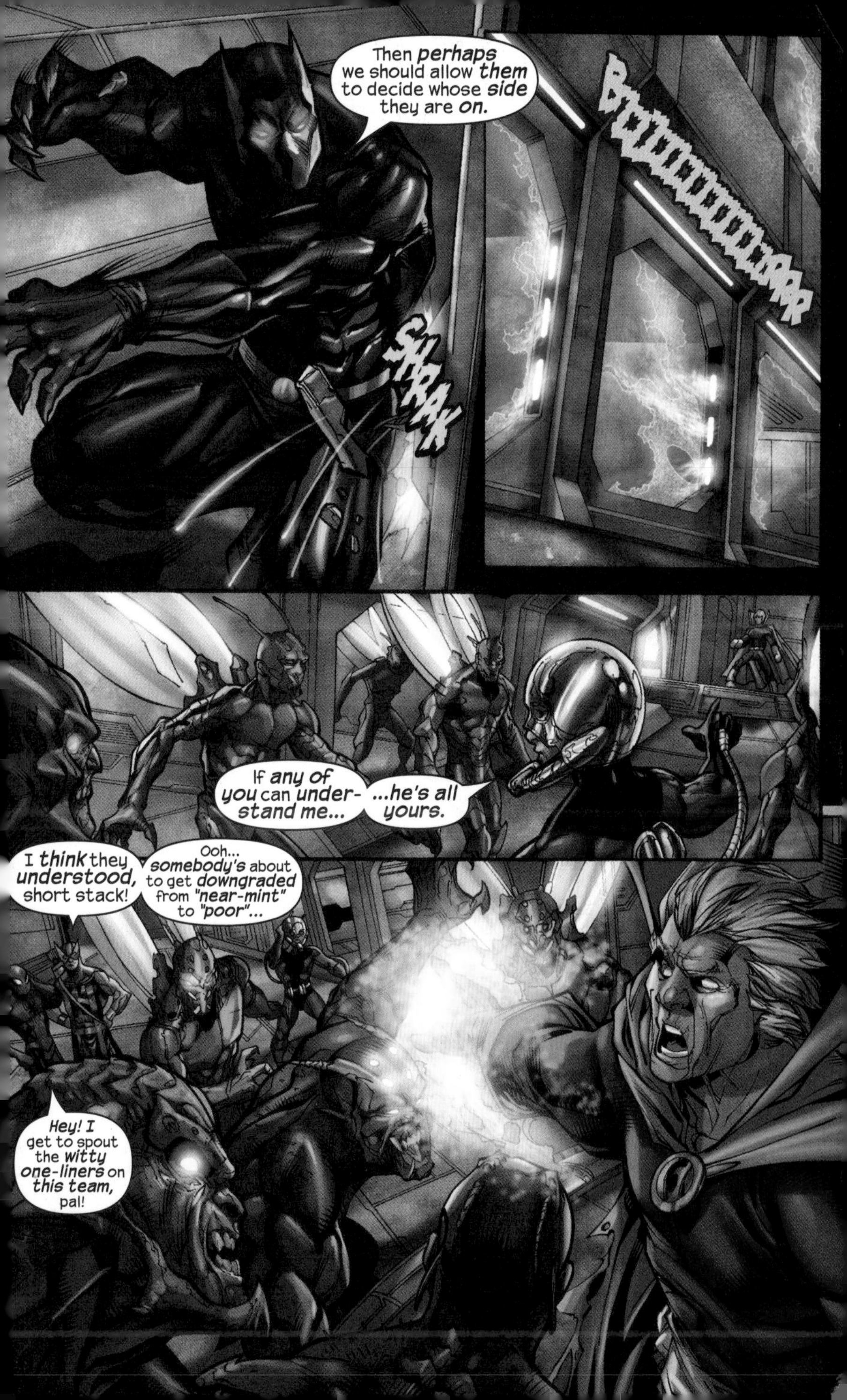
Then perhaps we should allow them to decide whose side they are on.
BDDDDDDDRRR
SHRAK
If any of you can understand me...
...he's all yours.
I think they understood, short stack!
Ooh... somebody's about to get downgraded from "near-mint" to "poor"...
Hey! I get to spout the witty one-liners on this team, pal!

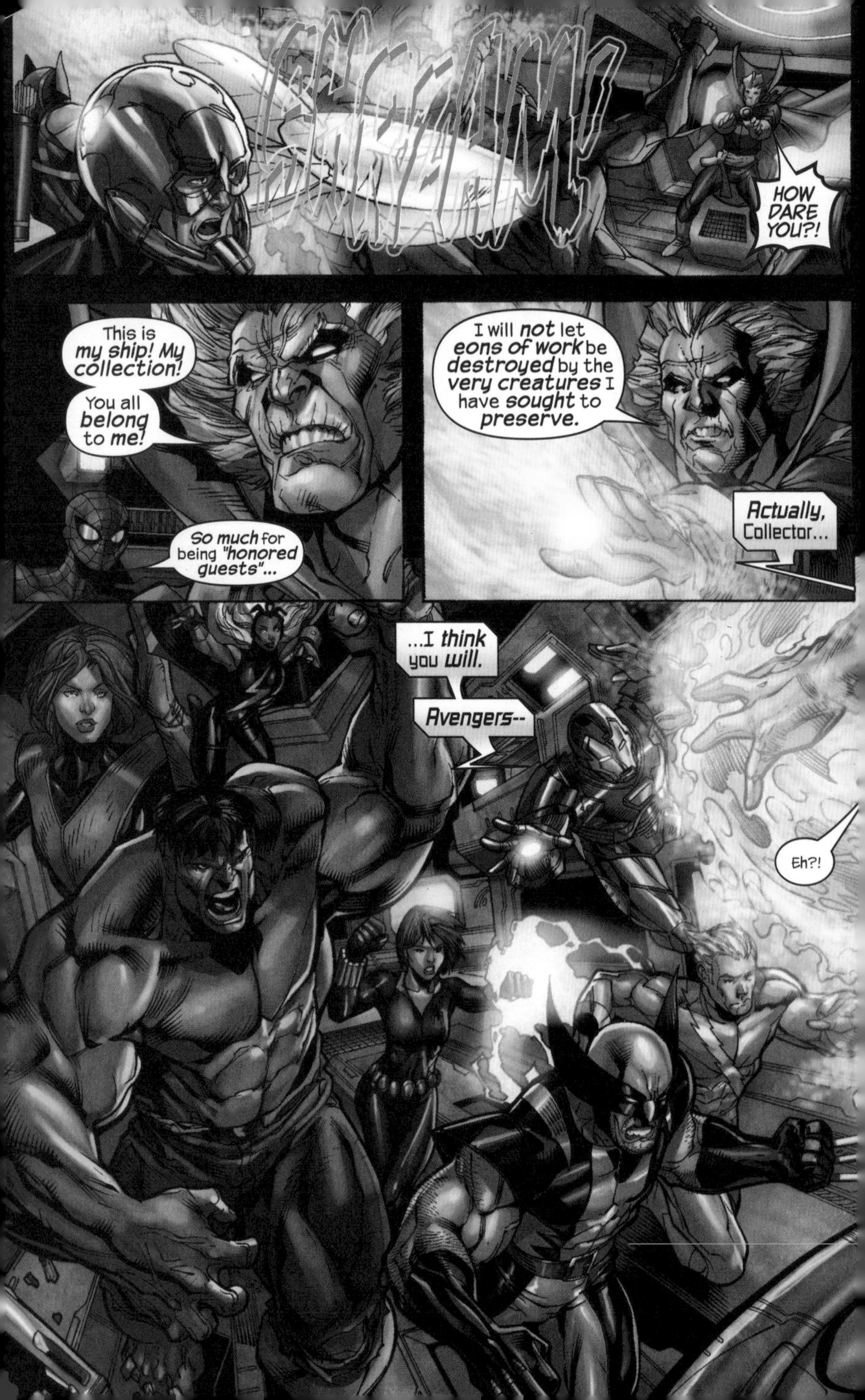
HOW DARE YOU?!
This is my ship! My collection!
You all belong to me!
So much for being "honored guests"...
I will not let eons of work be destroyed by the very creatures I have sought to preserve.
Actually, Collector...
...I think you will.
Avengers--
Eh?!

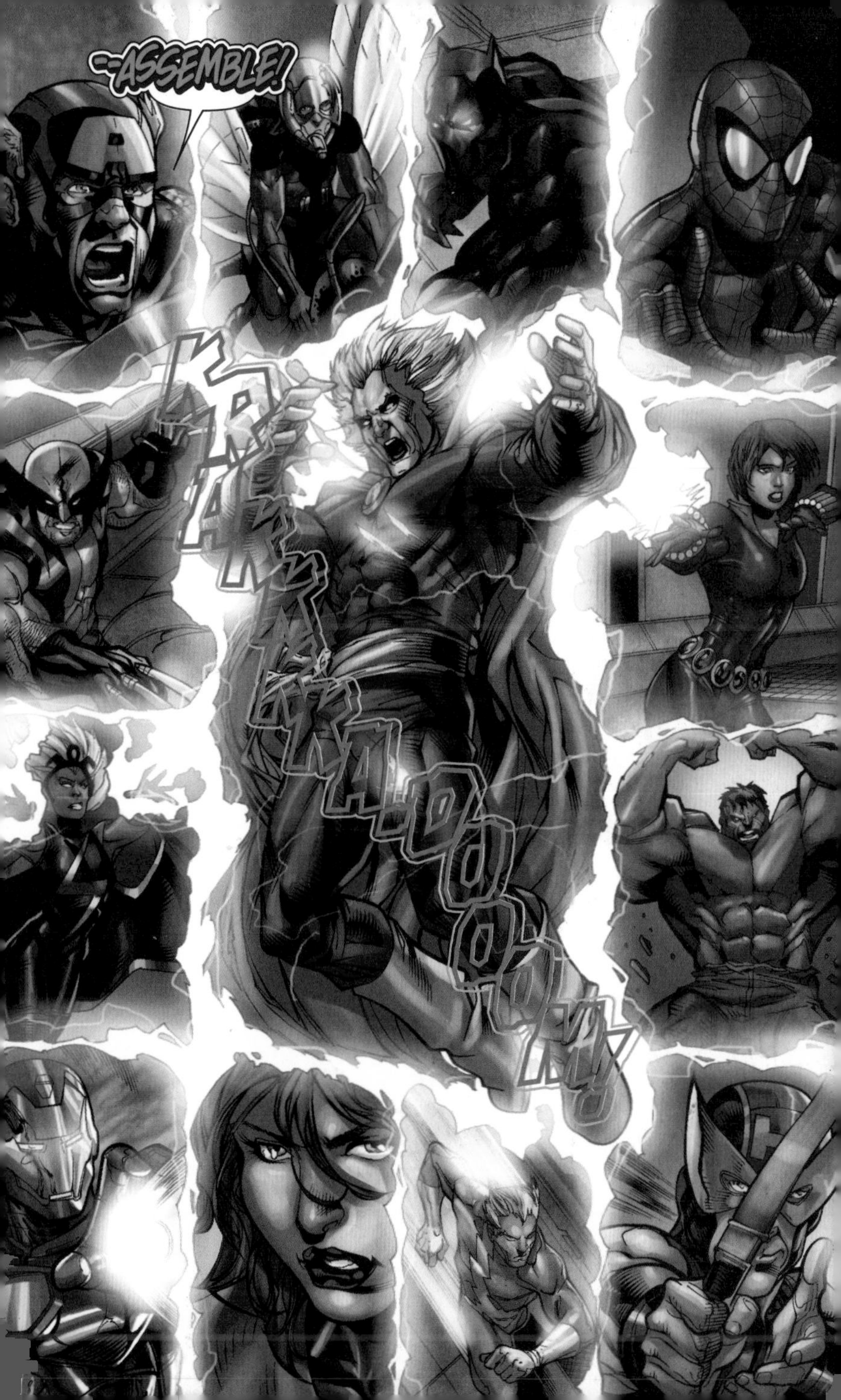
--ASSEMBLE!

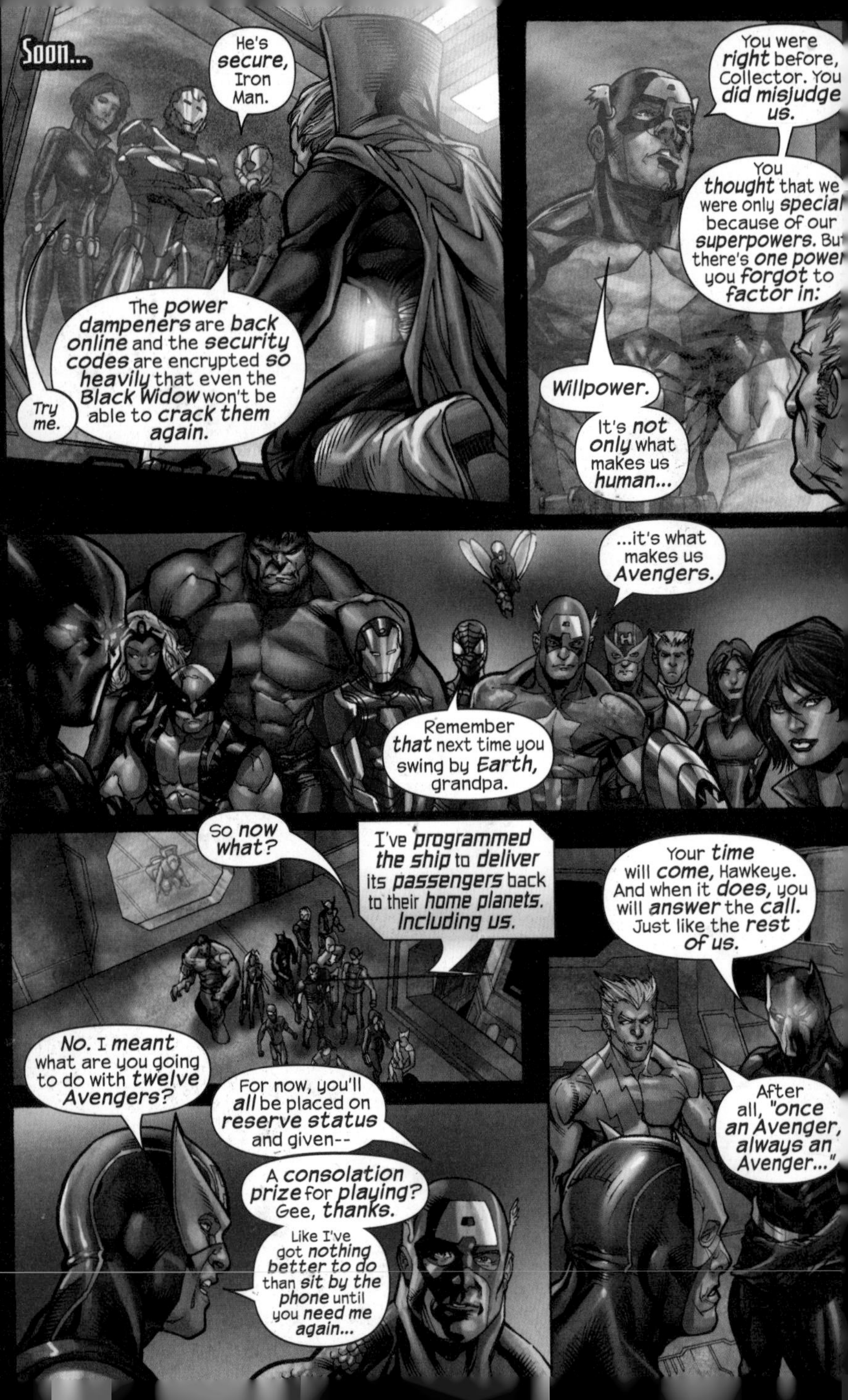
Soon...
He's secure, Iron Man.
The power dampeners are back online and the security codes are encrypted so heavily that even the Black Widow won't be able to crack them again.
Try me.
You were right before, Collector. You did misjudge us.
You thought that we were only special because of our superpowers. But there's one power you forgot to factor in:
Willpower.
It's not only what makes us human...
...it's what makes us Avengers.
Remember that next time you swing by Earth, grandpa.
So now what?
I've programmed the ship to deliver its passengers back to their home planets. Including us.
No. I meant what are you going to do with twelve Avengers?
For now, you'll all be placed on reserve status and given--
A consolation prize for playing? Gee, thanks.
Like I've got nothing better to do than sit by the phone until you need me again...
Your time will come, Hawkeye. And when it does, you will answer the call. Just like the rest of us.
After all, "once an Avenger, always an Avenger..."

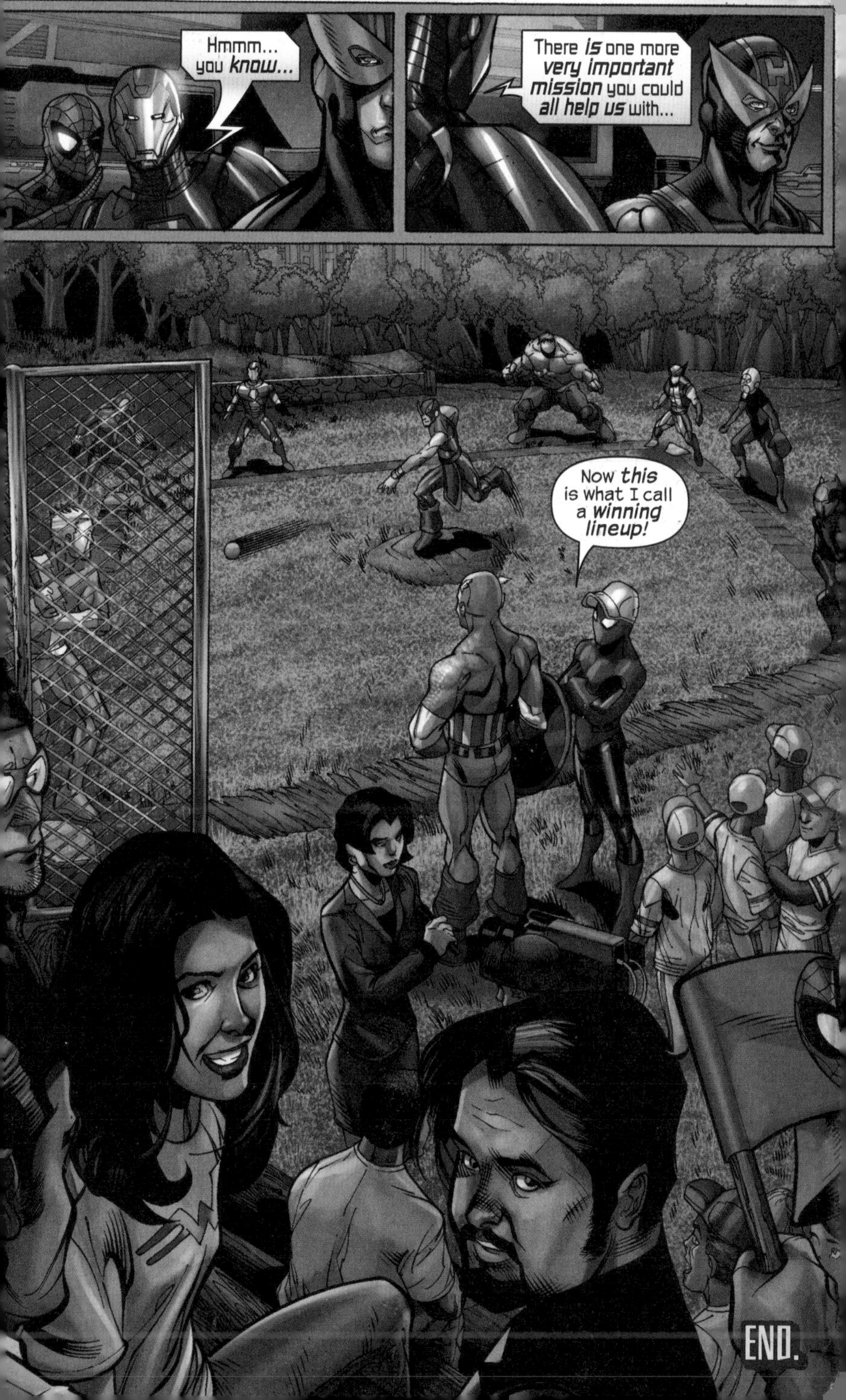
Hmmm... you know...
There is one more very important mission you could all help us with...
Now this is what I call a winning lineup!
END.